THE GANG OF ST BRIDE'S

Penny Green Mystery Book 9

EMILY ORGAN

First published in 2020 by Emily Organ

emilyorgan.com

Edited by Joy Tibbs

ISBN 978-1-9993433-9-2

THE GANG OF ST BRIDE'S

❧

Emily Organ

❧

ALSO BY EMILY ORGAN

Penny Green Series:
Limelight
The Rookery
The Maid's Secret
The Inventor
Curse of the Poppy
The Bermondsey Poisoner
An Unwelcome Guest
Death at the Workhouse
The Gang of St Bride's

Churchill and Pemberley Series:
Tragedy at Piddleton Hotel
Murder in Cold Mud
Puzzle in Poppleford Wood
Christmas Calamity at the Vicarage (novella)

Runaway Girl Series:
Runaway Girl

Forgotten Child
Sins of the Father

CHAPTER 1

M iraculous Discovery of Missing Plant Hunter

Thursday 19th February, 1885

Jubilant news was received from Amazonia at the weekend relating to the discovery of esteemed plant-hunter Mr. F. B. Green. Mr. Green was last seen during an ill-fated expedition to the United States of Colombia in 1875, shortly before he and his guide vanished within the dense jungle south-west of Bogotá. A search party led by explorer Mr. Isaac Fox-Stirling in 1876 discovered a hut Mr. Green had been staying in but uncovered no further evidence of his whereabouts.

Many feared that Mr. Green had met with an untimely end, and it is not yet clear how he has occupied his time over the past ten years. During this time no contact has been made between him and his colleagues or family on British soil. Neither the details of Mr. Green's condition nor the circumstances of his disappearance are yet fully known.

One of the most singular aspects of this incredible discovery is the fact that Mr. Green was discovered by a gentleman who was entirely unaccustomed to foreign climes. Mr. Francis Edwards was, before embarking upon this adventure, a clerk at the British Library. His aptitude for exploring foreign lands, with the assistance of a Spanish guide, has impressed even the most seasoned of travellers. Mr. Edwards was chosen to undertake the search by virtue of his acquaintance with Mr. Green's daughter, Miss Penelope Green.

Although Mr. Green's whereabouts are now known, it is not, at the current time, certain whether the intrepid explorer will return to English soil. Many questions remain, as yet, unanswered.

Mr. Fox-Stirling, who carried out the initial search for Mr. Green, said: "Perhaps he suffered some delirium and lost his mind, or perhaps he was imprisoned by the natives. I should like to extend my congratulations to Mr. Francis Edwards on finding the man."

Mr. Edwards embarked on his travels in September 1884, accompanied by Mr. Anselmo Corrales. A letter from Mr. Edwards containing a more detailed account is keenly awaited by the Green family.

Mr. Green's wife, Mrs. Harriet Green, resides in Derbyshire. He has two daughters: Miss Penny Green, a reporter for the Morning Express newspaper, and Mrs Eliza Billington-Grieg, who is estranged from her husband, Mr. George Billington-Grieg.

Miss Penelope Green told our reporter: "We are still struggling to believe the news; however, the whole family is overjoyed that our precious father has been found, and we are indebted to Mr. Edwards for finding him. We hope he is fit and well and hasn't suffered at all since he went missing."

CHAPTER 2

"This arrived with the morning post," I said to James as I passed him Francis' letter from Colombia.

"It was written a month ago," added Eliza. "Hopefully he's on the boat home by now."

The three of us sat in a clarence cab en route to an exhibition at the Grosvenor Gallery. The excursion had been Eliza's idea as she was keen to view some of the Gainsborough paintings. The traffic on the busy Piccadilly shopping street was so slow that it was tempting to alight and walk to our destination in the March sunshine.

"What does the letter say?" asked James, furrowing his brow in response to the number of pages it contained. "In summary?"

"It explains how he found Father," I replied. "He finally met with the European orchid grower based in Cali, who he'd written to us about before. He had hoped the man in question would be Father, but was disappointed to find out that he was, in fact, a German gentleman named Herr Hanzelback."

"What happened then?"

"Fortunately, Mr Hanzelback had come across an English plant-hunter living in the jungle nearby. He told Francis the location of his settlement, and just a few days later he came face to face with Father."

"What did your father make of that?"

"Francis explains it all in his letter if you'd care to read it."

I took the letter back from James and leafed through it, trying to find the relevant section.

"Here it is: 'Mr. Green regarded me cautiously, as if wondering what could possibly have brought me to this remote outpost in Amazonia. When I informed him of my great relief to finally find the gentleman I sought, he rose to his feet and greeted me warmly.'"

"But what has your father been doing there all this time?" asked James. "Does the letter explain that?"

"A little, though I get the impression there is far more for Francis to explain to us in person. He says at the end of the letter that he's about to depart for home, so it shouldn't be much longer before he's here."

"Your father doesn't intend to return with him?" asked James with raised eyebrows.

"It seems not," I replied, turning to look out of the window and doing all I could to ignore the heavy sensation in my chest. I distracted myself by watching two ladies dressed in furs strolling along arm in arm. A maid walked behind them carrying several boxes.

"Father cannot bring himself to face us!" cried Eliza. "Read the part which describes what Father said, Penelope."

I felt a lump in my throat as I turned back to the letter and read Francis' words aloud: "'I explained to your father that I was acquainted with his daughters and had travelled to Colombia to seek him with their blessing. At the mention of your names he became thoughtful and fell silent. Eventually the words came: "I hope they forgive me."'"

I placed the letter down in my lap, then removed my spectacles and dabbed at my eyes with my handkerchief.

"Oh, Penny," said James.

The softness of his words caused my chest to tighten. I held my breath and tried as hard as possible to prevent an outpouring of tears.

"I don't understand it," he continued. "Is he refusing to come home?"

I shook my head. "It doesn't matter. He's clearly happier where he is."

"It *does* matter!" James exclaimed. "You're his daughters!"

Eliza gave a loud gulp, then began to cry. I rested my hand on her arm in an attempt to comfort her.

"There must be a viable reason, which we will no doubt come to learn in due course," I said.

"It had better be an extremely good reason," retorted James. "I don't think there can be any excuse for abandoning one's family in such a way!"

"Let's hear what Francis has to say when he returns," I replied. "I feel we need to learn more before we become too angry or upset about it. I'm consoling myself with the wonderful fact that Father is alive and well."

"That's certainly something to be grateful for," added Eliza with a sob. "He may be a scoundrel, but at least he's not dead!"

"Maybe he's not a scoundrel at all," I suggested. "Maybe there's a reasonable explanation we should wait to hear before we make our minds up."

James shook his head and turned his attention to the window. I could tell he was angry with my father, but that he was doing all he could not to say any more for fear of upsetting Eliza further.

"I wonder if we could write to him," she said, drying her eyes. "We could tell him how happy we are that he's alive. It really is such a great comfort when you consider that, until recently, we had every reason to believe he was dead."

"How do you send a letter to someone in the jungle?" I asked.

"Oh, I'm sure a messenger could find him."

I mulled this over for a moment. "Hopefully Francis will be able to tell us how easy that would be."

"I wish we knew the reason why he has chosen to stay there," she said.

"Cowardice!" commented James.

"I think we need to know more before we can pass any judgement," I said. "We always knew the outcome of Francis' expedition might be difficult to accept."

"Yes, I suppose we did," said Eliza. "If Father wasn't dead there had to be some unpalatable reason as to why he hadn't sent any form of communication to us for ten years."

James shook his head again.

"Let's turn our attention to happier events!" said my sister, forcing a cheerful expression onto her face. "There are just nine weeks left until your wedding day!"

James and I exchanged a smile. "Mother is more excited than I've seen her in years," I said.

We had recently returned from a few days in Derbyshire to tell her the news of our engagement. I fondly recalled how she had embraced me, I was finally doing something that met with her approval.

"Hello, what's this?" James pulled down the window of the carriage and requested the driver to halt.

A well-dressed lady was sitting on the pavement outside a smart jeweller's shop. A small group of people stood around her, while several others were running, as if either attempting to escape or to chase someone.

"Something's afoot!" said James. He slid his hand into his

jacket pocket and took out a shiny florin, which he swiftly handed to me. "Here's some money for the fare."

"I'll come with you," I replied, passing the coin to Eliza.

"What?" She looked at the florin, aghast. "I don't need this – I can cover the fare myself – where are the two of you going?"

James jumped out of the carriage as we slowed to a stop.

"What's going on?" asked Eliza. "James, you can't get involved, it's your day off!"

"He can't really pass this sort of situation by and we both need to find out what's happening." I got up from my seat and prepared to follow him.

"But it's your day off too, Penelope!" my sister protested.

"I'm sorry, Ellie, but I don't want to miss out on a story."

"Must I go to the gallery by myself then?"

"We'll meet you there later!" I replied, hopping out of the carriage.

I gave Eliza a wave and shut the cab door. She pursed her lips and glared at me as the carriage pulled away.

CHAPTER 3

I could see the blue uniform of a police constable among the melee, and as we moved closer it became clear that he was trying to keep everyone calm. The lady sitting on the ground wore a smart moss-green dress with a matching hat and looked to be around fifty years of age. A young lady was crouched down beside her.

"I'm all right, I'm all right!" grumbled the older lady. "Just let me get up!"

"But you've had such a dreadful shock, Mother!" said the young lady.

"I've survived far worse."

"It's an absolute disgrace!" fumed a gentleman in a velvet-trimmed jacket and top hat. "This sort of thing keeps happening. Something needs to be done about them!"

"About whom?" I asked.

"The vagabonds roaming our streets! It shouldn't be allowed to happen on Piccadilly!"

"What's happened?"

"This lady's been robbed! Her purse was cut from her wrist!"

"Did you see who did it?"

"Three women," a lady called out from close by. "We saw them running away!"

"Which way did they go?" I asked.

Fingers were pointed in a westerly direction, toward the location of Hyde Park.

I joined James, who was talking to the constable.

"They've taken off," said the constable. "A member of the public has already gone after them. A woman, believe it or not!"

"I saw them turn up Sackville Street," added the young lady who had been tending to her mother.

"Right under the noses of the officers at Vine Street police station," said the man in the top hat. "It's a disgrace that the police keep allowing these people to get away with it!"

"Let's see if we can catch them," said James, dashing off in the direction of the three women and the lady pursuing them.

I followed after him, feeling burdened by my long skirts and tight corset.

James turned into Sackville Street and I followed suit. The street was home to a number of cloth merchants, with rolls of fabric filling the shop windows and covering the trestle tables laid out on the pavement.

"Did you see any women running this way?" I asked a lady with an oversized feather in her hat.

"Yes, they went that way," she replied, pointing up the street. "What's going on?"

"There's been a robbery."

"Oh, goodness. Not again!"

I felt many pairs of eyes on me as I continued running. I had to hold my spectacles in place to keep them from slipping off my nose.

"Is everything all right?" a gentleman with grey whiskers called out. "What the devil's going on?"

"There's been a robbery," I called back. "Did you happen to see any women running this way?"

"Yes, three or four of them!"

I eventually reached the crossroads at the top of the street, where James had stopped outside a public house. He was speaking to a lady in a blue flannel dress who looked about thirty years of age. She held her hat in her hand, and her brown hair had fallen loose from its pins. Her complexion was freckled and her face was flushed from the exertion of running.

"I did my best, Inspector," she puffed, "but somehow I lost them. I can only assume they ran into this public house here. That's the only explanation I can give for their sudden disappearance. But when I went inside there was no sign of them, and the fellow working behind the bar hadn't seen them either."

James glanced over at the crossroads. "I suppose there are a number of directions they could have run off in," he said. "There were three women, you say?"

"Yes. The first thing I knew of it was when an elderly lady fell to the ground and three others ran off, which instantly struck me as suspicious, Once I'd seen that there were people on hand to assist the old lady, I decided to give chase. I didn't expect them to take off as they did. They're clearly well-practised at scarpering."

"Can you describe them for me?" James asked, taking out his notebook.

"I'm afraid I didn't get a good look at their faces, Inspector. They were all wearing hats, which were quite dark in colour. Not particularly fancy hats, but smart. One of them had a dark feather in hers. Their clothing was dark, too."

"Any idea of the colour?"

"One was dark blue and I'm sure another wore dark brown. Well, it was more of a burgundy sort of colour, actually. They hitched up their skirts in the most unladylike manner and made a run for it. One of them glanced back at me, now I come to think of it. It was a very quick glance, but enough for me to see that she had a smirk on her face, as if she were amused by my attempt to chase them down. She urged the others on with some sort of encouraging cry, and they moved even more swiftly after that."

"What did this particular lady look like?"

"I remember her being young. She was the lady in the burgundy. Fair-haired from what I could tell, though most of her hair was pinned beneath her hat."

"Eye colour?" James asked.

"I wasn't close enough to see, I'm afraid."

"Height?"

"Well, let me think... I stand at five feet five inches. The woman who turned to look at me was the shortest of the three, and a bit shorter than I am. I'd hazard a guess that she was no taller than five feet."

"And the other two?"

"Somewhere between my height and the height of the smallest one. It's difficult to be more accurate than that, Inspector. Between five feet and five feet five inches, I would say."

"And the hair colour of the other two?"

"One had darker hair, probably a shade of brown. I'm certain she was the one wearing dark blue. The other was also wearing dark blue, but with a slight green tinge. I think her skirts were a dark blue and green plaid. I couldn't tell you the colour of her hair, though."

"You remarked that the shortest of the three called out to her companions while you were running. Did you hear any of the words she used?"

"No, I'm afraid not. I'm assuming it was something along the lines of 'Run faster!' given that she'd spotted me running behind them."

"You didn't hear her call either of them by name at all?"

"Sadly, no."

"And you heard no other words exchanged between them at any time?"

She shook her head. "None. I wish I'd been able to catch up with them, but I'm not accustomed to running as a general rule. The three women gave the distinct impression that they run a great deal. They're obviously used to evading capture by the looks of things."

"These ladies were well-dressed, you said. Did they strike you as being of a particular class?"

"An interesting question, Inspector. There was something about the manner in which the shorter one smirked and then urged her companions to run that seemed rather coarse in nature. It wasn't what you'd expect from a lady with refined manners. My impression was that they were women of a lower class who had assumed the dress of gentlewomen in order to blend naturally with the environs of Piccadilly. Members of a pickpocketing gang would surely do such a thing, would they not?"

"That would make sense." James wrote this down. "And you've already told me your name is Mrs Henrietta Worthers, is that right?"

"Yes." She reached into a small bag and retrieved a carte de visite. "Here, Inspector, please take this. If you need to speak to me again about this afternoon's incident, I shall be only too happy to oblige."

"Thank you, Mrs Worthers." James took the card and placed it in his pocket. "And thank you for trying to apprehend these thieving women. You've been a great help."

"I'd have been of even greater help if I'd managed to catch one of them!"

James and I walked back to the scene of the street robbery on Piccadilly.

"It'll be interesting to see how that information tallies with what the victim is able to tell my colleagues in C Division," he said. "I shall leave them to see to this case. There's no reason for the Yard to be involved in the case of a street robbery. C Division will be quite capable of managing it."

"Judging by the comments from some of the onlookers it sounds as though this sort of thing has happened several times before."

"Unfortunately, it has. We've known about a female pick-pocketing gang in this area for a while."

"And nothing has been done about them?"

"I can't be telling C Division how to manage their own cases. There are so many gangs in London these days, the work required to tackle them is never-ending."

"I can understand why people feel frustrated when nothing ever appears to be done about them."

"Work is underway, but its effects aren't always immediately obvious. I shall speak to Inspector Paget at C Division, he's at Vine Street. I'll find out how his work is progressing with regard to this particular gang and ask if he'd like some assistance. If it was easy to stop them, they wouldn't still be roaming the streets. Besides, you know how it is with these gangs. You think you've cracked one and arrested the ring-leaders, but then the remaining members reform and continue. It's akin to chopping off one of the Hydra's heads."

"Well, I hope the poor lady who was robbed will recover from her ordeal. She didn't seem to be injured, fortunately."

"That is fortunate indeed."

"Do we still have time for a trip to the Grosvenor Gallery?"

James checked his pocket watch. "Yes, I think so. I'd like to find Inspector Paget and have a quick word with him first, but after that we can continue on our way. Let's hope Eliza is still there by the time we arrive."

"And let's hope she won't be in a foul temper with us!"

CHAPTER 4

I sat at the typewriter in the *Morning Express* newsroom the following day, working on my report of the Piccadilly robbery. The newsroom was a shabby place, with piles of paper on every surface and a grimy window which overlooked Fleet Street.

"It won't be long now until the return of the great adventurer, Mr Francis Edwards!" said my colleague Edgar Fish. He was a young man with heavy features and small, glinting eyes. "Everyone's looking forward to hearing how he found your father, Miss Green. I understand your father won't be accompanying him, is that right?"

"Apparently not," I replied glumly. "It seems he prefers to stay where he is."

"Perhaps he's become the head of a tribe," chipped in another of my colleagues: the corpulent, curly-haired Frederick Potter. "Perhaps they even worship him. If they've never seen a European before they may consider the mysterious, white-skinned gentleman to be a god of some sort."

"Potter!" scolded Edgar. "Please be mindful of Miss

Green's feelings. I'm sure she has no desire to hear such idle speculation!"

"There is nothing I haven't already considered myself," I replied. "I've had plenty of time over the past ten years to consider what might have happened to him."

"While I appreciate that, Miss Green, it can't be nice to have others sticking their oar in. And besides, it's not particularly polite."

"You brought the topic up in the first place, Fish," said Frederick.

"I don't think I did... did I?"

"Yes, you did."

"I'm trying to recall exactly how the conversation went, but I'm quite sure you're mistaken, Potter."

"That's enough bickering from the two of you," said our editor, Mr Sherman, as he strode into the newsroom, leaving the door to slam shut behind him. He wore a blue waistcoat and his shirt sleeves were rolled up. His hair was oiled and parted to one side. "Where have you got to with that story on the Prince of Wales's visit to Berlin, Fish?"

"Was I expected to write an article about it?"

"Yes!" Mr Sherman scowled. "You haven't done anything on it?"

"I hadn't realised I was supposed to, sir."

There was an uncomfortable silence.

"I'm joking, sir!" said Edgar with a grin. "It's already completed. Here you go!" He got up from his seat and handed the editor his article.

"There's a time and place for jokes, Fish," said Mr Sherman tartly.

"And this is neither the time nor the place for them?"

"Exactly. Now, Miss Green." He turned to me. "I think something needs to be written about guarding oneself against street robbery in this week's ladies' column."

"Of course, sir. What sort of guarding measures did you have in mind?"

"Those are for you to come up with."

"I don't think I know of any, sir."

"You're a writer, Miss Green, just use your imagination! I should think that most of the advice would be common sense, such as not parading around with one's valuables on display and that sort of thing. All quite self-evident, but it's important to demonstrate to our readers that we provide timely and actionable advice in our ladies' column. A number of our readers will be feeling quite worried about shopping on Piccadilly in light of these thefts."

"Very well, sir."

"And I'd like you to attend this event." He handed me a pamphlet advertising a spring fair in Hanwell. "You'll be aware, no doubt, of the schools there that are used to house and educate destitute children. The fair is being held to secure much-needed income for the schools. As a reputable newspaper we must report on these philanthropic events to help instil the sentiment in our readers' minds. Reporting on such endeavours encourages members of the public to attend, and that adds to the coffers of these worthy causes. I'm growing increasingly aware of the responsibility our publication has when it comes to shaping the minds of the general public. There was a time when we did little more than report on parliament, the money markets and coroners' inquests, but I believe we have a duty to inform our readers more widely about the issues we're facing in society today."

"Well said, sir," said Edgar.

"Thank you, Fish."

"That's a style of reporting I can firmly agree with," I said. "How else will the public learn about the inequalities and injustices of this world?"

"It's important to recognise where the boundaries lie,

though, isn't it?" replied my editor. "It's one thing to report on the injustices in this world, Miss Green, and another to dive headlong into them and forget all about the ladies' column for this week."

I gave a knowing smile. "Quite."

"Very well. Oh, and I also need a quiet word with you in my office, Miss Green." Mr Sherman left the room with a slam of the door.

I felt an unpleasant tremor in my chest. *What could my editor possibly wish to speak to me about in private?*

"Hatpins," said Edgar.

"I'm sorry?" I replied, puzzled.

"That's what's needed to guard against street robbery. You're quite adept with a hatpin, isn't that so?"

I gave a wince as I recalled the unpleasant occasion upon which I had been compelled to use one in self-defence. "I would only recommend such a course of action in a life or death situation," I replied. "I think if you have something valuable you really couldn't bear to part with, it would be better to keep it tucked safely away somewhere."

"But some ladies like to go out wearing their jewels."

"I understand that, and ideally it should be safe to do so. Sadly, there are numerous vagabonds out there intent on stealing other people's precious things."

"My uncle has a walking cane gun," said Frederick. "Apparently, it can kill at a distance of one hundred yards."

"Good grief!" exclaimed Edgar. "Does he have a licence for it?"

"I don't know. But what I do know is that it looks just like an ordinary walking cane. He has a sword stick, too."

"I don't know about you, Miss Green, but I'm not walking down Piccadilly unless I've got Uncle Potter with me," said Frederick. "What do you think?"

"Uncle Potter sounds like a gentleman to be reckoned

with." I replied, standing up from my seat and heading over to join Mr Sherman in his office.

I took a seat in the cluttered room, its walls yellowed from years of stale tobacco smoke. Like the newsroom, every surface was covered with piles of books and papers.

Miss Welton came in and collected two empty coffee cups from the desk. Mr Sherman waited for her to depart before speaking.

"I'm extremely reluctant to discuss this with you, Miss Green, but I suppose I must." He gave a sigh and leaned forward onto his desk. "Please remind me of the date set for your wedding."

"The twenty-third of May, sir."

"I see." He sat back in his chair again. "Then I suppose we must discuss a departure date."

This was a conversation I had feared might happen yet hoped never would.

"Surely I don't have to give up my job," I protested.

He gave a shrug. "It's customary, Miss Green. You and I both know that."

"But Inspector Blakely is quite happy for me to continue working after we are married."

"As am I, Miss Green, but it isn't appropriate for a married lady. Before long you'll have a household to manage and children too, no doubt."

"I'm hardly the sort of person who craves a household and children, Mr Sherman."

"I realise that. But they go hand in hand with marriage, don't they?"

"They don't have to."

"I imagine it'll be rather unavoidable, Miss Green. It's the way things work in polite society."

"In *polite* society, perhaps, though I don't see why I can't do what a working-class married woman does and continue with my work."

He gave a laugh. "Working-class? I realise you've disguised yourself as such for certain reporting jobs, Miss Green, but you certainly don't belong to the lower classes. Those women work because they have to, married or otherwise. Your work has always been a choice."

"Because I enjoy it! I can't think for a single moment what I should do if I didn't have my work to occupy me."

"Your time will soon be taken up with managing a—"

"I have no desire for a household or children, sir."

"I see. They're usually somewhat inevitable for a lady who marries, but I won't pursue that argument."

"I sincerely wish to keep my job at the *Morning Express*. I've worked here for eleven years now."

"Yes, you have."

"And I have found it to be the most interesting and fulfilling role I have ever undertaken in my life. I've seen my sister manage a household and I know how much it has bored her. Some ladies enjoy it and are well suited to it, but we're not all alike, sir."

"No, I realise that."

"I should lose my mind if I were unable to do this job. And I know that my husband-to-be is fully supportive of me in that respect."

"It's wonderfully supportive of him, Miss Green, and it's safe to say that there aren't many husbands like him around. Most insist on their wives giving up any paid employment as soon as they're married."

"He's known for a while that I'm quite different to most ladies."

"Indeed. And while it's admirable to see, and a view I

share myself, I'm afraid that we must still agree upon a departure date."

"Because married middle-class ladies cannot work?"

"You could undertake some voluntary employment."

"But I wish to be a news reporter, Mr Sherman! That's all I've ever wanted to do."

"You could still write... no one can stop you doing that. And you have your own typewriter now, haven't you?"

"Yes, I can still write, but it's not quite the same as news reporting, is it?"

"I'm afraid my hands are tied regarding this matter, Miss Green, and we must agree on a departure date."

"But why?"

"Because Mr Conway will insist on it. You know how important the reputation of this newspaper is to its proprietor."

"You mean to say that employing a married lady would ruin the reputation of the *Morning Express*?"

"Not *ruin* it exactly, but you know what our rivals are like. A recent scandal concerning this newspaper has already taken place, for which I must take full responsibility."

Mr Sherman had been arrested six months previously during a police raid on the Hammam Turkish Baths in Soho, where it was believed activities of an immoral nature were taking place.

I laughed. "Between the two of us, we make rather an unconventional pair, don't you think, sir?"

"Perhaps. But defying convention always leads to gossip. We don't want to give people any further reason to talk about the staff working on this newspaper, Miss Green. It undermines our ability to report on events as we see them. It's no good at all if the newspaper itself becomes the news! That was the case for a short while and it was quite disastrous, as

I'm sure you'd agree. Now that we've restored ourselves to a steady equilibrium, we cannot afford to rock the boat again."

"And by that, sir, you mean that we've escaped one scandal but cannot be expected to escape another?"

"Yes."

I gave a sigh. "It's simply not right that it should be considered scandalous to employ a married lady."

"A workplace such as this is no place for a married lady, Miss Green."

"No, of course not. She should simply remain within the confines of her home."

"And visit the homes of other married ladies, and go on shopping expeditions and out to parties, and so on."

"How incredibly dull."

"I can't say that it appeals much to me, either. I consider myself quite fortunate to be a man at times like this. I shall miss you, Miss Green. You're the best reporter I have."

"Can't you ask Mr Conway whether he'd be prepared to change his mind about me? While I understand that he wants everything to proceed in the proper manner, surely there's a way for me to stay. I could ask Inspector Blakely to write him a letter explaining how happy he is for me to continue working after our marriage. Perhaps that would help."

"It might do."

"Will you speak to him?"

"Yes, I'll speak to him, but I think he'll be adamant about it. I imagine his wife will be quite disapproving, and you know how much he listens to her. Wives wield quite a bit of power, you see. No doubt you'll discover that for yourself before long."

CHAPTER 5

The fields gleamed an emerald green in the spring sunshine as the train pulled into Hanwell Station. The location was on the rural edge of West London, where rows of new homes were under construction among the farms and country houses.

A horse-drawn omnibus decorated with colourful flags was waiting at the station to take visitors to the fair at Hanwell Schools. I climbed the steps to the upper deck so I could enjoy the view and fresh air. It made a pleasant change to escape the smoke and busy streets of central London, though as I looked at the new construction taking place I wondered how long it would take for the fields around me to be swallowed up by the encroaching city.

After a short journey I stepped off the omnibus into the extensive school grounds. The neat brown-brick buildings overlooked an array of stalls and marquees. The mild breeze carried with it the strains of a brass band.

The children were dressed in their best clothes, the boys sporting shiny, buttoned boots and the girls wearing crisp white aprons and coloured ribbons in their hair. A range of amusements had been provided for their entertainment, from an organ grinder and his monkey to a Punch and Judy show and a coconut shy. There were stalls selling many items the children had made, such as fruit jams, knitted socks and needlework pieces.

I readied myself with my notebook and pencil, keen to signify to the school's proprietors that I was here to report on the proceedings. I found a group of dignitaries positioned close to the bandstand. A rotund man in striped trousers approached me as I wandered over.

"May I help you, madam? You appear to be looking for someone."

After I had introduced myself, he told me that he was Mr Richardson, the school's superintendent.

"A lady news reporter, eh?" he added. "Most interesting indeed. And not merely a writer for one of those ladies' journals, either, but for an actual daily newspaper! I can't say that I've come across your type before."

I smiled politely and began to ask some of the questions I had prepared about the school.

"We have almost fourteen hundred children here. That's quite an amount, isn't it? Each year we discharge around four hundred and fifty, but we also admit about the same number. Some of them are orphans, but most simply have drunk or idle parents; the sort of people whose parental mantle hangs rather loosely upon them. You know of the sort, I'm sure."

"What happens to the children when they leave the school?"

"For the most part they go into service, though a number of our boys enter the army. We do our utmost to ensure that each and every child is able to become a useful citizen, and that means providing them all with a meticulous routine of teaching and instruction."

"What does that involve?"

"Worship morning and evening, and also a daily walk, come rain or shine. The boys spend their afternoons in the workshops, where the younger ones make matchboxes and darn socks and the older ones learn woodturning, tailoring or shoemaking. The girls work in the laundry and are taught needlework and dressmaking skills, with cookery lessons once a week. All the children are instructed in gymnastics, swimming and military drills. In the summer we have picnics, and each August we take an excursion to the coast. Every Sunday the children attend church in the morning and Sabbath School in the afternoon. Those who have families visit them once a month. Ah, Mrs Sutherland!"

We were approached by a slightly built lady with brown hair, which was parted in the centre and neatly fastened at the nape of her neck. Her dark dress was modest and simple, but the gold rings on her fingers hinted at wealth.

"Mrs Sutherland is one of our most loyal benefactors," enthused Mr Richardson. "She has been wonderfully supportive of our efforts for some time now, and we are extremely grateful to her."

"Thank you, Mr Richardson," she said.

As he explained who I was, Mrs Sutherland regarded me with interest.

"I do so like to see fellow ladies taking on important work," she said with a smile. "Thank you for coming, Miss Green, and for reporting on this event in your newspaper. I realise a great number of similar events are held in London each week, competing for the attentions of the public. We feel very flattered that you have chosen ours."

I smiled, failing to mention that I was only here because my editor had ordered me to attend.

"How long have you been supporting Hanwell Schools?" I asked.

"About three years. I felt it was high time I began using

the income I've earned from my own business to help others."

"And what is your business?"

"It's the family business: commercial properties and shops, mainly. After the death of my parents the business was passed on to me."

"How do you find the work?"

"I enjoy it, and it keeps me busy."

"Why did you choose Hanwell Schools?"

"One of the ladies who works for me spoke very highly of the schools here, and at that time I was considering various charitable causes to assist. I visited this place and was so impressed with Mr Richardson and the other officers that I decided to devote some time and money to support the work. I believe every child deserves a good start in life, but sadly so many of them miss out on it for one reason or another. So I like to support organisations and institutions which are able to give those children another opportunity – a second chance, if you like – to make something of themselves. My interests are not just limited to children, however. I also helped found the North London section of the Women's Rights Society."

"Is that so? My sister runs the West London Women's Society."

"Does she?" Mrs Sutherland raised an interested eyebrow. "I've heard good things about that particular society. They keep themselves busy with all sorts of good causes."

"They do indeed. My sister's name is Eliza Billington-Grieg, and she has just been elected to the Paddington Union board of guardians. I think she would be extremely interested to talk to you about your philanthropic work."

"That is most excellent news! Your sister sounds like a fine woman. There's certainly something to be said for us holding a joint meeting of our respective groups."

As Mrs Sutherland continued to explain the work she did,

a group of passing ladies caught my eye. I felt quite sure that they looked familiar. I knew it was extremely unlikely, but they seemed to match the description of the three ladies James and I had chased.

Could it be possible?

It was then that I realised Mrs Sutherland was awaiting an answer to a question she had put to me.

"I'm sorry, Mrs Sutherland, I didn't quite catch what you said."

I detected a slight scowl between her brows as it registered that I hadn't been paying attention. I felt rather foolish.

"I asked how you felt about working as a lady news reporter."

"Oh yes. I suppose we're quite similar in some ways, aren't we? Both unusual in our choice of employment." I smiled.

"I'd say that it was more of a choice for you than for me, Miss Green."

"Yes indeed."

"How do you find it?"

"I enjoy it very much. Every day brings with it something different."

I couldn't stop my eyes from straying to the three women once again.

"I shan't detain you any longer, Miss Green. You appear to have other business to be getting on with."

I felt a little guilty at the end of our conversation that I hadn't given Mrs Sutherland my full attention, she must have considered me quite impolite. However, I kept recalling Mrs Worthers' description of the three women and, as I strode off in the direction in which they had walked, I felt extremely pleased to have them in my line of vision again.

Sure enough, one of the ladies was wearing burgundy as Mrs Worthers had described. Another wore dark blue and had dark hair, and the third also wore a shade of blue. All three women wore hats and they were conversing with one another as they walked.

Surely they aren't planning to pickpocket the attendees of a fair organised to raise funds for disadvantaged children...

They paused to buy a glass of lemonade each so I stopped beside a jam stall close by.

"It's only thruppence!" a young voice piped up.

"I'm sorry, what did you say?"

"The jam," said a girl at the stall. "Which flavour do you like?"

"Oh, strawberry please."

She gave me a jar topped with a pretty square of fabric. I found a threepence coin in my purse and handed it to her.

The three women remained where they were, quite absorbed in their conversation. They weren't glancing around as if to plan an assault.

Could I be certain they were the street robbers... or was I merely imagining it?

One of the ladies turned unexpectedly and caught my eye. I swiftly looked away but felt sure I hadn't been quick enough. I moved away from the stall, her eyes still resting upon me.

CHAPTER 6

"So when's he coming back?" my landlady asked as I prepared to leave for work the following morning. She wore her customary apron and bonnet as she dusted the table and looking glass in the hallway.

"Mr Edwards' boat should hopefully return to these shores any day now," I replied. "I don't know which ship he's on, otherwise we'd have been able to look up its progress in the shipping news."

"No, not him. I meant your father."

"Oh."

"You don't know when he'll be arriving?"

"I don't think he plans to return at all, Mrs Garnett."

Her mouth dropped open. "He's not coming back?"

"I don't think so."

"After all that trouble the lovesick librarian's put himself to?"

"He's not lovesick any more, Mrs Garnett. That was a long time ago."

"But he still went to all that trouble, didn't he? All the way across the seas and all that searching in the jungle, and now your father's not even coming back!" She sucked her lip disapprovingly.

"I don't suppose anyone can force him to return."

"No, I don't suppose they can. He should be ordered to, if you ask me. The Queen should command it."

"I don't think the Queen could involve herself in an affair of this kind."

"Course she could. He's got a duty to his family and to his country. A man's risked life and limb trying to find your father and it's his duty to return. And if he won't, the Queen's soldiers should go out there and bring him back by force!"

"I'm not sure that would resolve anything."

"Of course it would. You'd have your father back!"

"Against his will, though. Once I've ascertained his reason for staying there, perhaps I shall understand it a little better."

"There's nothing to understand as far as I'm concerned. The man has a duty—"

We were interrupted by a knock at the door. Mrs Garnett answered to find a telegram being thrust into her hand by a messenger boy.

"It's for you, Miss Green," she said.

I hurriedly opened the envelope.

Come to Thames Police Station, Wapping.
James

About twenty minutes later, my cab stopped on Wapping High Street. Brown-brick wharves and warehouses, six or seven storeys high, towered above the narrow, cobbled road. A smaller, more attractive building of brown and cream sat between two of them. A sign beside the door announced that it was Thames Police Station, one of the stations belonging to the Thames River Police Force. The river itself lay just beyond the row of warehouses.

A small group of people gathered outside the police station, its members asking questions of a police officer wearing a black uniform and peaked cap. The symbol of an anchor was embroidered next to the number on his collar. He patiently ignored the restless group of people but admitted me to the station when I mentioned James' name.

I found him in a room overlooking the river and speaking with a police officer whom he introduced to me as Sergeant Bradshaw. He was an upright man with broad shoulders and dark whiskers, and he regarded me through narrowed eyes.

"The body of a young woman has been pulled out of the river," James explained. "It's not an altogether uncommon occurrence, but this poor girl has had her throat cut."

"How awful!" I exclaimed. "Have you any idea who she is?"

"None whatsoever," replied Sergeant Bradshaw. "There was nothing on her person that could give any clue as to her identity."

"Sergeant Bradshaw believes she hasn't been in the river for long," said James.

"Not long at all," added the sergeant. "The effects of water on a corpse are relatively swift, not to mention the damage caused by passing boats. The seabirds like to have a go too, if they get the chance. We're lucky we got hold of the body quickly enough to find her relatively intact."

James glanced at me, as if he felt wary that such talk should enter a lady's ears. I calmly wrote a few words down in my notebook.

"Her dress might give some indication of her background," I suggested, hoping as soon as I had said the words that her body had been retrieved fully clothed.

"Yes," said James. "Her clothing is quite simple and well-worn. Skirts, a blouse, a bonnet and a shawl. Her boots are also quite worn and show signs of having been repaired several times. She's young... between the ages of sixteen and twenty-one, I'd say. The slit in her throat strikes me as the obvious cause of death, but it's always best to await confirmation from the police surgeon, who is taking a look at the body now."

"Do you think she was already dead when she was thrown into the river?"

"It's difficult to tell at this stage, but my thoughts are that she was. Would you agree, Sergeant Bradshaw?"

The sergeant nodded.

"We'll know more once the police surgeon has carried out the autopsy," continued James.

"Do you know where she entered the water?" I asked.

"Impossible to say," replied the sergeant. "With a tidal range of twenty feet or more the river is very unpredictable." He gestured at the fast-flowing brown water in view beyond the window.

"What is tidal range?" I queried.

He gave an impatient sigh and explained. "It's the difference between low and high tide. It's usually about twenty feet, but it can be as much as twenty-three or so when there's a spring tide. The river's tidal down to Teddington Lock, about fifty-five miles from the mouth of the river. The last high tide was at around twenty minutes after one o'clock this morning, it makes sense that someone would have put her in the river around then rather than during low tide. The mud banks are exposed at low tide and a fair bit of effort would have been required to get her into deep water. Unless she was thrown from a bridge, of course."

"Could she have been left lying on the mud and then the river covered her?" I asked.

Sergeant Bradshaw gave a thoughtful nod, as if he hadn't considered this possibility. "We can't rule it out," he said. "But would someone do such a thing? If she'd been left lying on the mud she might have been seen. I believe whoever it was threw her into the river to hide her body. Perhaps they hoped she would remain in the water much longer than she did."

"Where was she pulled out?"

"Just off Cherry Garden Pier, across the river from us over on the Bermondsey side."

"So if high tide was at twenty minutes past one, the river would have begun flowing back into the estuary after that time."

He gave another nod, as if impressed by such reasoning from a lady who knew little about rivers.

"Then the water would have taken her out toward the sea," I continued, "but presumably the flow changed as low tide was reached. What time would that have been?"

"At ten minutes to eight this morning. She was found shortly before low tide. As she hadn't been in the water long, my guess is that she was carried in an easterly direction after high tide."

"And you think she was put into the water during the night?"

"Most certainly within the past twenty-four hours. Any longer than that and it would show. The river isn't kind to the dead, you see. I'm fairly sure she was in there for less than twelve hours. My guess is that she went in west of here, possibly in the centre of town but not much further upstream than that." He turned to acknowledge a constable who had been trying to attract his attention. "Excuse me one moment," he said, heading off to speak to him.

"A single cut to the throat," I said to James. "Is that the only injury she suffered?"

"The only *apparent* injury," he replied. "The police surgeon may be able to tell us more."

"She didn't appear to have been involved in a fight, though?"

"I saw no injuries on her person that might have suggested a scuffle. There were no wounds to her hands to suggest she had tried to defend herself. It seems to me that she was taken completely by surprise by the attack. It's possible she was approached from behind."

"Or restrained so that she couldn't fight back."

"Yes, that's another possibility. That would imply that there was more than one assailant. Her clothing shows no sign of having been disturbed, which to my mind rules out an attack of a more depraved nature."

"Her clothing suggests a woman of limited means, so robbery is unlikely to have been a motive, wouldn't you say?"

"She was wearing a gold locket containing a lock of hair," said James. "I'd say that had robbery been the motive, the locket would have been taken along with anything else she was carrying. She didn't strike me as the sort of lady who would have been carrying anything valuable. Money perhaps? It's possible she was working as a prostitute and was robbed for her money. But cutting someone's throat in that manner is unusual during a street robbery, and it still doesn't explain why the perpetrator went to the trouble of throwing her body into the river."

"It's as if they didn't want anyone to discover her."

James nodded. "There was no way of gleaning an identity from her surroundings or personal belongings. I recall a case similar to this one a few years ago, where a gentleman murdered his maid because he'd discovered she was carrying his unborn child."

I gave a shudder. "That could be a possible motive in this case, I suppose."

"The post-mortem will tell us whether she was with child," said James. "Oh, goodness! I'm so sorry, Penny. I should have been more careful with my words. This is hardly a conversation I should be having with a lady."

"It's me, James." I gave him a reassuring smile. "It isn't a pleasant conversation, but that's because it isn't a pleasant incident. Both you and I know that many unfortunate women and girls have lost their lives for that very reason. I'd rather forget about pleasantries for the time being and openly discuss who the perpetrator might be. It certainly appears as though the poor lady had either become an inconvenience or had upset someone. Maybe that someone wanted to silence her. Or maybe it was an act of revenge."

James gave a shrug. "I hope we learn more details about the case soon. Perhaps someone saw an altercation taking place down by the riverside last night, or perhaps some of her belongings were left there. There isn't a great deal for you to publish in the *Morning Express* as things stand, but when more people hear of this sad discovery we should hopefully see someone coming forward with information."

CHAPTER 7

I returned to the scene of the Piccadilly robbery the following day. I couldn't stop thinking about the gentleman in the velvet-trimmed jacket and top hat who had claimed that nothing was being done about the street robbers. The three women also intrigued me. *How were they managing to get away with their crimes?*

"Fewer customers are visiting me now," said the jeweller, Mr Sowerby, who was a squat man with oily hair. The latest robbery had taken place just outside his shop. "People are staying away from Piccadilly; I've never known it so bad. Last week a lady had her purse snatched as soon as she stepped out of her carriage! People are afraid to walk along the street in case they get robbed."

"Gentlemen as well as ladies?"

"Everyone! If these women can snatch a watch chain, they'll do just that. It seems to be purses and jewellery they're really after. Oh, and rings and necklaces. They'll take rings from gentlemen as well, you know. It happens so quickly, and these women are difficult to spot. They're always smartly dressed and they don't stay together. Instead, they converge

on their chosen victim and then pounce without warning."
The tinkle of the bell above the door sounded "Oh, good
morning, Mrs Worthers!"

We were joined by a lady in an olive green dress. She had
brown hair and freckles, and I recognised her as the woman
who had chased the three thieves a few days previously. She
greeted us both.

"I was just telling this news reporter, Miss Green, about
the scourge of Piccadilly."

She shook her head in dismay. "Something needs to be
done about them."

"I've been telling Miss Green how efficiently this gang
operates," he continued. "Everything is carefully co-ordi-
nated, and they blend into the crowds extremely well. They're
almost indistinguishable from my regular customers. These
women are very skilled, I must say. I like to think that I could
spot them, but I can't. And if I can't, how can my customers
be expected to?"

"They're outwitting us all at the moment," added Mrs
Worthers.

"I'm receiving calls to visit customers' houses so they can
purchase their jewels within the safety of their own homes. I
oblige, of course, but I always feel rather nervous carrying so
many valuables around with me. My son accompanies me
with his pistol, but what is the world coming to when we're
forced to take such precautions? I'm sure my shop will
become a target again before long."

"Have thefts taken place here before?" I asked.

"Oh yes, we've seen a few distraction burglaries. We once
had a lady in here with a male companion, and they asked to
see some diamonds. He was a very talkative gentleman, and
well he might be. No sooner had I laid them out than the
diamonds had gone up the lady's sleeve and they were running
out of here! I don't fall for it any more. In fact, I've most

likely turned legitimate customers away on account of it. A friend of mine owns a trimming shop up on Oxford Street and has women going in there wearing capes and dresses with all manner of hidden pockets. Gloves, lace, silk, ribbons... they take them all. At this rate he'll have to close it down."

"It's a disgrace," added Mrs Worthers.

"Have the police visited you recently?" I asked.

He gave a nod. "They've been in all right, but I can't say I'm confident they're on the right track. Lady Bellingham was apprehended last week by a constable who had mistaken her for a member of the thieving gang! She and her husband were absolutely horrified by the incident. She happened to be walking along Piccadilly with a friend and for some reason the constable considered them suspicious. I suppose it's not an easy job for the police. We complain they're not doing enough about the problem, but when they apprehend someone who happens to be innocent we complain about that, too!"

"So true!" added Mrs Worthers with a laugh.

"I and some of the neighbouring establishments have decided to pay for a beadle to patrol the stretch in front of our shops," said Mr Sowerby. "It shouldn't be necessary, but the police aren't coping well with this situation. And these women are so brazen! They're not afraid of the law one bit. Years ago, they'd have been hanged for such a crime but these days it's a spell in Newgate instead. It's not nearly enough of a deterrent.

"And in the meantime the business is struggling. Time is money, and if I'm having to travel to my customers instead of them visiting me here I'm not making good money. I'm looking at premises in Kensington now. This part of London attracts too many criminals if you ask me."

"May I ask about your circumstances, Mrs Worthers?" I said. "Do you own a shop on Piccadilly?"

"No, I—"

We were interrupted by the tinkle of the bell above the door as an elderly lady dressed in dark blue silk entered the shop.

"Good morning, Mrs Falkland!" said the jeweller jovially. "How are you this morning?"

"Nervous, Mr Sowerby."

"These robberies are giving you cause for concern, are they?" I asked.

"Absolutely! You can see my carriage waiting out there. My husband's valet travelled over here with me and he's waiting inside the carriage, armed with a revolver. We shouldn't have to do such things, but that's the sad state of affairs at the moment, unfortunately. Lawlessness, that's what it is." She eyed my carpet bag. "Have you come here unaccompanied? You ought to be very careful, you know. Someone could snatch that in a brief moment."

"That has happened to me before," I responded.

She made a tutting noise.

"I'm careful not to carry anything valuable around with me now," I added. "It would be a great inconvenience if someone were to take my bag, but at least I wouldn't lose anything important."

"But you could be injured! These women have pushed ladies to the ground before."

"I understand the risk, but I have no intention of letting people like that force me to stay at home. I want to get out and about. It'll be very sad indeed if people become too scared to venture out."

"I agree," said Mrs Worthers. "I won't allow them to interfere with my daily routine."

"And that's why I'm here today," added Mrs Falkland. "We want to show those fiends that life must continue as normal for us, albeit with a little extra protection. You wouldn't believe this was Mayfair, would you? It's like something from Buffalo Bill's Wild West!"

I left the jeweller's shop and walked in a westerly direction along Piccadilly toward Sackville Street. As I did so I pondered Mrs Falkland's words. I didn't like the thought of people carrying guns to protect themselves against this thieving gang, few people who carried pistols or revolvers were well-practised at using them. I shuddered to think of one being fired on a busy shopping street and innocent bystanders being hit.

I spotted a familiar figure speaking to a police inspector just beyond the junction. It was James.

I felt a grin spread across my face as I crossed the road and joined them. I recognised the police officer as Inspector Paget of C Division. He was a tall, thin man with a dark, wispy moustache. I had encountered him while investigating a murder in St James's Square.

"Penny, what a surprise," said James. "You remember Inspector Paget, don't you? He's been telling me more about the gang."

"We suspect it's the Twelve Brides," explained Inspector Paget. "There are one or two others it could be. The Bolsover Gang is quite active in the area and there's also the Portman Mob. But we think it's more likely to be the Twelve Brides. Theirs is a notoriously secretive gang solely made up of females from the vicinity of St Bride's."

"On Fleet Street?" I said.

"Yes. St Bride's Church is at the eastern end of Fleet Street, as I'm sure you well know. We've tried to make arrests but it's difficult because the gang members have proved themselves so adept at ridding themselves of stolen items. Now and again we round up the fences – the stolen goods handlers, I mean – that we know about, but it's difficult to prove who passed the stolen goods on to them. Despite our suspicions we have very little firm evidence. We've managed to arrest a few gang members over the past year but we've received almost nothing from them."

"They wouldn't talk?" asked James.

"It's partly that but, to be honest, they don't appear to know a great deal about the gang themselves. Ask them who's in charge and they can't tell you. It appears as though the foot soldiers are kept completely in the dark. We have a few informants on the streets, though, and the name Rosie Gold has been mentioned several times. It's possible she's the ringleader... or the *queen* as leaders of female gangs are often known."

"Queen Rosie Gold," I said. "She sounds interesting."

"We'd be very interested to have a word with her. I can't say that I've ever clapped eyes on her myself. She's said to change her appearance on a regular basis; she disguises herself, if you like. There are reports that she dresses as a lady, as her street robbers do, and at other times she dresses as a woman of the lowest class. Apparently she's extremely convincing whichever dress she assumes."

"So perhaps you've clapped eyes on her without realising it," James suggested.

Inspector Paget gave a nod. "It's possible, I suppose."

"Could there be eleven others?" I asked.

"What do you mean?" replied Paget.

"Perhaps Rosie is one of the twelve brides, and there are eleven more to find."

"I sincerely hope not," he replied. "I couldn't honestly tell you how the number twelve comes into it."

"A lot of people around here feel unsafe," I said. "I've just spoken to Mr Sowerby, who runs a jewellery shop. I spoke to one of his customers, too. Rather worryingly, they both said that people are beginning to arm themselves. Aren't you concerned that people have begun carrying weapons when they visit the shops on Piccadilly?"

"Yes, it worries me a great deal. We want people to feel safe."

"But they don't."

"I realise that, but my men are doing all they can, Miss Green. There's one of our constables now." He pointed over my shoulder. "I've just been explaining to Inspector Blakely that we've put a few extra men on the beat around here, and we've also been given some assistance by D Division. It's difficult to spot these thieving women before they pounce, and one of my constables regrettably tried to arrest an innocent lady as a result. You can't blame the man really, he was only trying to do his job."

"The shopkeepers are far from happy themselves," I said. "They've decided to employ their own man to keep guard."

"So I've heard, though I wish people wouldn't take matters into their own hands. We'll put a stop to these robberies and we're working extremely hard on it, but we can't do it overnight. I must say that it doesn't help to have every single incident reported in the press. It merely serves to fuel the hysteria."

"People need to know about these things."

"But it doesn't help the police, does it? We've come in for rather a lot of unfair criticism that we're not doing enough. If we could just be allowed to do the job at hand, I'm sure we'd be able to put an end to the problem sooner rather than later."

"The Yard will do what it can to assist," said James. "We'll speak to our informants and see what we can find out about this mysterious Rosie Gold. Someone must know something."

CHAPTER 8

Once Inspector Paget had continued on his way, James and I walked together along Sackville Street, looking out for anyone who appeared suspicious. I observed each lady we passed but it was impossible to judge whether any of them could have been a member of a gang.

"All things considered, any of these ladies could be criminals, couldn't they?" I commented.

My remark was overheard by a lady who happened to be passing, and she gave me a sharp look in response.

"I suppose we can rule out the older ladies," said James. "The descriptions we have gathered so far have all been of younger women. They would naturally find it easier to run at a fair speed when making their getaway. Those women we followed last time also had a clear route in mind. I wonder where they ended up."

We reached the top of Sackville Street and stood outside the public house James had inquired within on the previous occasion.

"From here they could either have turned left or right," he said, glancing around him. "Right leads into Regent Street, which is a busy thoroughfare. Three running women would likely draw attention to themselves there."

"Unless they slowed to a walk and simply blended in with the crowd."

"That's a possibility."

We turned left, heading away from Regent's Street.

"The jeweller told me about a friend of his who owns a trimming shop on Oxford Street," I said. "Apparently, the lady thieves hide the items inside their clothing."

"I've heard about them," replied James. "Does the jeweller think it might be the same gang?"

"He didn't say. There is a difference, though, isn't there? The Oxford Street gang is stealing from shops, whereas the Piccadilly gang is robbing people."

"It could be two separate gangs; however, both seem to have female members. It's possible we're dealing with a large gang consisting of separate teams that carry out different types of robbery. Perhaps this Rosie Gold character sits at the top of them all. We need to learn more about this gang but, unfortunately, Inspector Paget hasn't uncovered a great deal as yet. In the past, we've been able to send in constables disguised as gang members to infiltrate them but that can be rather difficult when it comes to dealing with female perpetrators."

"You need some lady constables."

"Perhaps that'll become a reality one day, but for now we must work with what we have. And before you even suggest it, Penny, I won't allow you to disguise yourself as a gang member. It would be much too dangerous."

"You forbid me?"

"I know I can't completely forbid you, but my advice to you, as a police inspector, would be that you mustn't even consider it. If they found you out, it's unlikely you would live to tell the tale. Just contemplating that thought upsets me dreadfully."

"I won't consider it, then," I replied. "After all, I should like to be around for our wedding day."

James grinned. "I'd rather like you to be around for it, too."

We found ourselves at the junction of Savile Row and Burlington Gardens, which was home to a number of smart four-storey townhouses.

"Let's walk up Savile Row," said James. "It'll take us in the direction of Oxford Street."

We made our way along the elegant street, walking past shops with the names of tailors proclaimed in gold lettering above windows filled with men's suits and hats.

"Talking of our wedding," I ventured, "I hope you haven't forgotten about our appointment with Reverend Crosbie."

"How could I forget?" James turned to me and grinned. Reverend Crosbie was the vicar of St Giles Cripplegate, which was close to my home. "I'm looking forward to it," he added.

"I must confess I've been rather remiss recently with regard to my Bible study," I said. "Is he likely to question us on it?"

"He'll expect us to know the most pertinent passages about marriage, I should think."

"Oh dear. Which ones are they?"

"I can't remember."

"And to think you've done all this before!" I laughed.

"Please don't remind me," said James. "And besides, I didn't pay much attention last time round because I was too distracted by the thought of marrying you instead!"

"I hope you'll be able to pay more attention this time."

"Of course." He took my hand and gave it a gentle squeeze. "I shall dedicate every moment of my time to it.

Besides, Reverend Crosbie won't allow us to marry if we can't recite the necessary Bible passages by heart."

"Won't he?"

"No. So you'd better start devoting every evening to Bible study from now on, Penny."

"Now you're just teasing!"

I pulled my hand away and James laughed.

The properties were smaller at the top end of the street, which soon became a narrow, covered walkway. We walked on through it until we reached Conduit Street; another bustling high street, and no doubt a lucrative area for the street gangs. We crossed it and made our way toward Hanover Square.

"It seems my days at the *Morning Express* are numbered," I said, telling James about my conversation with Mr Sherman.

"That's a great shame," he replied, "and it seems rather unreasonable of him."

"It's not his idea, of course. I like to think that if the decision were his to make, Mr Sherman would let me stay. He says Mr Conway would refuse to employ a married lady, even though I've worked there for eleven years!"

"Perhaps you could find work at another newspaper."

"If the *Morning Express* won't continue to employ me as a news reporter, I can't see why any other newspaper would. I expect I shall be limited to writing occasional musings on seasonal changes for ladies' periodicals."

"What's wrong with that?"

"It's dull!"

"It's better than not writing at all."

"I suppose it is, though everyone seems to have assumed that I'll be happily managing a household and children once we're married."

James smiled. "I can't imagine you being happy with that at all."

I took his arm. "I hope you don't expect it of me."

"Of course I don't. I knew long before I proposed that you had no intention of stopping your work."

"Unfortunately, it seems as though no one wishes to employ me any longer."

"I'm sure someone will."

"Why would they? There are plenty of other good reporters out there. Most of them are gentlemen, but there are a number of lady reporters, too now... *unmarried* lady reporters. I don't see why anyone would waste their time employing me when it's considered inappropriate by most people."

"But you're good at your work, Penny. You're an accomplished reporter."

We reached Hanover Square, where a number of large houses with classically styled facades overlooked a square piece of green, bordered by a line of neat iron railings. A bronze statue of William Pitt the Younger surveyed the environs.

"I'm happy to hear that you consider me to be accomplished at my work, James," I said, "but so are many other people. Increasingly so, I should add. During my time as a reporter I've noticed an improved level of professionalism among my colleagues."

"Surely you're not talking about Edgar Fish?" he said with a laugh.

"He does all right at his job," I replied tactfully, "but I was really referring to reporters from other publications, with the exception of Tom Clifford at the *Holborn Gazette* of course. And there are more ladies involved now. The progress is wonderful, but I'm beginning to wonder whether I'm to be left out of it from now on. Perhaps fate has decreed that it's time for me to stop."

"Of course it hasn't."

"What sort of wife will I be if I'm not seeing to the

household and bearing children? Surely you deserve a woman who is prepared to do those things?"

James stopped beside the Pitt statue and turned to face me. "Not at all, Penny. I'm marrying you because I wish to spend the rest of my life with you. I couldn't care less whether you choose to spend it managing our home or reporting for a newspaper. Either way I would love you just the same and feel equally honoured to be your husband."

"Would you really, James?"

"Without a doubt!"

"Thank you. If we weren't standing on a busy street, I would embrace you!"

He looked round about him. "Where can we go to enjoy a little more privacy, I wonder?"

I smiled. "There isn't time for that now. We both have plenty of work to be getting on with."

CHAPTER 9

"Who'd have thought it?" said Edgar. "Everyone seems to be running scared from a group of ladies! I can't say I'd object to being pounced upon by a flock of the fairer sex."

"Yes, I think it would make for quite an enjoyable afternoon," added Frederick.

I rolled my eyes. "Don't flatter yourself that they would have any interest in you," I replied. "They'd steal your pocket watch and be off before you even knew about it."

"I'm sure I could charm them with a word or two," replied Edgar.

Frederick laughed.

"Why don't you offer the Vine Street police your assistance?" I suggested. "It would be news indeed if a newspaper reporter single-handedly put an end to this wave of crime."

Mr Sherman entered the newsroom with a slam of the door.

"I like your ladies' column this week, Miss Green. You've

put together some good tips on protecting oneself against thieves and a nice description of the Hanwell Schools Fair."

"Edgar has an idea about how to protect oneself against lady street robbers, sir," said Frederick.

"What might that be?"

"By using his charm, sir."

Frederick and Edgar broke out into giggles.

The editor shook his head despairingly. "On a more sombre note, Miss Green, have you heard anything more with regard to the unfortunate girl who was pulled out of the river?"

"I've received no word with regard to her identity yet, sir."

"Let's hope they message her name to us if it's discovered before deadline so we can include it in tomorrow's issue. On yet another note, you must be overjoyed to hear that Mr Edwards is to arrive back in London this weekend."

My eyes widened. "Is he, sir? How do you know that?"

"I thought everyone knew it. The Press Association received a wire. The public will be very interested to hear all about his travels."

"As am I."

I felt an uneasy sensation in my stomach. *Why wasn't my father returning with him? What might his reason for not contacting his own family be?*

"Yes, Mr Edwards' story will make for interesting reading indeed," my editor continued. "Now then, Fish and Potter," he snapped, "no more larking about. This is a newsroom, not a school yard. I need a final draft on the German emperor's eighty-eighth birthday celebrations an hour from now, Fish."

"But the deadline is three hours away, sir!"

"And I suspect a good number of edits will be needed before then."

The editor left the room with another slam of the door.

Edgar sighed. "At least you won't have to put up with this slog for much longer, Miss Green."

"I wouldn't mind it if I did."

"You're only saying that because you're about to leave us. We shall miss you, of course."

"I might just miss you both, too."

"*Might?*"

"Oh, all right. Perhaps I will miss the two of you."

"Only perhaps?"

"You're more sensitive than I realised, Edgar."

"It's true." He adjusted his collar. "What will you do with all your spare time after you've left us, Miss Green?"

"I really don't know. If truth be told I've no wish to leave at all, but it seems the respectable thing to do."

"It's the way of the world," said Edgar. "A married lady shouldn't be out to work unless it's strictly necessary. I expect you'll keep yourself extremely busy, anyway."

"With what?"

"With all the things married ladies do. I'm convinced Mrs Fish works much harder than I do."

"It wouldn't exactly be difficult to work harder than you, Fish," said Frederick.

"And as for Mrs Potter, I've never met a more industrious lady! How many children is she rearing now?"

"Six at the last count."

Edgar laughed. "At the last count! I swear Potter forgets how many children he has sometimes!"

"I believe there'll be another one arriving in the summer," added Frederick.

Edgar laughed again and slapped his desk. "He *believes* there's another one arriving. As if he has nothing to do with it!"

"Sometimes I wonder whether I do. I must confess to

feeling quite superfluous in the Potter household these days. They're all girls, you know."

Edgar laughed even louder. "Isn't it funny, Miss Green? Six daughters for Potter here, and probably soon to be seven! The chap is most assuredly outnumbered."

The thought of bearing seven children left me feeling rather cold. I drew comfort from the fact that a good number of my childbearing years were already behind me. But there was still an opportunity for children, and I wasn't sure that motherhood was something I was either prepared for or would enjoy.

"My nieces and nephews are quite enough for me," I said. "I can't imagine devoting my time to child-rearing."

"You wait until you're married, Miss Green," replied Edgar with a wink. "Your life will change completely."

"That's what I'm afraid of."

"Why don't I ask Mrs Fish to invite you to some of her ladies' lunches? The pair of you have met a good few times now, haven't you? And I know that you get along well."

"That's very kind of you, Edgar, though I'm still holding out a bit of hope that I won't have to leave the *Morning Express*. I'm praying Mr Sherman will be able to persuade Mr Conway otherwise."

CHAPTER 10

I excitedly opened the telegram awaiting me on the hallway table when I arrived home that evening. It bore the news Mr Sherman had mentioned. Francis had just arrived in Liverpool and would be travelling to London by train in two days' time.

I climbed the stairs to my attic room pondering what he would have to tell us. I wondered whether he would be able to explain why my father hadn't returned home with him. Although I was keen to hear the explanation, I felt worried about what it might be.

Was I prepared to hear the truth?

I let my cat, Tiger, in through the window. She stood on my writing desk and rubbed her head against my hand. I gave her some sardines and buttered myself a thick slice of bread before settling down to write.

I was soon interrupted by a knock at the door, followed by my sister's voice.

"Penelope!" she beamed as I answered. "Wonderful news!" she added, waving a telegram at me.

"Francis?" I ventured.

"So you've heard too!"

"Yes, I also received a telegram."

"Isn't it marvellous?"

Eliza strolled into my room and sat down on my bed. She was dressed in her customary tweed jacket and matching divided skirt, which she wore when riding her bicycle.

"And before you ask, Penny, yes I did leave my bicycle next to the privy so Mrs Garnett cannot complain about it blocking the steps or the passageway. I'm sure it'll offend her in some other way, though." She pulled her hat off and rested it next to her on my bed. "I can't wait to hear what Francis has to say."

"Me neither. Aren't you a little nervous as well, though?"

"A bit, I suppose. But I just want to hear a proper explanation for everything. We've waited so long. It's been ten whole years!"

"It doesn't seem real, does it?"

"You don't sound as enthusiastic as I feel, Penelope. What's the matter?"

"I just feel rather nervous about whatever it is Francis is about to tell us. Why isn't Father returning home? Why doesn't he want to see us?"

"Oh, I'm sure he does. There must be a good reason why he can't."

"That's what I'm nervous about. It might be something that would be difficult to hear."

"I'm sure it will be. It hasn't been easy since Father vanished, has it? Aren't you the least bit excited about seeing Francis again, though?"

"I shall be very pleased to see him," I replied. "I must admit that I've missed him."

"Oddly enough, I have too. I wonder if he's still the same man he was before he left."

"I'm sure he can't have changed too drastically in six

months. It will be lovely to see him, but I think it might be rather difficult for him if he's to be the bearer of bad news."

"Bad news? What are you talking about, Penelope? Father's been found!"

"But there must be a reason why he isn't coming home, Ellie, and I can't imagine it's a happy one. Perhaps he has decided never to see us again." I heard a crack in my voice as I said these words.

"Oh, I see." Eliza gave a deep sigh. "I suppose we just don't know, do we? I can't see any use in upsetting ourselves before we've even spoken to Francis. Let's hear what he has to say for himself first. I shall invite him to tea as soon as I receive word that he's in London. His return is a happy occasion, Penelope, you must remember that."

"I will."

"I must thank you, by the way, for your introduction to the delightful Mrs Sutherland."

"You met with her?"

"She called on me at home after you mentioned my name to her at the fair for Hanwell Schools. We spent a happy hour talking about the work of our respective societies and have arranged to meet for dinner next week."

"That's excellent news, Ellie."

"She's a fascinating lady, isn't she? A lady of industry, I should add. She has a lot to do, what with the running of the family business. How she finds the time to involve herself in so many charitable causes I really don't know. She told me all about how she established the North London section of the Women's Rights Society. She said she would greatly appreciate an introduction to my employer, Miss Barrington, as she's interested in the work we do to provide homes and assistance for the poor."

"Perhaps she would consider establishing a similar scheme herself if she has the money to invest."

"Yes, I think that may be her plan, Penelope. Social causes rely on philanthropists like Mrs Sutherland. How else can any progress be made?"

"It is very important indeed."

"Anyway, how are your wedding arrangements progressing? I'm so excited about it, Penelope. And we can invite Francis now that he has returned!"

"Yes, of course."

It struck me that my father could also have attended if only he had chosen to return with Francis. Eliza's face became solemn for a moment, as if the same thought had just occurred to her.

"Mother will have such a marvellous day!" she enthused, attempting to brighten her expression with a smile. "She can stay with me, of course, and it'll be lovely to have her here in London with us. I'm looking forward to the ceremony at St Giles Cripplegate. And the reception is to be held at your home, is it not?"

"James' home," I said.

"Well yes, but it's to be *your* home as well. You're to be married, remember?" She laughed. "You won't be living alone in this little attic room for much longer."

I glanced around the small, cosy loft which had been my home for many years. "No, of course not, but I sometimes forget."

James lived in a tidy little terraced house on Henstridge Place in St John's Wood. I liked the house very much, though the area was a little quieter, and possibly less interesting, than the street I had been living on under Mrs Garnett's roof. "It'll take me a little longer to get to and from work," I added.

"Has Mr Sherman agreed to let you continue, then?"

"No, he hasn't, good point. I'm not sure what I'm to do about it, Ellie."

I wasn't sure whether it was the talk of our father or the

sadness I felt about stopping my work, but tears welled at the back of my eyes. Much as I loved James and wanted nothing more than to be his wife, my life was about to change quite drastically. It would take some time to grow accustomed to everything.

"Perhaps it's more difficult when you're older," I said.

"What on earth are you talking about, Penny?"

"I'm thirty-five, Ellie. I've lived my life a certain way for a long time. The change will be difficult to adjust to, I think. If I were twenty years old and still living with my parents, I should be enormously excited by the prospect of moving to a new home with my husband, but given that I'm so much older..." I trailed off, not sure how to finish the sentence. "What if Tiger hates our new home?" I asked. "I shall feel so terribly bad if she's unhappy."

Eliza stood and walked over to me. "Oh, Penelope." She put an arm around my shoulders. "Tiger will adore her new home, I feel sure of it. An impending wedding is daunting for everyone, no matter your age. It's entirely normal to feel apprehensive about it, even if you're marrying the person you love more than anyone else. You want to feel certain that you're marrying the right person, and I feel absolutely sure that you are. James will be a wonderful, devoted husband and the perfect father."

The mention of motherhood caused an uncomfortable lurch in my stomach. "I'm worried enough about my pet cat as it is," I replied. "I don't want to start considering children as well."

CHAPTER 11

The inquest into the death of the woman found in the river was held in an upstairs room at the Town of Ramsgate public house just a short distance from Thames Police Station. Heavily laden carts lumbered along the cobbles, and rough-faced boatmen touted for business beside the narrow passageway which led to Old Wapping Stairs.

"I'm sure Execution Dock was located somewhere around here," I said to James as we approached the public house.

"Where they used to hang pirates? Yes, I believe it was. And there they hung until three tides had washed over them. If they'd been really bad, their bodies were subsequently dangled off Blackwall Point in cages. There's a strong argument for bringing back such severe punishments."

"Ugh, do you think so?"

"Reserved for a select few of the very worst, perhaps." He smiled.

Before the inquest had even begun, the sombreness of the occasion was interrupted by the merriment of sailors in the bar rooms downstairs.

"I've had a word with the landlord about the noise," said the coroner's assistant. "These chaps have just arrived from the island of Saint Lucia, apparently."

"They could be a darn sight quieter about it," grumbled the coroner. "A proper courthouse is what's needed for an official inquest."

"There's talk of them building one at Poplar," replied the assistant.

"That doesn't help us this morning," retorted the coroner, rearranging his papers irritably. "Let's get on with it."

I was extremely pleased to learn that the girl in the river had been identified. Having realised she was missing, her family had called at a police station in Ladbroke Grove. We were told her name was Josephine Miller, and that she had been nineteen years old.

Her mother, Lily Miller, was a careworn woman who wore an eye patch. Her faded shawl was wrapped firmly around her shoulders as she stepped forward to give her deposition to the coroner and the jury, all of whom were seated around a large, well-polished table.

"Where do you live, Mrs Miller?" asked the coroner.

"Brandon Street."

"That's in North Kensington, am I right?"

"Yeah, Your Honour."

"And did your daughter reside with you?"

"Nah, she lived over Clements Road way."

"Which is close to your home in North Kensington?"

"Yeah."

"When did you last see your daughter, Mrs Miller?"

"Friday last."

The coroner consulted his papers. "That would be Friday the twentieth of March. Is that correct?"

"Yeah."

"And where did you see her?"

"She come over ours."

"At what time?"

"Jus' after midday."

"And how was she when you saw her?"

"She needed money." Mrs Miller gave a laugh, as if this had been a common occurrence.

"A lot of money?"

"She said a shillin' would see 'er right, but she'd 'ave taken sixpence if I'd 'ad it."

"Did you give her any money?"

"I didn't 'ave none!"

"Did Josephine have any form of employment?"

"Yeah, she was workin' down the dye works but she gave 'em too much cheek so they let 'er go."

"She was disrespectful to her employer?"

"Yeah, but it weren't just them. She give ev'ryone cheek, she did. I told 'er summink bad'd come of it. I told 'er yer can't go round talkin' like that. People don't like it!"

"Then Josephine was no longer employed at the time of her death?"

"None that I knowed of."

"And she relied on you for money?"

"Yeah. She must 'ave got it from other people an' all, cos I ain't got none 'alf the time."

Mrs Miller described how she had given birth to nine children, and how her husband had been a heavy drinker and regularly beaten her. He'd drowned in the Grand Junction Canal when Josephine was thirteen years old. Mrs Miller wiped her eyes with the corner of her shawl as she spoke and refused to be drawn on any suggestion that her daughter might have worked as a prostitute. She maintained that her daughter had been 'better than that'.

A sombre, sallow-cheeked man named Bill Chambers was called up next. He told the inquest he was an employee from the dye works and was aged twenty-one. He held his cap in his left hand and shifted uncomfortably from one foot to the other.

"You had been keeping company with Josephine Miller. Is that correct, Mr Chambers?" asked the coroner.

"Yeah."

"How long had you been doing so?"

"Since last summer."

"And when did you see her most recently?"

"The day afore she died."

"And where was that?"

"At 'ome."

"You lived together as man and wife, did you?"

"Yeah."

"At what time did you see her?"

"Abaht five o'clock. She told me she were off ter meet a friend."

"She left your shared home at about five o'clock?"

"Yeah."

"And do you know who this friend was?"

"Nah."

"She didn't tell you?"

"Nah."

"Did she often meet up with friends?"

"Yeah. She told me she were tryin' to get work off of 'em."

"Can you name any of these friends?"

"Some of 'em, but not all. I've told the coppers everyfink I know."

"You mean the *police*, Mr Chambers," corrected the coroner.

"Yeah." He gave a toothy grin, then resumed his sombre expression.

"And you have an alibi for the night of the twentieth of March, is that right?"

"Yeah. I were down the Unicorn on Princes Road. Lotsa folk can vouch for me, sir."

"So I understand. You returned home at what time?"

"I din't. I went round a friend's 'ouse, Tom Clavell. I told the p'lice abaht that an' all."

"When did you first realise that Josephine was missing?"

"I got 'ome at four o'clock next day and there weren't no sign of 'er but I thought as she could of came back earlier that day an' gone out again. When she din't come back that night I got worried." His brow furrowed and he wiped a rough hand over his eyes.

"What did you do at that juncture?"

"I wen' to 'er ma's 'ouse next day, and she said 'I ain't seen 'er neither', so we've went round askin' ev'rybody an' then we've went ter the coppers."

"The police."

"Yeah."

I watched Bill Chambers closely as he spoke and wondered whether he was telling the truth. There was little doubt in my mind as he stood fidgeting with his cap that he had an air of criminality about him.

Did he have a motive for murdering his common-law wife? Although he had alibis for the night Josephine had died, had he persuaded them to lie?

After hearing further depositions from Sergeant Bradshaw, the police surgeon who had performed the autopsy, and two of the men who had found Miss Miller's body, the coroner summarised all the details for the jury. They didn't take long to return their verdict: murder by person or persons unknown.

"I can't say we're any closer to discovering who murdered

Miss Miller now that we know her identity," said James as we left the Town of Ramsgate public house and walked along Wapping High Street. "And we have no idea where she was thrown into the river. If we could find the murder scene, there might be more clues as to what took place."

"Do you think Mr Chambers could have done it?" I asked.

"It's possible, yes, and his friends may be covering up for him, but the alibis he has for that evening are quite convincing, including one from the Unicorn's landlord. Besides, the couple lived in North Kensington and the closest section of the river, over in Hammersmith, is two miles from there. If Mr Chambers murdered Miss Miller at their home, I'm not sure how he would have transported her body such a great distance. In addition to that, officers from T Division have already visited the home and found no evidence of a struggle there."

"They could have gone down to the river together, and perhaps he murdered her right there on the riverbank."

"It's possible. The river loops north at Hammersmith and he could have thrown her in at that point. Poor Miss Miller's body was found at Cherry Garden Pier, which is opposite Wapping and around eight miles east of Hammersmith. However, we worked out that it's closer to twelve miles when you follow the river's winding route. Sergeant Bradshaw doesn't think her body could have been carried that far during the short period of time she was in the water."

"So she was put in closer to Wapping?"

"The next place to consider would be Chelsea. After the northern loop of the river at Hammersmith it loops south around Fulham. Travelling north again it reaches Chelsea and the riverside at that point is three miles from the home Mr Chambers and Miss Miller shared. Perhaps they went to Chelsea together. That's about six-and-a-half miles by river to Wapping."

"You think she could have gone into the river there?"

"It's possible."

"Your knowledge of river distances is quite impressive," I observed.

James laughed. "I discussed it at considerable length with Sergeant Bradshaw. He's the knowledgeable one. I would say that six-and-a-half miles is still a long distance for such a short period of time in the water. Miss Miller was last seen at around five o'clock in the evening and her body was recovered from the water shortly before eight o'clock the following morning. During that time she presumably travelled down to the riverside, where she was killed and thrown into the water. But where was she before she ended up in the river? That's what I want to know. She was either with Mr Chambers, who has provided a fairly reliable alibi for that evening, or she was with the mysterious friend he mentioned. Sergeant Bradshaw and his men are making enquiries at every public house along the riverside."

"There must be a great number of those."

"Indeed. But someone visiting one of those public houses that evening might have seen Miss Miller with her unknown companion. Perhaps the pair were seen drinking at a public house together, or maybe they were involved in an altercation down by the riverside. There must be at least one witness, though night fell shortly after half past six that evening, which doesn't help matters."

"Someone may have heard an altercation in the dark even if they didn't see one. They might have heard someone crying out or a splash in the river."

"They may have. And there are the bridges to consider, too. Sergeant Bradshaw tells me there are nineteen of them between Hammersmith and Wapping. Five are railway bridges but some have pedestrian access. And there is also Grosvenor Road train station on Victoria Bridge to consider.

This is where we need your help, Penny. We need to publish an appeal for information from members of the public. Someone must have seen something on one of the bridges or down by the riverside that night."

"I can do that."

"Thank you. I'll ask some of the other newspapers too, just so we can appeal to as many people as possible. I might even need to ask the *Holborn Gazette*," he added with a sheepish smile.

"Treachery!" I laughed. "Joking aside, this crime may only be solved with the help of witnesses."

"You're right, and at the moment we have none at all. We need to find out where the murder scene is. Without going into too much detail, a person's throat cannot be cut without making a great deal of mess. If the scene was cleaned up, a significant number of rags would have been needed to do so. And the culprit's clothing would also have been stained."

"And there must also be a murder weapon somewhere."

"Exactly! And we haven't managed to find it in Mr Chambers' possession. He's the most likely person to have harmed Miss Miller, but we have no evidence at all to suggest that he did so. Neighbours of the couple tell us they heard no argument between them on the day of the murder or in the days leading up to it."

"I suppose it's easy to judge a man of his class and character, and to simply assume he's the murderer," I said.

"I try not to do that, but you're right. It's easy to imagine how someone like him could do such a thing. What's crucial now is that we uncover the identity of the mysterious friend Miss Miller went to see that evening. The men from T Division are working on it, but they've had no success as yet."

CHAPTER 12

"He's here!" exclaimed Eliza, peering out of her drawing room window. "I can see him getting out of the cab!"

My heart began to pound. *How would it feel to meet Francis again?* My face flushed warm as I thought back to the moments when I'd felt sure he was about to propose marriage to me.

Eliza clapped her hands together excitedly. "Open the door, Mrs Burroughs!" she instructed her housekeeper. "Let him in!"

I glanced at James, who had given a bemused snort. "Poor chap won't know what's hit him once he steps through that door," he said.

Eliza was too impatient to wait in the drawing room any longer. As soon as she heard the front door open, she dashed out into the hallway. James and I smiled at each other as a shriek of delight echoed through the house.

"It's lovely to see you again, Eliza," came Francis' voice from the hallway.

"Come in, come in!" she shrilled. "Penelope and James are

here, too!"

Eliza stepped back into the drawing room with a man I barely recognised. Francis' skin had been darkened by the sun and his fair hair had been cut shorter than before, so that his fringe no longer draped over his spectacles. There was a leanness in his face, which had given rise to more defined smile lines around his mouth and eyes, and he looked older, wiser and taller than I remembered. He also appeared a little more handsome.

"Penny!" he grinned.

I dashed over and embraced him. As I did so, I recalled our fond farewell at Euston station six months previously. It was difficult to comprehend that he had travelled all the way to South America and back since then.

And found our father.

"I can't quite believe it!" I said, releasing myself from his embrace. "Look at you! You seem so different. And yet... somehow still the same!"

"An interesting observation, Penny," said James wryly. He stepped forward and shook Francis heartily by the hand. "Welcome back, Francis. It's good to see you safely returned from your travels."

"Good to see you too, James," he replied with a broad grin.

"Penelope and James are engaged to be married," my sister interjected.

"Is that so? Well, congratulations to you both! What wonderful news."

I smiled at James, feeling pleased that Francis seemed so genuinely happy for us.

"When is the wedding to take place?" he asked.

"The twenty-third of May."

"I'm sure it'll be a lovely celebration."

"We'd love you to attend," I said. "Wouldn't we, James?"

"We would indeed."

"Thank you," said Francis. "How exciting to have such a happy event to look forward to."

"Come and sit down, Francis," said Eliza. "Mrs Burroughs is fetching us all some tea. You must have missed drinking tea on your travels."

"I certainly did," he replied, waiting for Eliza and me to sit before he and James did the same. "They mainly drink coffee in Colombia, along with one or two other intriguing concoctions."

"Have you fully reacclimatised yet?" asked my sister. "It must feel like quite a shock to be back in this damp, chilly weather."

"I adore the damp and the chill," he responded. "I've missed it enormously! We had our fair share of cloud and rain in Colombia, but the altitude takes some adjusting to. When we first arrived in Bogotá I felt perpetually out of breath. It was most disconcerting."

"Oh, Francis, I could listen to your tales all day," enthused Eliza. "You must have so much to tell us!"

"I have, but all in good time." His face fell. "I need to speak to you about your father first."

"Yes, of course." Eliza grew sombre. "He doesn't wish to return home?"

"He may do in good time, but he wasn't willing to come with me right away. I think my discovering him came as quite a surprise. He's still growing accustomed to the realisation that everyone knows he is alive and well after all this time."

"Is he in good health?" I asked.

"He appeared to be and having spent some time with him I must say that he is a charming, intelligent gentleman."

"How did he look? What was he wearing?" I probed.

"He was dressed appropriately for the climate in a collar-less shirt and trousers which were cut off at the knee. His feet were bare, and around his neck was a necklace strung with the teeth of a wild animal. He told me they were jaguar teeth."

"Goodness!" exclaimed Eliza. "Do they have jaguars in Amazonia?"

"Yes, and a number of other large cats."

Francis' description was puzzling to hear. It didn't fit with what I knew of my father at all.

A maid wheeled in the tea trolley and began arranging the tea set on a table at the centre of the room along with plates of sandwiches and cakes.

"How would you describe his manner?" asked Eliza.

"He was extremely welcoming when I first arrived. Europeans do pass through that part of the world from time to time, so my appearance there wasn't entirely strange. However, his manner changed rather abruptly when I revealed that I was well acquainted with his daughters."

"In what way?"

"He became rather subdued and requested that we speak alone."

"He wasn't alone when you found him?" I asked.

"No. He lives in a jungle settlement approximately twenty miles from Cali."

"He lives with a tribe?" I asked.

"Yes."

"Are there any other Europeans with him?"

"No."

"How odd," commented Eliza. "I cannot understand why he would choose to live with them rather than returning home."

"After a while he told me his story. It all began when he and his guide fell down a ravine near the Falls of Tequendama."

"Oh, goodness!" cried Eliza. "Was he badly hurt?"

"Fortunately, he came off extremely well, especially when you consider that the poor guide lost his life. Your father believes himself to have been unconscious for some time, and then he lay on the ground for a while longer, unable to move himself. He still had enough water in his pouch to last a day or two or he would likely have died. He told me he had just about resigned himself to death from starvation, thirst or wild animal attack when he was discovered by a group of natives."

"Thank goodness for that," I said. "He must have been very frightened."

"He admits that he was, but your father is a brave man. The natives took him to a small settlement deep in the jungle. He had suffered a number of injuries during the fall, including a broken leg, broken ribs and a blow to the head. They nursed him back to health, though he continues to walk with the aid of a stick. Despite the natives' apparent care, they were rather suspicious of him and took away all of his belongings. He was left only with the clothes he had been found in, and they kept him shackled to a tree while they decided what to do with him."

"Why didn't they just set him free again?" I asked.

"He believes the tribespeople may have considered holding him for ransom, but he worked quickly to establish a rapport with them. The leader was an abrupt man, by all accounts, but one of his sons – a lad of about thirteen – was quite intrigued by your father, watching him intently from a distance for several days. It was then that your father began to entertain the boy with some of his parlour tricks."

Eliza gave a laugh. "I remember those!" she exclaimed. "Don't you, Penelope?"

I felt my eyes grow damp. "Yes, I do."

James handed me his handkerchief.

"A trick that enabled him to pass a pebble through a piece

of wood proved particularly popular," said Francis, "and before long the lad encouraged some of his friends to come and watch. Word soon spread that their European captive had magical powers."

Eliza and I both laughed this time.

"Gosh!" she exclaimed. "Did the parlour tricks save his life?"

"Your father believes so. He was asked to perform for the senior members of the tribe, who were quite amused. From that point onwards a mutual trust began to develop. Perhaps the parlour tricks impressed the tribe a little too much, they began to believe the arrival of your father was a good omen so they kept him."

"Like a pet lap dog?" asked James with a smile.

"I suppose so," replied Francis. "He was kept shackled most of the time, then after a while he was allowed some freedom during the day but remained shackled at night."

"Why didn't he try to escape once they had taken the shackles off?" I asked.

"He told me there was always someone watching him."

"Do you mean to say he's been shackled by this tribe for the past ten years?" asked Eliza. "Surely there must have been plenty of opportunities to escape during that time."

"No, this was right at the beginning," said Francis. "I think his detention lasted only a month or so."

"What has he been doing since then?" asked Eliza. "Why has he not returned home?"

Francis shifted uncomfortably in his chair.

"Did he tell you, Francis?" I asked. "He must have explained why he has decided to stay there."

"He did explain it."

"What was the reason?"

Francis cleared his throat before replying. "I'm afraid to say that your father fell in love."

CHAPTER 13

"W ith whom?" snapped Eliza. "A *native?*"

"Yes," replied Francis quietly, unable to meet her eye. I felt sorry that delivering this news to us was making him so uncomfortable.

"*How?*" said Eliza. "How on earth could he fall in love with a native woman while he was shackled?"

"He didn't relate it all to me in great detail, and I must say this is the part of our conversation I've been fearing the most since I discovered your father alive. I reminded myself that at the time of his capture he had been travelling through the jungle for approximately five months. And when one has spent that length of time in the jungle, one's ordinary existence here in England would naturally seem very far away. So far away that it would feel like another lifetime altogether, I imagine. Those who become acclimatised to the jungle soon adapt themselves to life there. It's quite different from anything we might experience here. In fact, it's not dissimilar to a fantasy world one might read about in a tale such as *Gulliver's Travels*. Although perturbing, and often dangerous, there is something incredibly intoxicating about the jungle. I suppose it's rather like being at sea for a long time. It wouldn't take long for a chap to forget about the former life he might have led back home—"

"But his family!" interrupted Eliza. "How could he forget about his family?"

"He never did. When I spoke of you and Penny, I could see that the topic caused him great anguish."

"Why couldn't he just return home with this... this woman he fell in love with?" Eliza asked.

"I don't think anyone on these shores would have considered such a thing acceptable. But, as odd as it may sound, he told me he had always intended to return. Perhaps he considered the love he felt for this native lady to be nothing more than a fleeting fancy caused by the unusual circumstances of their meeting. My impression is that he didn't only fall in love with this native woman, but also with the jungle."

I sighed. "He must have always loved the place, and maybe that's why he kept returning. It wasn't just for the sake of the orchids. He probably preferred the jungle to his own home."

"How utterly selfish!" fumed Eliza.

She slammed her cup and saucer down on the table, stood up and strode over to the window. Although I didn't feel the same anger, I shared the sentiment behind it. A heavy sadness weighed down upon me.

"He has betrayed us and our mother!" continued Eliza. "His own wife! We've been waiting patiently for him to return all this time, and to think he even allowed us to imagine he was dead! He spared no thought at all for our feelings!"

"The jungle can do strange things to a man's mind," said Francis.

"That's no excuse!" shouted Eliza, spinning around to face him. "Don't try to defend his actions, Francis! He was used to travelling in the jungle; he'd been there many times before. To forget his family the way he has and offer us no reassurance whatsoever that he was alive is inexcusable!"

Silence followed.

I fidgeted with the cuff of my sleeve as I struggled to absorb what Francis had told us.

"I have no desire to defend your father," he ventured, "I only wish to impress upon you the effects life in the jungle can have on a person. He had also suffered quite a serious accident, which may have altered his mind a little. Although I cannot agree with what he's done, I can almost see how he made this enormous mistake—"

"*Mistake?*" snarled Eliza. "It's more than just a mistake! He's completely ruined our lives!"

"I wouldn't say ruined, Eliza," I interjected.

"We thought he was *dead*, Penelope! We mourned for him!"

"I agree that the word '*mistake*' plays down the effects of his actions a little," said Francis, "but it certainly wasn't something he purposefully set out to do. It was initially his intention to return home then, after a while, it became his intention to send some sort of communication. However, the longer he stayed there, the greater his shame became."

"Good!" responded Eliza.

"The enormity of his shame became something he simply couldn't face. He wasn't sure how to go about explaining to his daughters why he hadn't returned home, or indeed how he had managed to fall in love with a native woman."

"Coward!" my sister cried scornfully.

"Please don't direct your anger at Francis, Ellie. He is merely the messenger," I said, feeling sure that Francis would eventually grow impatient from having to bear the brunt of Eliza's anger.

He gave an amused laugh. "It's said that Tigranes the

Great cut off the head of a messenger who had come to warn him the Romans were approaching. At least that fate hasn't befallen me just yet."

"I must apologise, Francis," said Eliza. "I'm just struggling to control my anger! Ten years have passed, Penelope. *Ten years!* All that time and Father never once sent word to us that he was safe and well. He allowed us to mourn for him... to believe he was dead! If he doesn't care about us, then I will no longer care for him. He is no father of mine!"

She marched back toward her chair and slumped into it before promptly bursting into tears. I walked over to her side and put my arm around her.

"Perhaps we've heard enough for now," I said. "We knew there was a possibility that finding out what had happened to Father might lead to upset. If he wasn't dead, we knew there had to be another explanation as to why he hadn't sent us any form of communication. And now we have discovered it. It wasn't easy to hear his story, but our questions have been answered. I'm sure Francis will be able to elaborate more over the coming days—"

"But why aren't you angry, Penelope?" She glared up at me from her tear-streaked face.

"I feel a profound sense of disappointment instead, Ellie. Perhaps I had long prepared myself for this eventuality. Whatever Francis had found could never have been completely good news. I'm comforting myself with the thought that Father is alive and well, and that he hasn't suffered a dreadful death. He's simply chosen another life. It's true that he thought only of himself, but that's the choice he has made. There was nothing you or I could have done about that, nor does it reflect any shortcoming on our part. He simply decided to become a different person and forget about us. I cannot deny that it is an immensely hurtful situation, and one that has caused great pain to us both. And to Mother, too."

"Oh, goodness!" Eliza let out a wail. "How on earth are we to tell Mother about this?"

"Let's not worry about that for today," I replied. "We have enough to be thinking about at present."

"He has never forgotten about you," said Francis. "I mentioned earlier that his manner became rather subdued when I told him I was acquainted with you both. He feels terrible about what he's done; he can barely bring himself to think about it. I could see by the expression on his face that the thought caused him great pain. I suspect he has tried not to dwell on memories of the family he left behind. My arrival served as a stark reminder of his responsibilities, and he found it all rather difficult to cope with." He put down his cup and saucer and rose to his feet. "I think it might be best if I take my leave of you all now. I've probably told you enough for one day."

"Oh no, Francis, there's really no need for you to go. I apologise for losing my temper," said Eliza sorrowfully. "It won't happen again, I can assure you."

"You are perfectly within your rights to lose your temper," replied Francis. "I'd have said much the same thing had my father behaved in such a manner. But I must insist on leaving now and allowing you all to get some rest. There is a great deal for you to consider and it's important that you take a little time to accustom yourselves to the news. There is much more to tell, and I shall be happy to do so in due course, but that's quite enough for today."

"Thank you, Francis," said James. "I think that sounds very sensible. We're all deeply indebted to you for finding the answers to the questions Penny and Eliza have had for so long."

I stood to my feet. "Let's meet again soon, Francis, so you can tell us more. If you're feeling brave enough, that is!"

"I promise not to shout again!" added Eliza, drying her eyes.

"I consider it my duty to tell you about everything I encountered during my travels," said Francis. "I know it wasn't easy to hear what I have said but, despite it all, I still feel pleased that we finally found him."

CHAPTER 14

My colleagues in the newsroom listened quietly as I told them the news of my father.

"I'm sorry to hear that he's chosen to remain where he is for the time being," said Mr Sherman sombrely.

"It's preferable to him being dead, I suppose," said Edgar.

Mr Sherman glared at him. "I'm not sure that's what Miss Green needs to hear at this very moment, Fish."

"Oh! I am sorry, sir. My apologies, I—"

"Please don't worry about apologising, Edgar," I said. "You're absolutely right. I'm relieved that he's not dead, and glad to know why he has been missing for ten years, even though the reason was quite difficult to hear."

Frederick remained uncharacteristically quiet, as if he felt fearful of saying something which might upset me. I had the distinct impression my colleagues were treading on eggshells around me, and it made me feel irritable.

"I've had long enough to think about all this," I continued. "I managed to consider just about all the possibilities during the ten years he was missing."

"Including the native woman?" ventured Edgar.

"The thought may have crossed my mind once or twice, but I refused to dwell on it. I had no wish to think ill of my father."

"And yet you probably do now."

"I won't pass judgement until I've heard everything Francis Edwards has to say. He has plenty more to tell us."

"He'd better get on with it," said Edgar. "We all want to hear it! Why hasn't he told you everything yet?"

"My sister has been rather upset by it all, as have I. It's just that she becomes a little more visibly upset, if you understand what I mean."

"I know exactly what you mean. Mrs Fish has similar tendencies."

"Hysteria!" said Frederick with a shake of his head.

"Not exactly," I retorted, "and Eliza is quite justified in being upset. I felt sorry for poor Mr Edwards who had to impart the shocking news to us."

"The jungle will have made a man of him," said Edgar. "Don't worry about Mr Edwards, Miss Green, you already have enough to think about. When will you learn the rest of it?"

"My sister intends to host a special dinner for Mr Edwards."

"We'll need to publish an article about this," said my editor. "Our readers will want to know why Mr Green has chosen to remain in Amazonia despite being discovered alive. We'll need to interview the chap at Kew Gardens who Mr Green was collecting orchids for at the time of his disappearance. I can hardly expect you to cover this, Miss Green, when the whole thing is so close to your heart. Edgar, do you think you could make a go of it?"

"I'd be delighted to, sir."

"And there's that explorer fellow who tried to search for Mr Green years ago and failed," added my editor.

"Mr Fox-Stirling," I said.

"That's the chap. It'll be interesting to hear what he makes of this new development. Seek him out, Fish, and see what he has to say for himself."

"You won't have any difficulty getting information out of him," I said disparagingly. "He certainly likes to talk."

"I hope you don't mind Edgar writing about your father, Miss Green," said Mr Sherman. "I realise this is a difficult time for you, but it's also a newsworthy story. The fact he has refused to return home is quite compelling."

"Everyone will want to read about the European plant-hunter who turned native!" said Edgar.

I gave a sad nod. Although it was painful to hear, my profession had made me well aware of the inevitable public interest in such stories.

"In the meantime, perhaps you'd like to write something more on the subject of philanthropy for this week's ladies' column," suggested my editor. "It's a popular theme at the moment. I'd like five suggestions as to how a gentlewoman can do her bit for good causes. Oh, and we'll need something on Easter bonnets, too."

"What, in particular, regarding the Easter bonnets, sir?"

"The newest shapes and how they should be trimmed. No doubt there'll be particular flowers or feathers that are popular this year. No lady should be without a fine bonnet this Eastertime!"

It had been apparent to me for some time that Mr Sherman had far more enthusiasm for the ladies' column than I did.

It was a pleasant surprise to find James waiting for me when I left work that evening. The buildings of Fleet Street glowed a deep yellow in the setting sun.

"I thought I'd come and find out how you were after Francis' visit yesterday," he said.

"I didn't sleep well."

"That's not terribly surprising. There was an awful lot to take in, wasn't there?"

"I suppose some of what Francis had to say was expected. His news overlapped slightly with some of the thoughts I'd had myself. The confirmation can be disquieting, nonetheless. Ultimately, I feel relieved that Father is alive and living a life that makes him happy."

"With all due respect to the fact that he's your father, Penny, what he's done is absolutely shameful! I'm not a father yet, but I cannot imagine how someone could abandon two daughters in such a way, and without a single word as to his welfare!"

"I suppose it all comes down to the shame he felt, as Francis suggested."

"Well, it's devastatingly selfish. How can one's own sense of shame ever become more important than one's family? I just cannot understand it. I feel worried about whatever it is Francis intends to impart next."

"I should imagine he's told us the worst of it now."

"I'm not convinced he has, Penny. Do you remember his words? *'There is much more to tell,' he said.* And judging by the expression on the poor chap's face at the time, he's not looking forward to it."

CHAPTER 15

"Tell yer what, why don'tcha block the 'ole road while yer at it?" a cabman shouted at the driver of a cart laden with barrels.

"It ain't me what's blockin' the road, it's the coppers!" the cart driver shouted back as he tried to turn his horses and vehicle around at the junction of Wapping High Street and Church Street.

A slew of curse words followed as I hurried along in the direction of Thames Police Station. A sizeable crowd had gathered outside it, and a group of blue-uniformed constables was attempting to maintain order. They had clearly been drafted in to assist the river police, as I could see from their collar numbers that they were from Stepney's K Division.

I had received another telegram from James, and the talk I heard on the street confirmed that another murdered woman had been pulled from the river. Word appeared to have spread quickly this time, with the death of Josephine Miller still fresh in people's minds. An early morning mist hung over the rooftops and my stomach was clenched into a tight knot.

"Why does *she* get to go inside?" yelled a pressman as one of the constables permitted me to enter the police station.

I found James and Sergeant Bradshaw inside. They explained to me that the woman had been found in Rotherhithe at first light that morning.

"This one's been in there much longer," said the sergeant. "Could have been a week or so." He gave an apologetic grimace, as if he felt he should have found her sooner.

"Is there no clue to her identity?" I asked.

"None. She appears to be a woman of low class, like the last one. It's difficult to be completely sure, given the condition of the body, but it looks as though there may have been an injury to the throat again. The police surgeon will need to carry out an examination to confirm it. The river isn't kind to human flesh, you see."

"As you've suggested before," I replied, hoping he wouldn't go into further detail. "Do you think her death might be connected to the murder of Josephine Miller?"

"The circumstances seem rather similar so far. She may have gone into the river at the same time as Miss Miller, but it just so happens that we found Miss Miller and not this one."

"Instead, her body was carried on up to Rotherhithe," I said.

He gave a nod. "Absolutely. They often get stuck in that loop of the river."

"I'm surprised she's only just been discovered," I said. "Shouldn't someone have spotted her sooner?"

"Not necessarily. Some float better than others, you see. Some get trapped among the bridge piers beneath the water for a time. The river only gives them up when it's ready, Miss Green."

The idea that the Thames played a deliberate part in

these tragic events lent a menacing character to the fast-flowing water beyond the window.

"In that case, might Josephine Miller and this woman have been together when they died?" I asked. "I can't see how a single assailant could murder both and throw two bodies into the river."

"He would presumably have met with significant resistance from the two women while they were under attack," replied the sergeant. "Which means they were either murdered separately or there was more than one assailant."

"Then the men you have looking for witnesses along the riverside must consider the possibility that the two women were together and may have been accompanied by at least two companions. They may need to look for witnesses who saw a group of people that evening."

Sergeant Bradshaw gave a nod. "It certainly means we need to consider more scenarios."

"Let's not forget the possibility that these two deaths are completely unrelated," added James. "It could just be a coincidence that two women were murdered and thrown into the river at around the same time."

I gave a sigh. "There's a great deal of work to do here."

"There certainly is, Miss Green," replied the sergeant. "Inspector Blakely has suggested that another appeal in your newspaper might help us find witnesses to one or both of these murders. Liaising with the press isn't something I'm personally accustomed to doing, but he told me you've had some success in previous cases after asking the public for help."

"We have indeed," I replied. "I'd be more than happy to write up the details of this second case and to ask whether anyone has seen anything suspicious down by the riverside recently. I should get back to the newsroom right away and make a start. With a bit of luck, the piece will make it into the second edition."

I bid James and Sergeant Bradshaw farewell and left the police station, making my way through the crowd of onlookers on Wapping High Street.

I hadn't travelled far when someone shoved me to one side. Before I could fully register what had happened, I saw a boy taking off with my carpet bag in his hand.

"Oi!" I shouted, giving chase. As I ran, I was reminded of the time my bag had been stolen in St Giles. "There's nothing valuable in it!" I called after the running boy. "Drop it now!"

I had little chance of catching up with him, but I ran as swiftly as I could. The boy had almost reached the swing bridge at Wapping Basin when a young woman stuck her foot out and tripped him up. He fell to the ground, his arms and legs sprawled out.

The woman bent down and gripped his ear. "Give it back, yer little gutter rat!"

The boy yelped with pain.

"Give it back ter the lady!" she ordered again as I reached them.

The boy reluctantly released my bag and the young woman let go of his ear. She grabbed the bag as he stumbled to his feet before taking off down the lane as fast as his legs could carry him.

"There yer go," she said, handing it back to me. She wore a shabby bonnet and shawl and her face was gaunt, but she only looked to be about twenty years of age. She had sandy hair and her eyes were a piercing shade of blue.

"Thank you so much." I took the bag from her, then reached for the purse at my belt. "Let me give you something for your trouble."

"I don't want nothin'."

"Please take it. You've been very kind."

"There weren't nothin' to it. I always do it when I see 'em robbin' people."

"That's brave of you."

"Them little urchins can't 'urt no one. They jus' run fast, that's all. Yer don't 'alf carry a large bag fer a lady."

I smiled. "It has my papers in. I'm a news reporter for the *Morning Express,* you see."

She gave a nod and glanced in the direction of the crowd outside the police station. "Yer bin reportin' on them girls they found?"

"Yes, I have. I don't suppose you know anything about them?"

"Nope." She began to stroll off.

"Thanks again!" I called after her.

CHAPTER 16

"There's a monster on the loose," said Eliza, shaking her head in dismay. She folded up the *Morning Express* and placed it on the table next to her chair. "How many more poor women does he intend to slay? You need to find this man quickly, James!"

We were sitting in my sister's drawing room awaiting the arrival of Francis, who had been invited for dinner. Eliza had dressed for the occasion in a loose-fitting scarlet gown which required no corset. Her dress reminded me of those worn in Pre-Raphaelite paintings.

"Everyone's doing their best," replied James. "The case has been extremely frustrating so far, and the police are hampered by the fact there is currently no crime scene to examine. If only we could find out where the two women were pushed into the river, we might be able to track down some witnesses."

"Hasn't anyone responded to the appeals for information published in the newspapers?"

"Many have done. Rather too many, in fact. The problem we have now is finding witnesses who have something useful to tell us among all those making wild claims about their own ability to solve the crime. I think we've lost count of the number of clairvoyants who've contacted us."

"Perhaps there might be something in it," suggested Eliza.

"In what?"

"Clairvoyance."

"I doubt it very much. I certainly don't know of any crimes that have been solved in such a way."

"I assume evidence like that wouldn't be admissible in court anyway," said Eliza, "but if they gave it a chance—"

"There's no need for that," interrupted James. "The methods we're using at the present time will serve us well."

"But you still haven't caught him!"

"Not yet, but we will."

I noticed James' jaw clench and decided to intervene. "It'll be interesting to hear what Francis has to tell us this time, won't it?"

"I'm not sure '*interesting*' is quite the word I'd use," replied Eliza, perching on the edge of her chair. "I'm feeling rather nervous."

"I feel sure he's already told us the worst of it," I said. "The rest of it is probably just... extra detail."

"What sort of detail?"

"I don't know. Just more information about his circumstances and so on, I should think. But whatever he tells us, Ellie, please don't shout at him again."

"I was upset!" Spots of colour appeared high on my sister's cheeks.

"I realise that. We *all* realise that. But he's only passing on the information he has found out. None of this is his fault."

"Oh, I'm sure Francis can cope with it," said James. "He's just travelled all the way to South America and back. I'm sure he can handle a little upset on the part of the Green sisters!"

"*I* shan't get angry with him," I retorted.

"Well, let me congratulate you, Penelope, on your remarkable composure," snapped my sister. "Perhaps my blood runs a little warmer than yours!"

"It merely comes down to having a little self-control!" I shot back.

"Self-control? How ridiculous! When I think of all the scrapes—"

"I think that's quite enough for now," said James. "It wouldn't do to upset ourselves before Francis even arrives."

"It's your fiancée's fault," said Eliza. "She has a habit of—"

We were interrupted by the housekeeper. "Mr Francis Edwards is here," she announced.

"Goodness, is he?" Eliza smoothed down her hair and patted her cheeks. "Very well. Do show him in."

Eliza seemed keen to make small talk before dinner, as though she were steadily preparing herself for Francis' next instalment. I felt impatient to hear what he had to say but decided to let the hostess steer the conversation.

"Well then, Francis," she stated as we began our first course of mock turtle soup. "What else do we need to know about our errant father?"

"I have a photograph of him," said Francis. "Would you like to see it?"

Eliza and I exchanged a surprised glance.

"Yes," I said firmly. "I'd like to."

He put his soup spoon down and retrieved an envelope from his pocket. Eliza was seated next to him, so he handed the photograph to her first. I sprang up from my seat and looked at it over her shoulder. We both stared down at the sepia print of a thick-whiskered man looking out at us. The shape of his brow was familiar, but there was little else about him to confirm that he was truly our father. The lower half of his face was hidden beneath grey whiskers and his skin was dark. He wore the collarless shirt and shortened trousers Francis had described to us, along with a wide-brimmed straw hat and the necklace of teeth. His feet were bare. He stood with one hand on his hip and the other holding a large, roughly hewn walking stick.

"This is him?" I asked incredulously. Then I felt a smile appear on my lips.

Surely this picture showed my father in native costume. This couldn't really be how he looked now.

His eyes were large and dark, just as I remembered. I recalled the same eyes smiling down at me when I was a child and a sudden sob caught in my throat.

Eliza put her hand on mine. "That can't really be him... can it, Penelope?"

"No." I gulped back tears. "Only... only it is."

"Ten years in the jungle can take quite a visible toll on a man," commented Francis.

"An enormous toll!" replied Eliza. "I'm struggling to believe it's really him. And I have many more questions besides," she continued, placing the photograph beside her soup bowl.

I returned to my seat next to James.

"Ask away," said Francis. "We have all evening."

Eliza cleared her throat before speaking. "Was my father living with this native woman when you found him?"

"Yes. They live together as man and wife." Francis' reply was perfunctory, as if he had resolved to impart the pure facts without passing judgement.

"Do you have any idea how this romance began to blossom?"

"As I understand it, there was interest between the two from a fairly early stage. Once word of his parlour tricks had spread, most of the tribe members came to enjoy his performances."

"He met this woman, yet was unable to speak to her?"

"That's right."

"Presumably he has learned some of her language by now," mused Eliza.

"Yes, and she has learned some English. They speak to each other in a combination of the two."

"You have met her, then?"

"Yes." He gave an awkward cough.

"What's she like? Is she a beauty?"

"She's a native woman of a similar age to mine."

"Then she is about twenty or thirty years younger than Father," I said.

"I believe so, based purely on my observations. I didn't ask the lady's age."

"Is she a beauty?" asked Eliza again.

Francis gave an awkward laugh. "I've always considered beauty to be a subjective matter, though she is relatively fair of face. She is a native lady, of course, and therefore dresses accordingly. It takes an Englishman a while to accustom himself to the manner in which these women present themselves. They wear very little in the way of clothing, of course."

Eliza tutted. "I see now why Father was attracted to her."

"She seems to be a pleasant and polite lady, and she is kept rather busy with her..." He paused to remove his spectacles, giving them a quick polish with his handkerchief. "I suppose now would be as appropriate a time as any to inform you that they have children together."

CHAPTER 17

I choked on my mouthful of soup.

"Children?!" exclaimed Eliza. "How many?"

"Four."

"*Four?* Are you hearing this, Penelope? We have *four* half-native siblings!"

She slammed her soup spoon down on the table and shook her head.

I somehow managed to swallow my mouthful and compose myself. "I suppose if they have been living as man and wife it's only to be expected that children would be born," I said quietly, still trying to comprehend this latest piece of news.

"The children are very polite," said Francis. "Their ages are nine, eight, six and four. The six-year-old is a girl and the others are all boys."

"Then he has heirs," commented Eliza bitterly, "albeit illegitimate ones. Excuse me for a moment." She got up from the table and left the room.

"Oh dear," said Francis, wiping his brow with his serviette.

"This is so terribly difficult. Poor Eliza. And poor you, Penny. I must say you're bearing all this news extremely well."

"It still doesn't seem completely real," I replied. "It sounds like a tale from a book of adventure stories. Next you'll be telling us he explored some caves and found the world's largest diamond."

"Perhaps he did," said Francis. "It wouldn't surprise me, truth be told."

James shook his head. "The man is a disgrace. Fancy setting up home in the jungle with a replacement family, and not a word to his wife or daughters about it! He has a lot to answer for. It's no wonder the coward refuses to return to these shores and face the music. It's no way to behave as a husband and a father. No way at all!"

"Perhaps there's another explanation," I ventured, still struggling to believe what I had heard. "Maybe the man you found wasn't Father after all, Francis. Perhaps it was someone else. He does look rather different in the photograph, I must say. I feel sure that Father would never have found himself a new... well, wife, I suppose she is. And children, too. It's just not something he would have done."

Francis said nothing but his eyes offered me a kind, almost sympathetic, gaze.

"If it isn't him, Penny," said James, "how do you account for your father's silence over the past ten years?"

"I don't know." I felt fresh tears pricking my eyes. "Oh, I don't know at all. I know it's him really... I just don't want to believe it!"

"This is what makes me so angry!" erupted James. "How could he do such a thing to you and your sister? He doesn't deserve to be called your father any more."

"Please don't be angry, James," I implored. 'There really is no need. Perhaps there's another explanation—"

"Impossible!" he snapped. "You must stop making excuses for him, Penny."

I removed my spectacles to wipe my eyes.

"It'll take you all a little while to grow accustomed to this news," said Francis. "That's the reason I imparted only a fragment of the story during our first meeting. There is an awful lot to understand, and perhaps some of it will never be fully understood."

"Not unless the fiend travels back to England and answers to his actions!" fumed James. "However, I don't suppose that'll happen any time soon. Or ever, in fact. I've a good mind to travel to Amazonia and have a word with him myself."

He fell silent as Eliza returned to the room.

"Is there anything else, Francis?" she asked curtly as she took her seat at the table.

"I could tell you more about his living conditions if you wish to hear it."

"I meant to say, is there anything else in the way of scandal we need to be aware of?"

"No. That is all the scandalous news I had to impart."

"Good. We have siblings, Penelope! Little jungle-native brothers and sisters! What do you make of it, James?"

"I've already shared a few thoughts on the matter, but I don't think now is the time for me to be drawn any further on it. Suffice to say that at the present time I consider your father's behaviour despicable!"

"Good," replied Eliza. "And do you agree, Francis?"

"Yes. I'm not sure why my opinion on the subject matters, but I do think it a most unfortunate situation. I can only repeat what I said the last time, however, that the jungle can do very odd things to a man's mind."

"Were you tempted by any of the native women, Francis?" asked my sister.

His face turned red and he gave an awkward laugh. "My, what a question to ask! Erm, no. I was far too busy with my mission to find your father to be distracted by other matters. He was imprisoned for some time to begin with, so he started off on quite a different footing. My visit, on the other hand, was only fleeting."

"What did Father say when you demanded that he return to England?" asked Eliza.

"I didn't order him to return. I could see that the man had established himself where he was, so I didn't immediately assume he would be ready to come back with me."

"What did you ask of him?"

"I asked whether he would consider returning home."

"Whether he would *consider* it?"

"You couldn't expect Francis to order Father to do anything, Ellie," I said. "We only asked him to search for Father."

"But I'd assumed that if Francis was successful, Father would return with him!" retorted Eliza. "I never, not even for one moment, imagined Father would willingly stay there."

"I don't think any of us did," I said. "I suppose the reality we all have to accept is that he was never waiting to be found. He has established a new life there. Had he wanted to return, he'd already have done so."

"What were Father's exact words when you asked him to consider returning home?" Eliza asked Francis.

"He told me he would give it some thought."

"That's all he said on the matter?"

"He went on to say that he hadn't done a good job of things—"

"He's certainly correct on that account!"

"And that whatever he did now, someone was bound to be upset by it."

"He's well aware of what he's done, then."

"Yes, he is. I explained how worried his daughters had been about him, and how they'd feared the worst for a number of years. He remained quiet in response, and then he left the shelter we were sitting in and walked away for a little while to spend some time alone."

I felt tears at the back of my eyes again.

"How long was he gone for?" asked Eliza.

"About fifteen minutes, perhaps. I waited for him and when he returned, he was quite visibly upset. He told me then that he felt he would never be able to face his family again. I sensed he was experiencing an overwhelming sense of shame."

"And so he should!" snapped Eliza.

"Maybe he just needs more time to consider it," I ventured. "It must have been an enormous surprise to suddenly be discovered after all these years. He probably hadn't given his home here much thought for a long time. He'd been keeping himself busy with his new family instead."

"But what about his *real* family?" asked Eliza.

"He simply forgot about us for a while... or tried to, at least," I replied. "I shouldn't think he ever completely forgot about us; he just didn't wish to keep reminding himself of his betrayal."

"That's what it is, Penelope. You've chosen exactly the right word there," said Eliza. "It is a betrayal."

"He's not the first to do it," I said, "and he won't be the last, either."

"I realise human nature is far from perfect, but he's our father!"

"An imperfect father. Much as we like to think our loved ones will never betray us, I'm afraid there's always the possibility it will happen. Perhaps, after Francis' visit, he'll spare some thought for the family he left behind. He might even write us a letter."

I didn't know what else to say. The thought of my father living in the Amazonian jungle with his new family was utterly bewildering.

Francis and James also seemed rather lost for words.

CHAPTER 18

Eliza sighed. "We shall have to go and explain everything to Mother, and it won't be easy."

"I'm not looking forward to it at all," I replied.

"Perhaps there's no need for you to go, Penelope. Out of the two of us I'm the one who has a more harmonious relationship with her, and you and James have only recently visited to tell her the news of your engagement."

"Let me come with you instead, Eliza," said Francis. "I'd be more than happy to explain my meeting with your father to Mrs Green. In fact, I insist upon it. That way if she has any questions, I shall be there to answer them."

"Thank you, Francis, though I must warn you that our mother isn't an easy person to deal with," Eliza replied.

"She deserves to hear as much of the story as possible from someone who has recently spent time with her husband. Or as much as she's able to contend with, at least."

"That's very kind of you, Francis," I added.

"With Francis with me I shall manage the visit perfectly well, Penelope," said my sister. "There's no need for you to come as well."

"Are you sure?"

"Absolutely. We don't want to overwhelm Mother with visitors, after all."

"No, we don't," I responded, feeling quite relieved not to have to face any more difficult conversations.

"We'll need to visit her within the next few days," Eliza continued. "I'll make arrangements with my employer, Miss Barrington, and then investigate the train times." She gave another sigh. "Well, I have no wish to discuss Father any more this evening. If he really cared about us, he would have come home or sent a letter at the very least. Besides, I have some good news I wish to discuss instead."

"Progress with your divorce?" I asked.

"Divorce?" queried Francis. "Goodness, I'm very sorry to hear about that."

"There has been no progress on that front at all," replied Eliza.

"May I ask who is petitioning for divorce?" asked Francis.

"I am," replied Eliza. "After George got caught up in that unpleasant criminal enterprise last year, I realised I no longer wished to be married to such a man."

"I can understand that."

"I've been trying to petition on grounds of cruelty. However, as George wasn't physically cruel to me, it's proving rather difficult. I want to make it clear that his cruelty related to the exposure of our family to the dangers of criminal behaviour, but my solicitor doubts that will get me very far. Apparently if I can add another charge, I may experience more success, so I've been trying to find evidence to show that George has committed adultery."

"Goodness, how awful!" exclaimed Francis.

"It isn't particularly awful, as I can find none whatsoever that he ever did such a thing. Which leaves me rather stuck. I can only hope that his failed attempts at a reconciliation will lead to him petitioning for divorce himself. It's much easier for a man to divorce his wife than the other way around."

"Just one instance of adultery on the wife's part is sufficient for the husband to petition for divorce," I added.

"Is that not the case for the husband?" asked Francis.

"No. A woman commonly needs more than one cause," replied Eliza. "It's all rather hopeless, anyway, given that George appears to have been entirely faithful to me throughout our marriage."

"A tricky dilemma indeed," said Francis.

"And not at all what I intended to talk about. I was about to tell you all that Mrs Sutherland and I are to found a new society together: the London Women's Rights Society."

"That's wonderful news, Ellie!" I sat back in my chair and grinned, relieved that we finally had something happier to discuss.

"Our inaugural meeting will be held on the twenty-second of April. I'd like you to attend and report on the proceedings, Penelope."

"I should love to."

"We intend to campaign on issues such as suffrage and employment rights," continued Eliza. "There's a great deal to do, but between us we're familiar with a good number of influential ladies. As Mrs Sutherland and I talked, we realised how much we could achieve if we simply drew upon the membership of our respective societies."

"Congratulations!" said James.

"I'm sure you'll achieve a great deal as a result, Eliza," said Francis.

"Mrs Sutherland is a very busy lady," Eliza continued. "She has generously agreed to provide a little capital, while I will devote any time I have outside the work I do for Miss Barrington."

"You'll be rather busy from now on by the sounds of things," said Francis.

"That's probably just as well, isn't it? I must say a little distraction is just what I need."

"Before you enter into that period of distraction, I should add that there is one further matter I must discuss with you ladies regarding your father," said Francis. "I'd like to seek your permission, if I may. The Royal Geographical Society has asked me to speak about my travels at a dinner. I could refuse it, of course, but I have received a number of similar requests to date. With the news of your father being found still occupying multiple columns in the newspapers it's proving rather difficult to escape the public's attention. It seems they all wish to hear about the excursion."

"You mustn't turn down the invitation on our account, Francis," I said. "If you'd like to speak, I think you should. As you rightly say, people will want to hear all about how you found our father."

"But the details of the discovery are not so easy for you to stomach, are they? It should really remain a private matter for the Green family."

"Father chose not to follow a private profession," said Eliza. "He courted attention when he needed it to fund his overseas travel."

"But that's no fault of yours either," said James.

"No, but we can understand the public interest. If you tell people all they want to hear in the coming weeks, you'll hopefully be left alone in due course."

"Whereas if you turn down each and every invitation people will only pester you until you relent," I added.

"There is that, I suppose."

"As long as we're already aware of everything you intend to speak about, that is," said Eliza. "It would be quite upsetting if anything were to come out at one of these appearances that you hadn't divulged to us."

"I won't disclose anything I haven't told you about first," replied Francis. "You have my word on that."

CHAPTER 19

News of my father's indiscretions spread a little faster than I had anticipated. As I passed by the newspaper reading room at the British Library, I was surprised to read how detailed the reports were. The news of his common-law wife and children had been relayed with great sensation.

The *Illustrated London News* caught my eye. It bore a large illustration on the cover based on the photograph Francis had shown us of my father. Within its pages were countless imagined scenes of him going about his daily life in the jungle with his new family. I was only able to view a few before my stomach gave a sickening twist. *What right did any publication have to speculate on my father's life in this way?*

I reluctantly turned to *The Holborn Gazette* to see how the *Morning Express'* embittered rival had decided to report on the discovery of my Father's indiscretions.

Scandalous news has emerged from the depths of Amazonia where once-renowned plant-hunter, Mr. Frederick Brinsley Green, has been discovered living as a native. It is reported by the explorer Mr. Francis Edwards that Mr. Green has made a comfortable living for himself with a common-law native wife and four native children. The discovery has put an end to the mystery surrounding the fate of Mr. Green, following his disappearance in the jungle ten years ago.

The initial encounter between Mr. Edwards and Mr. Green brings to mind the famous meeting of Dr. David Livingstone and Mr. Morton Stanley on the shores of Lake Tanganyika in Africa in 1871. One can only speculate as to whether Mr. Edwards repurposed the immortal greeting and uttered the words: "Mr. Green, I presume?" Unlike the diligent and industrious Dr. Livingstone, however, Mr. Green has opted to pursue a life of languor among the kapok trees.

Perhaps unsurprisingly, the former paragon of plant-hunting has chosen not to return home but prefers to remain in the jungle rather than face his legitimate wife and children. And well he might. With one daughter, Miss Penelope Green, causing a breach of promise action to be brought against an inspector at Scotland Yard, and the other, Mrs. Eliza Billington-Grieg, petitioning to divorce her husband, Mr. Green would be well advised to remain within the relative peace of the Amazonian jungle.

These barbed words were no more than I expected from the *Holborn Gazette*. I gritted my teeth and folded the newspaper away. As I did so, a headline caught my eye: '*Another Robbery on Piccadilly*'. This time a lady had required the attentions of a doctor after receiving injuries to her face during the robbery. I sighed deeply and wondered how Inspector Paget was faring with his investigation.

In the meantime, I had to get word to Eliza urging her to visit Mother as soon as possible. The quickest way to communicate this to her was by telegram from the post office on Great Russell Street. I left the newspaper reading room and scurried toward the exit. In doing so I almost hurtled directly into Francis.

"Penny!" he exclaimed. "Goodness, you're in a terrible hurry!"

"Hello, Francis. Yes, Ellie needs to go to see Mother right away. The papers are printing the news about Father's common-law wife."

His suntanned face paled a little. "Oh gosh, already? Word has spread very swiftly indeed!"

"When were you and Eliza planning to visit?"

"Tomorrow, but it sounds as though it must be today instead. We cannot have your mother finding out what has happened from the newspapers. I'm at a loss to understand how they already know so much."

"Who have you told?"

"Apart from you, Eliza and James, I have told only Mr Price at Kew Gardens and a chap called Mr Smith at the Royal Geographical Society."

"They've clearly shown no hesitation in spreading the news. It's all rather scandalous and entertaining to them, I suppose."

"I came here this morning to revisit my old stomping ground, but that can wait. I'll take a cab to Bayswater immediately and summon your sister."

"Thank you, Francis. I was just about to send her a telegram. How lucky it is that I bumped into you here this morning."

"Very fortunate indeed! I shall be on my way."

"Thank you, and good luck with Mother. You'll need it!"

I worked in the reading room for the remainder of the morning and, as I walked toward the *Morning Express* offices at lunchtime, I hoped Eliza and Francis had already boarded the train bound for Derby. The journey only took two hours from Euston station, so with any luck they would be with Mother by late afternoon.

"Miss Green!" Edgar greeted me as I arrived at the office. "Are you all right?"

"Yes," I replied. "Why wouldn't I be?"

"Well, in light of these, er... these rather unfortunate revelations about your father being made public... It can't be particularly pleasant for you."

"I'm mainly thinking of my mother," I replied. "Francis' story was published before we had a chance to tell her everything."

"Oh dear. Why did he allow that?"

"He didn't do it on purpose. He just happened to have spoken to a couple of people, who then presumably decided to inform the press. The *Illustrated London News* has published countless made-up illustrations of him! Fortunately, Mother won't be able to buy a copy of that up in Derbyshire."

"I'm so sorry, Miss Green. I really don't know how it must feel to discover that one's father is a bigamist."

"Is he a bigamist?" asked Frederick. "He hasn't married the native woman, has he?"

"She's his common-law wife, so it's more or less the same thing, isn't it?" replied Edgar. "But even if he had married her, I don't suppose it would be recognised here in the eyes of the law, would it? I can't imagine marriages in the Amazonian jungle being legally binding in England."

"And now there are four little Green natives running about!" added Frederick. "Are you tempted to travel over there to meet your new family, Miss Green?"

Although I had resigned myself to the topic being openly discussed, I found Frederick's comments a little too flippant.

He smiled awkwardly in response to my steely stare, then quickly apologised.

Mr Sherman marched into the newsroom. "I hear young Francis Edwards is to address the Royal Geographical Society about his travels to Colombia."

"Yes. He's received a great deal of interest from people who wish to hear how he went about finding Father."

Mr Sherman must have noticed something in my expression that suggested I was growing tired of the topic. "Well done with the tips for ladies on guarding themselves against street robbery, Miss Green," he said. "We've received several nice letters from ladies who were very appreciative of the advice. What's the latest on the two young women found in the river?"

"The second girl's identity remains unknown," I said. "And there is no explanation yet as to how either of them ended up in the river."

"Then the latest news is that there is no news."

"Unfortunately, no. I shall visit Inspector Paget at Vine Street this afternoon to find out what progress he has made with the street robberies, if any."

"Good. It would be helpful if the police could make a bit of progress with something."

CHAPTER 20

"We have found a young lady who's willing to lead us to Rosie Gold," said Inspector Paget. We stood in the parade room of Vine Street station just outside the doorway to his office. "She's an informant who was introduced to us by the Yard."

"A brave lady from the sound of things," I commented, quickly scribbling down some notes in my notebook. "What has she been able to tell you so far?"

"That Miss Gold often frequents the Mondragon Hotel. My men have now become regular visitors to the place. In plain clothes, of course."

"Have they seen her there?"

"Not yet. They're working on making their faces known in the establishment, so that once they become more familiar with the staff they can begin to earn their trust. These things take time."

"Can't your men just go in there one evening and arrest her?"

He stroked his wispy moustache. "I'm afraid it's not that simple, Miss Green. For one thing we need to be certain she's at the hotel when we raid it. And we can't always be sure what the woman will look like. As I've explained, she regularly changes her appearance."

"What do you know about her so far?"

"That she is between the ages of twenty-five and thirty-five. She's slight in stature and the colour of her hair is said to vary from fair to brown. She also wears wigs when it suits her."

"Anything else?"

"There's a rumour that she's the daughter of a timber merchant, but we have no idea who he might be. Rosie Gold isn't her real name, of course."

"And you don't know her real name?"

"She's used a number of different ones in the past, including Emily and Jane with the surname Bartlett."

"Has she ever been arrested before?"

"If she has, it was under a name we're not yet aware of."

"Do you know where she lives?"

"We have a number of possible addresses, though these people typically move around to escape detection. My men are quietly investigating the houses we know about, but we need to make sure she doesn't get wind of what we're doing or she's likely to take off."

"And all the while the street robberies are still occurring."

"Yes, unfortunately they are. It appears to be business as usual for the Twelve Brides, which I suppose is a good sign as they don't appear to be aware that the net is closing in around them."

"Is it closing in around them, Inspector?"

"It will do soon, Miss Green, without a doubt. This informant is proving rather useful, I must say."

"I hope she's being careful. If the Twelve Brides find out what she's up to she could find herself in serious trouble."

As I left the newsroom and stepped out onto Fleet Street that evening, I noticed a young woman standing nearby, as if she were waiting for someone. On second glance I felt sure that I recognised her. She had the same piercing blue eyes as the sandy-haired girl who had rescued my carpet bag in Wapping. My first thought was that she had changed her mind about accepting some money for her trouble.

"Are you waiting for me?" I asked.

"Yeah."

"If it's money you want..." I reached for my purse once more.

She gave a laugh. "I don't want none of yer money."

"What is it you want?"

"I think we can 'elp each other."

"With what?"

She glanced around, as if worried that someone might overhear.

"Let's step inside," I suggested. "We can talk in there."

We climbed up one flight of stairs to get away from the rumble of the printing presses in the basement, then stood together on the little landing.

"Is here all right?" I asked.

"Yeah."

"How can we help each other?" I asked.

"I weren't quite honest with yer last time I saw yer."

"What do you mean?"

"I said I didn't know nothin' about them girls in the river, and I don't know 'em as such. But I know who they was working for."

"Who?"

"The Twelve Brides." Her voice was barely louder than a whisper now.

"Really?" My heart skipped at this revelation, but I tried to remain calm. "Both girls were members of the gang?"

"Yeah. And they stepped outta line."

"What did they do?"

"I dunno exactly."

"Are you also a member of the Twelve Brides?" I asked.

She gave a nod. "But I wanna leave. I don't like what's bin 'appenin', I don't want no more murders."

"My good friend is a police inspector at Scotland Yard—"

She took a step back. "I ain't talkin' to no one else. I chose yer cos yer a news reporter and yer know about a lot o' stuff."

I laughed. "I'm not sure about that."

"You gotta be clever ter be a reporter, an' that's why I called on yer. And yer a lady. I trust women better 'n men."

"What do you want from me?"

"I need someone clever ter look at somethin'. I ain't got it 'ere with me now, but I'll bring it yer."

"What is it?"

"Yer'll see."

"When?"

"I'll come find yer."

"Will you tell me more about the Twelve Brides?"

"Mebbe." She started walking back toward the staircase.

"I'll help you if you help me," I said. "Do we have an agreement?"

She nodded.

"At least tell me your name before you go!" I called after her.

"Sarah," she called back.

"I'm Miss Green," I replied.

And then she was gone.

"I've read all the newspapers, Miss Green, and I must say I'm terribly sorry about it all," said my landlady, Mrs Garnett.

She was standing in the hallway when I returned home that evening, and I suspected she had been waiting there for me.

"Thank you, Mrs Garnett, though it's hardly your fault, so there really isn't any need for you to say sorry."

"I meant it as a token of sympathy," she said. "It really is terrible news. What a way for your father to behave!"

"None of it sounds particularly honourable," I agreed. "However, the jungle is a different world altogether. Francis Edwards told us it can quite easily alter a man's mind."

After hearing such regular criticism of my father's actions, I was beginning to feel as though I should try to defend him in some way.

"That's no excuse," she retorted. "He's a married man with a family!"

"I know that only too well, Mrs Garnett. I wish we'd received an explanation directly from him, but I don't suppose that will ever happen now."

"He should write you a letter and explain himself."

"Yes, he could do that. It's not easy to send letters from the jungle, though." I realised I was just making excuses, as if attempting to soften the blow.

Mrs Garnett sucked her lip disapprovingly. "If he really wanted to send you a letter he'd travel to a civilised place and send one from there! There really is no excuse for it."

"No, I suppose not." I felt a heavy sensation in my chest as I turned away and began to climb the staircase to my room.

"Miss Green?" ventured my landlady. "I'm sorry. I didn't mean to direct my anger at you. I just can't understand why someone would do such a thing."

"Neither can I," I said, continuing to climb the stairs. "But I'm a little tired of hearing about it now."

"Miss Green?" she called again, clearly aware that I had been upset by the encounter.

"Yes?" I stopped on the top stair and turned to face her.

"I'm sorry," she said again. "You deserve better."

I cuddled Tiger when I reached my room and felt immensely grateful that she was unable to speak and was therefore incapable of pouring further scorn on my father's actions.

I glanced at the typewritten pile of notes on my desk which I had put together for the unfinished book I was writing about his life. I had begun the work as a tribute to him. My frame of mind had been quite different back then, when we had assumed he was dead. I wondered if I would ever find the enthusiasm to resume my work on it again. If only he had decided to return home, I could have spoken to him face to face. It was difficult to make up my mind about it all without hearing an explanation directly from him.

I pictured Eliza and Francis sitting on the uncomfortable settee in Mother's parlour. *What on earth would Mother make of what they had to tell her? Was it possible that such unexpected news might affect her health?*

CHAPTER 21

I told James about the mysterious Sarah as we walked along a busy Fore Street toward St Giles Cripplegate for another discussion with Reverend Crosbie about our forthcoming marriage.

"The Twelve Brides again," he mused. "This girl Sarah suggested the gang was responsible for the murders of the young women found in the river, is that right?"

"Yes. And that's why it's even more important that Rosie Gold is found right away," I said. "It sounds as though Inspector Paget is getting closer."

"The Yard could assist him if it transpires that the woman is a murderer. We can't be entirely sure Sarah is telling the truth, though. Did she tell you her surname?"

"No, and I don't suppose we can be certain her name is Sarah, either. She may have given me a false name."

"It's imperative that we speak with her again."

"I realise that, but I have no idea where to find her."

James shook his head. "How very frustrating."

"She told me she wants me to help her with something."

"What is it?"

"I don't know yet. She said she'd bring it to me, so that suggests I shall hopefully see her again. She told me she wants the murders to stop."

"We all want the murders to stop! She'd be a darn sight more helpful if she'd just speak to us about it. She didn't tell you anything more about the second girl who was murdered, did she?"

"No."

"I'm not surprised but if she agreed to help us, we could go some way to protecting her."

"Shall I tell her that the next time I see her?"

"If there is a next time. I'll share the information with Paget as soon as we've finished with the reverend this morning."

We walked through a passageway which opened out into the churchyard. Ancient walls separated this small haven from the surrounding huddle of buildings.

"How do you feel about your father now you've had some time to absorb Francis' revelations?" James asked.

"I think he's a fool," I replied, "but I'm holding out hope that he'll return home at some point."

"Do you really think so?"

"Yes, I have to believe it. I imagine Francis' visit will have prompted him to reflect on his actions, in any case."

"But he didn't send any form of communication for ten years."

I sighed. "I realise that. Perhaps it's just a vain hope of mine that he'll return one day."

"I think it quite honourable of you, Penny, to think that, despite everything he's done, your father might attempt to make peace with his family again."

"His *first* family," I added.

"Ah, yes." James shook his head. "It's all quite astonishing."

"I hope Francis and Eliza's meeting with Mother went as well as could be expected yesterday. It was extremely brave on Francis' part to tell her the news about her errant husband."

James laughed. "Your mother isn't that bad!"

"I suppose Francis handled Eliza's anger well, so hopefully he'll be able to cope with Mother in the same way."

"Yes indeed. He has a certain sangfroid about him, doesn't he?"

"I suppose you have to remain calm when you find yourself facing life-threatening situations in Amazonia."

"Was he ever in a life-threatening situation?"

"He nearly died of the fever."

"That's true."

"And he must have had altercations with people who didn't take kindly to yet another European exploring their land. Nothing seems to bother him, does it? He's able to remain calm in any situation life throws at him."

"In which case, talking to your mother shouldn't trouble him at all."

"I suppose not. Still, it's extremely kind of him to offer. He didn't have to."

"Brave and kind Francis."

"What do you mean by that?"

"I'm merely stating his qualities."

I stopped and turned to face him beside the door to the church. "You're not merely *stating* them. You mentioned them as though you felt put out by something."

"Such as?"

"Perhaps you're envious because he's been the centre of attention over the past few days."

James gave a dry laugh. "That's something to be envious of, is it? Francis Edwards being the cynosure of all eyes? I can tell you now that I'm not even a tiny bit envious of the chap, nor have I ever been!"

"So why make the comment in the first place?"

"To be frank with you, Penny, I'm a little tired of hearing all the eulogies to Francis. I understand he's achieved a tremendous amount, and I'm incredibly pleased that you finally know what happened to your father, but I think the hero's welcome is dragging on a little."

"I've waited a long time to find out about my father, James."

"I realise that."

"It's the fact that it's Francis, isn't it?" I said. "I don't believe you'll ever truly like him."

"You misunderstand me, Penny; I like the chap enormously! But he did wish to marry you at one time."

"That's long forgotten about now. No one has even given it any further thought... apart from you, it seems. At least I wasn't engaged to marry him!"

"Oh come now, there's no need to mention *her*."

"Why not? If you're determined to keep mentioning the fact that Francis once wished to marry me, I shall occasionally mention the fact that you once agreed to marry Charlotte Jenkins."

"I don't ever want to hear that woman's name again!"

"Then stop all this nonsense about Francis. He's a good man."

"Of course he is."

"And if everyone seems to be full of praise for him at the present time, it's for an extremely good reason. You'll simply have to endure our high opinions of him for a little while longer."

At that moment the church door swung open and Reverend Crosbie greeted us with a smile. "I see the happy couple has arrived!"

CHAPTER 22

There was a knock at my door that evening.

"Miss Green?" came Mrs Garnett's voice. "There's a young lady here to see you."

I opened the door with Tiger in my arms. As soon as she saw the two women the cat leapt down onto the floor with a thud and ran away to hide.

"Sarah!" I greeted the girl with a grin, relieved she had come to see me again. "How did you know I lived here?"

"I looked yer up in the direct'ry."

"I see." I realised she must be extremely keen to have my help, whatever form that might take. "Come in," I said, stepping aside.

Mrs Garnett gave us a bemused glance, clearly wondering who the girl was and what she was doing visiting her house at such an hour.

"Thank you, Mrs Garnett," I said, nudging the door as if to close it.

"You'll be all right, will you, Miss Green?" she asked.

"Yes, fine, thank you." I shut the door and turned toward my guest. "Please take a seat. There aren't many places to sit but there's a chair here beside my writing desk."

She perched on the edge of the chair. "Where'd yer cat go?"

"She's under the bed," I replied. "She always hides there when visitors come."

Sarah gave a crooked smile and bent down onto her knees, lowering her head to peek beneath the bed.

"Oh yeah, I think I see 'er! Timid, ain't she?"

"She is."

Sarah sat back up on the chair. "I love cats, I do."

I sat down on the end of my bed, deciding I needed more information from her before I agreed to help with anything. "What can you tell me about the Twelve Brides?" I asked.

She scratched behind her ear. "We nick money and jewellery off the toffs."

"What happens to the valuables you steal?"

"We give 'em to Miss Danby."

"Who's she?"

"She's the one who looks after us."

"Is she the ringleader?"

"Nope. She ain't the queen, if that's what yer thinkin'."

"Who *is* the queen?"

"She 'asn't never told us."

"Why twelve brides? Are there twelve people in charge?"

"I dunno."

"What do you receive in return for the items you steal?"

"A place ter stay, and some coins now and again."

"Where do you stay?"

"I ain't sayin'. What if yer tell the coppers?"

"I won't."

"Yer don't need to know where I stay."

"Is it near St Bride's Church?"

"I ain't sayin'."

"And you have no idea who runs the gang?"

She shook her head. "Nope."

"Perhaps it's Miss Danby?"

"She jus' passes on the orders. She 'ad a black eye once."

"Someone hit her?"

"Yeah. She got beat quite bad."

"Do you know if it was a man or a woman who did it?"

Sarah shrugged. "Couldn't tell yer. Miss Danby wouldn't say nothin'."

"Do you think Miss Danby would be prepared to meet with me?"

She gave a laugh. "Not a chance! An' if she ever finds out I've bin 'ere, I'll be for it."

She'd beat you?"

"Oh yeah."

"Has she beaten you before?"

"No, but I seen 'er do it ter the others."

"Do you think she might have murdered Josephine and the other girl?"

"Nope. She never would of done that."

"Do you know Rosie Gold?" I asked.

A half-formed smile lifted her lips. "'Ow d'yer know about Rosie?"

"Is she the queen?"

"I told yer, I dunno."

"But she is, isn't she?"

Sarah shrugged and said nothing more.

"The police are looking for her," I said. "Do you know where she might be?"

"Nope."

"But you've heard of her?"

"*Ev'ryone's* 'eard of 'er."

"Have you ever seen her?"

"Nope. And I don't know nothin' about 'er, neither, so don't go askin' me no more questions about 'er."

"Does Miss Danby ever mention her?"

"No, she don't."

"She runs the gang, though, doesn't she? With the help of eleven others, perhaps?"

"I dunno. Like I told yer before, I only know Miss Danby."

"But you also knew the murdered girls?"

"I've seen 'em about."

"How do you know they were murdered by gang members?"

"Cos we got warned! We've bin told the same thing could 'appen to us."

"Then you're quite sure the two girls were murdered by the gang?"

"Yeah, that's what I told yer."

"And you've no idea who the second girl was?"

She shook her head. "Nope."

I gave a frustrated sigh. "I think you could be of enormous help to us, Sarah, but there must be something more you can tell me. Where can we find Miss Danby?"

"I ain't sayin'. I won't go gettin' meself in no trouble." She lowered her voice. "I didn't come 'ere to 'ave all these questions asked o' me. I come 'ere cos there's summat yer might wanna see. I need yer 'elp, but it'll 'elp yer, too. I'm sure of it."

She lifted her shawl, revealing a small purse tied around her waist. She unbuttoned the purse and pulled out a folded piece of paper.

"What is it?" I asked.

"'Ave a read."

She handed the paper over. I opened it out and smoothed it flat on the eiderdown covering my bed. At first glance, I appeared to be looking at a poem. Written out in a careful, almost childlike hand, it read:

There's a friendly hostelry on every corner,
  Call at the one with our best-known mourner.
  From the Order of Preachers, cross the Thames,
  The Lapis Milliaris is one of our gems.
  A letter to the Galtans is widely read,
  And the Earl of Pemboke rests his head.
  But Hamlet no longer treads the boards,
  What can you poach for royal rewards?

"A riddle," I said, "but what's it for?"

"To 'elp us find 'em. The ones who's runnin' the gang."

"But how? I don't understand."

"Yer 'ave ter solve each line, and when yer've done that yer can find 'em."

"How?"

"I dunno. I s'pose yer find out after yer've done it."

"You don't know the answer yourself?"

"Course not! That's why I've come 'ere with it."

"Where did you get this from?"

"I took it off Miss Danby, only she don't know I've got it. I'll be in fer it if she finds out."

"Why did you take the risk?"

"Cos the riddle leads to a place... I know that much. It's an 'ideaway. If yer can get to all the people who's there yer got yerself the murderers."

"Why does the riddle exist in the first place?"

"It's fer members o' the gang to prove 'emselves. If they can work it out, they get ter be one of 'em."

"One of whom?"

"Them ones in charge. Like Rosie Gold."

"You're admitting she's the queen now?"

Sarah shrugged.

"Did Rosie Gold write this riddle?" I asked.

"I dunno who's wrote it, but I ain't clever enough fer it. I got no chance o' workin' it out. But I can tell yer clever, Miss Green. I reckon yer can do it."

I glanced down at the riddle again. "I'm not convinced that I can."

"Sure yer can! Yer write for the noospapers. Yer one o' them clever folks."

I gave a laugh. "There are many people who are far cleverer than me."

"Yer went to school, didn't yer?"

"I did. Didn't you?"

"I went to one o' them industrial schools where yer gotta live there. Me ma was bad wi' the drink and I was fendin' fer meself."

"And your father?"

"I never known 'im."

"Have you any brothers or sisters?"

"Yeah, two brothers, but they got sent off some other place. Dunno where they are now. I ran away from school cos the teachers bin cruel there. Beat us even when we 'adn't done nothin' wrong jus' cos they felt like it."

"That's not right."

"I know it ain't! That's why I 'ad ter run away. Then Miss Danby found me an' told me she 'ad some work fer me. Weren't no one else gonna 'elp me, were they? Anyone else woulda tried ter send me back ter that school again. I started thievin' cos that's what Miss Danby wanted off me. She's gave me a roof over me 'ead, so I 'ad no choice. It were either thievin' or 'ave men pay fer me company and I weren't doin' that."

"I'm sorry to hear you've had such a difficult time, Sarah."

"It ain't your fault, Miss Green, and I ain't gonna feel sorry for meself neither. At least I ain't in the river like them two girls. But I don't want no part in that gang no more. I wanna make a better woman o' meself one way or another. I don't want no more o' them girls gettin' murdered. What's 'appened ter them could of 'appened ter any of us! We're livin' in fear and it ain't right!"

Her eyes were round and impassioned, and I felt great sympathy for her plight.

"More of 'em's gonna die, I jus' know it."

"The police will help," I said. "They'll put a stop to it."

She gave a shrug. "If yer say so. What d'yer think o' the riddle? D'yer reckon yer can solve it?"

I read through it again. "No solution immediately comes to mind. 'Earl of *Pemboke*' is surely meant to read 'Earl of *Pembroke*', don't you think?"

"I got no idea."

"You've given me this so we can find out who leads the gang and then they can be arrested for murdering the two girls, is that right?"

"Yeah."

"It would be far easier if I could speak to Miss Danby directly."

"But she don't know I got it!"

"I could pretend that I know nothing about the riddle."

"I ain't tellin' yer where she is, neither. I've given yer the riddle and that's the end of it. I don't wanna be endin' up in the river meself."

"The riddle may take a long time to solve," I said. "Why not speak to my good friend Inspector Blakely? He can protect you from the gang."

"I don't want nothin' to do wi' no coppers."

"But you wouldn't be in any trouble."

"I don't speak to 'em!" She jumped to her feet.

"All right, Sarah." I wondered if there was anything I could do to persuade her otherwise, but she seemed quite resolute. "You'll need to tell me where I can find you in case I need your help with this."

"I won't be no 'elp." She walked over to the door. "I'll come find yer if I need ter."

CHAPTER 23

"Inspector Paget from C Division and Sergeant Bradshaw from the Thames River Police are meeting today to discuss the two murders," said James as we travelled on the underground railway toward Gower Street station. "They're working on Sarah's suggestion that the two girls in the river were members of the Twelve Brides gang, but we have to be careful as we only have her word for it. We need further evidence."

"She seemed quite adamant about it, and I must say I believe her."

"Why so?"

"Because she clearly knows about the gang. I pulled the riddle out of my bag and handed it to him. She gave me this."

He glanced down at it. "A poem?"

"No, not a poem," I laughed. "It's a riddle. Sarah visited yesterday evening and gave it to me. She said it would lead us to the senior members of the Twelve Brides gang. I'm sure that would include Rosie Gold."

Once I had explained all that Sarah had told me, James read though the riddle again with a furrowed brow.

"We don't have time for silly puzzles," he said, handing the piece of paper back to me.

"But it may help us find Rosie Gold!" I protested.

"And you really believe that, do you? This Sarah woman may just be playing a game with you. She claims to be a member of the Twelve Brides, then refuses to reveal anything worthwhile about herself and gives you a riddle that was probably copied from the pages of *The Family Gazette*."

I stared down at the piece of paper in my hand, suddenly feeling rather downcast.

"Why is she involving you in the first place?" continued James.

"She thought I might be able to help with the riddle, not that any of it makes any sense to me. Sarah told me she doesn't trust the police, like a good many other people from her background, but if you could just meet with her—"

"She won't allow me to. She obviously mistrusts me."

"But if you could, you would see her for what she is: a young woman recruited by a gang she no longer wishes to be a part of. She heard about the murders of the two girls and feels worried that the same fate might befall her. And I can't say that I'm surprised. She's rather similar to them, wouldn't you say? She's young and vulnerable, and she became part of the gang because there were so few choices available to her. Now she's doing what she can to help without getting herself into trouble. By solving the riddle and reaching the gang's senior members we can find whoever murdered the two girls."

James' face softened a little as he listened. "It all seems rather odd to me."

"It is rather odd, but what if I choose to ignore her? How do we know whether to dismiss the riddle or not? We could end up missing out on something."

"I'd be very careful about placing any trust in Sarah if I were you."

"I never said that I trusted her."

"But you believe her?"

"Only because of the riddle. Sarah couldn't have written it herself; she doesn't have the level of education required to do so."

"She might have copied it from somewhere."

"I suppose we can't rule the idea out, but does that mean we should completely ignore it? Aren't you at least a little intrigued to find out where it leads us?"

The train pulled into Gower Street station and we disembarked.

"I really think we should try to find the answer to the riddle," I shouted to James over the sound of slamming carriage doors and jets of steam. "We have nothing to lose."

"Other than time," he shouted back.

"I'll make time," I replied as we jostled our way toward the steps leading out of the station.

❦

We arrived at Euston station with plenty of time to meet Eliza and Francis on their return journey from Derbyshire. Eliza had sent me a telegram to let me know which train they would be travelling on, and James and I were keen to hear how their visit had gone.

A porter told us the train had been held up and would be arriving twenty minutes late. We waited in the station's high-ceilinged dining room, within which murmured conversations mixed with the clatter of crockery and cutlery.

"Let's have another look at it, then," James said resignedly.

"At the riddle you believe to be a waste of time, you mean?"

"It is a waste of time when there are more important things to be getting on with, but seeing as we've some time to kill it makes sense to take a quick look."

"I agree." I pulled the piece of paper out of my bag and laid it down on the table between us. "And who knows? Perhaps we'll have it solved before Eliza and Francis arrive."

James gave a cynical laugh. "I doubt that very much."

We both read through the riddle again. "'There's a friendly hostelry on every corner'," said James. "That first line is rather meaningless, isn't it? There's not a lot we can do with that."

"'Call at the one with our best-known mourner'," I added.

"Who would the chief mourner be?"

"I've no idea. The Order of Preachers... have you heard of them?"

"I can't say I have."

"'Cross the Thames'. That must be a bridge."

"Or a ferry of some sort."

"Yes, it could be. There's the Tower Subway to consider, too. That's close to the Tower of London. Could the tower have something to do with the Order of Preachers?"

"The Order of Preachers has religious connotations," said James. "Was there ever a religious order at the Tower of London?"

"I don't know."

I skimmed through the rest of the riddle, searching for something that looked familiar.

"'*Pemboke*' must be '*Pembroke*'," I said. "The Earl of *Pembroke* is well known, isn't he? He was a politician at one time and continues to air his views publicly in speeches and periodicals. 'Rests his head'. Do you think that could be a reference to his home?"

"Quite possibly."

"I suppose we'll need to find out where he lives, in that case. He no doubt owns a property in London as well as a family seat somewhere else. But I still don't understand the riddle. Even if we succeed in finding out where the Earl of Pembroke lives, what then?"

"I'm not sure," replied James. "And as he no doubt has more than one home, how do we know which the riddle refers to?"

"'Hamlet no longer treads the boards'. The play must have been performed at one of the theatres recently. I can look up the listings in the *Morning Express*."

"Is Lapis Milliaris a type of jewel?" asked James. "Perhaps it refers to a famous diamond of some sort. The name sounds Latin to me, but unfortunately Latin wasn't my strongest subject at school."

"We could ask Francis. He knows Latin."

"Of course he does."

"He may be able to help us with the rest of the riddle, in fact," I said. "We haven't done particularly well with it so far, have we?"

"Riddles are supposed to be difficult. There's a method to these things, and it often involves reading between the lines."

"How does one do that, exactly?"

"Mull it over, dwell on it for a while and something will eventually come to mind."

"I see. Who are the Galtans?"

"I have no idea."

"A family? A colony?"

"I can't say I've ever heard of them."

"I think we should ask Francis to have a look at this for us. I'm sure he'll be able to help."

"He may be able to identify what the riddle refers to, but can he surmise what is to be done with it? That last line means nothing at all. to me It says, 'What can you poach for Royal rewards?'"

"I'm sure it'll mean something once we've deciphered the rest."

"Hopefully it will, but what are we supposed to do with it then?"

"I'm hoping it should be fairly obvious by that stage," I said. "Once we've solved the riddle, we can tell Sarah the solution and then she can gain access to the secret headquarters of the gang. Perhaps Rosie Gold will be there herself."

"It sounds like a fair arrangement if she keeps her promise," said James. "We'll need to offer her some sort of protection when the time comes. Given the deaths of the two girls in the river it's quite evident what Sarah's fate would be if they heard she had shared this riddle with people from outside the gang."

"We must look after her if she's willing to help us."

"I'm still not sure how she'll benefit from the riddle being solved."

"She told me she wants justice. The deaths of Josephine and the other girl have upset her greatly and she wants it all to stop."

James gave a laugh. "I'm quite sure there must be a quicker way of telling us what we need to know without passing on this bewildering riddle!"

"I agree, but she feels too afraid to talk openly about the gang at the moment. Giving us this riddle was all she felt safe with at the moment, and I think it's the only option left open to us."

"The only option is to spend hours puzzling over this incomprehensible rhyme? Let's not forget about all the other work we need to be doing, Penny. We don't have a great deal of time to spend looking at this."

"Francis can help us."

"Francis Edwards comes to the rescue again!"

"There's no need to be facetious. If he's willing to help we'd be foolish to turn him down."

"Let's wait and see whether he's survived his visit to your mother first."

CHAPTER 24

"**W**e were too late, weren't we, Francis?" said Eliza. The newly arrived pair had joined us in the station dining room.

"Yes, we were," replied Francis. "A neighbour of Mrs Green's had visited her with a copy of the *Derby Telegraph,* which had, unfortunately, spilled the beans about Mr Green's indiscretions."

"Oh goodness," I said, feeling a horrible heaviness in my chest. "And how did Mother respond to it?"

"She was in surprisingly good spirits," replied my sister, "although she called him a lot of unpleasant names. I wasn't aware Mother even knew some of those words!"

"It was quite astonishing to hear," added Francis. "But fairly well justified, given the circumstances."

"She was pleased to hear that Father isn't dead," continued Eliza, "and she wasn't quite as angry as I'd expected."

"That is a surprise!" I said.

"In actual fact, Mother had something rather interesting to say to me, Penelope. She told me she had wanted to mention it before but it wouldn't have been appropriate given the possibility that Father wasn't dead."

"What was it?"

"She said, 'If people thought I would do nothing with my time other than sit and wait for him to return they don't know me very well.'"

"I see! And what did she mean by that?"

"She meant to say that she has carried on with her life. She told me that after Father had been missing for about two years, she made up her mind that he was never coming back."

"She never told me that."

"Nor me! We were obviously more optimistic than she was."

"She felt sure that he was either dead or would never return, then?"

"Yes, and that's not to say she didn't miss or grieve for him dreadfully, because she did. However, she told me she was already used to him being away a lot. Mother even confessed that she tended to allow him to slip from her mind when he went away on his travels."

"How very sad to hear it!" I exclaimed. "I recall him being away for long periods, but whenever he returned there was always great happiness. We took such lovely family excursions together and went fishing for minnows in the stream and ate picnics. I loved those times when Father returned."

"As did I, Penelope," my sister replied, her eyes damp. "It doesn't mean those times weren't happy. But Mother and Father's marriage was rather unconventional, wasn't it? It had to be because he spent so much time away."

"But no more so than a chap in the army or with other duties overseas," said James. "He can't use the absence from his family as an excuse for his misbehaviour!"

"Perhaps he doesn't intend to use it as an excuse," said

Eliza, "and perhaps he never has. Perhaps he simply isn't a good husband or father."

James gave a snort of laughter. "I think you may be right there!"

"It's not an easy thing to accept," said Francis. "We all like to think our parents are perfect, but sometimes it's just not the case."

"Oftentimes, I would say," said Eliza. "You would only need to meet some of the families I come across in the course of my work to see that. Distracted, drunken parents... Absent parents... Men who beat their wives and children... I could go on. I've had to remind myself that whatever his sins may be, Father isn't as bad as all that."

"He simply took himself off to the jungle for ten years and allowed his family to believe he was dead," commented James sourly. "The families you encounter in your work are often poverty-stricken, Eliza. I don't believe poverty can be held entirely to blame for their poor behaviour; however, it is a significant factor. As for your father, he's an educated, intelligent, middle-class man!"

"You believe he should have known better, do you?" asked Eliza.

"Of course he should. I accept that no one is perfect, and I include myself in that description – I've committed my own transgressions, and I'm not proud of them – but to abandon one's wife and children...!"

"Berating Father won't get us anywhere," I said. "I'm more interested in finding out how Mother is coping with it all. Could it be that she has found these past ten years a little easier than she's been letting on?"

"It would seem so," replied Eliza. "And I believe Mr Horace Dunhill has been of great assistance to her."

"Who on earth is he?"

"A gentleman she's acquainted with."

"I've never heard of him!"

"Neither had I until Mother told me about him. He's a widower, and it seems he's been a good friend and companion to her in recent years."

"Did you meet him?"

"No."

I quietly pondered this for a moment. "I suppose Mother is perfectly entitled to enjoy the company of another gentleman. As she said herself, she couldn't wait forever for Father to come home. And in light of everything that's happened I suppose it's just as well she didn't."

"Indeed. But it's an awful shame, isn't it? I feel extremely sad that what was once a happy marriage has come to this. Mother appears to have managed as well as she could have done, however."

"With the help of this Mr Dunhill."

"I imagine he's helped her through some rather difficult times."

I gave a hollow laugh. "I still can't imagine her having any companion other than Father!"

"Times have changed," replied my sister, "and she deserves a bit of companionship. Father never returned to her, so I suppose she was entitled to seek it elsewhere. Still, it'll take some getting used to. I must say I am extremely grateful to you, Francis, for everything you've done." She gave him a broad smile. "You accompanied me all the way to Derbyshire, tactfully explained your encounter with Father, demonstrated enormous patience with Mother and then put up with my company on the journey home again!"

"There's no need to thank me," he replied. "I considered it my duty to explain everything to Mrs Green as well as I knew how."

I noticed they held each other's gaze, and when she finally looked away Eliza was still smiling. I couldn't help but smile myself at the sight. *Was it possible that they were developing some sort of affection for one another?*

"Thank you, Francis," said James. "I realise it hasn't been easy to return with such difficult news. You've been enormously helpful to the Green family."

"It's a pleasure, James. I feel content that I've been able to help Eliza, Penny and Mrs Green discover the truth about Mr Green."

We all sipped our tea.

"While we're gathered here, perhaps I could ask you both for some assistance with a rather unusual riddle," I said, unfolding the piece of paper.

"Oh, I'm no good at riddles," said Eliza dismissively.

"But you may know something or other about the content of this one," I said. "I've been unable to make head nor tail of it so far."

"Where's it from?" asked Francis.

"It was given to us by a gang member."

"A gang member?"

"Yes, someone from the Twelve Brides. Apparently, the riddle is some sort of initiation challenge for new recruits," I said.

"How does it relate to your work?" asked Francis.

"That's a good question," said Eliza. "Penelope's employment has always been rather unconventional, though. Surely you've realised that by now, Francis?"

"I'm hoping that by solving this riddle we'll be able to work out who was behind the river murders," I said.

"Please be careful!" exclaimed Eliza.

"I'm not sure I like the sound of this," said Francis.

"Despite the certainty I have that my colleagues and I will find a more conventional way into this gang," said James, "Penny is intent on solving the riddle."

"Let's forget about all that for now," I said. "Take a look at this for a moment, Francis, and let me know your initial thoughts."

I passed the piece of paper to him and he stared at it for a while, his brow furrowed.

"What do you make of it?" I asked. "Does any of the riddle make sense to you?"

"No, I can't say that it does."

"But you're the clever one!" said Eliza. "Penelope expected you to solve it in an instant!"

"Not quite," I responded. "Is there nothing at all in the riddle that means something to you, Francis? What about the Latin part? That is Latin, isn't it?"

"Yes, it's Latin all right. Lapis Milliaris refers to a type of Roman milestone, I believe."

"Not a jewel?"

"No, I'd definitely say a milestone."

"Let me have a look," said Eliza, peering down at the piece of paper. It says, 'The Lapis Milliaris is one of our gems.' How puzzling."

"Why would it be described as a gem?" I asked.

"I'm not sure," replied Francis. "A gem is a precious stone, but a *precious* stone is quite different from a *mile*stone."

"Of course." I thought of the type of weatherworn milestone one typically saw at the side of the road and struggled to understand why it might be described as a gem.

"Is that what we're to look out for?" asked James. "A milestone?"

"There are hundreds of milestones lying around," I said. "Perhaps it relates to a particularly important one." An interesting thought occurred to me. "Perhaps it's Charing Cross. Isn't that the official centre of London, from which point all distances are measured?"

"Close by," replied Francis. "The actual location is just

south of Trafalgar Square, where the statue of Charles I on horseback stands."

"Is there a milestone there?"

"Not that I recall. Only a statue."

"We'd have to go and look," I said.

"It's spitting distance from Scotland Yard," said James, "but I don't recall ever seeing a milestone there."

"It says, 'From the Order of Preachers, cross the Thames'," Francis mused. "The Order of Preachers refers to the Dominicans, I think."

"Really?" I asked. "How sure are you about that?"

"Reasonably certain," he replied. "I can't think what else it might be."

"'Cross the Thames'," said James. "We think that could be a bridge or a ferry."

"It sounds as though you need to visit the Dominicans, then cross the River Thames," Eliza suggested with a smile. "You see, I can be of help with these things."

"But where are the Dominicans?" I asked. "Do they have a priory of some sort?"

"That's a good question," said Francis. "I'm sure a priory has been built in North London since the time of the Catholic Emancipation."

"Can you remember where?"

"I'm afraid not, but we could look it up."

"But North London is nowhere near the Thames," said James.

"That's a fair point," replied Francis. "This riddle points to the existence of a priory on the riverside."

"Has there ever been a priory by the river?" I asked. "Before the Dissolution of the Monasteries, perhaps?"

"Blackfriars!" announced James.

"Yes, of course!" said Francis with a grin. "That's what it must be."

"How did you come up with that?" I asked James.

"I don't really know. It must have been resting at the back of my mind somewhere. I simply thought of monks besides the river and then I thought of Blackfriars. It has to be right, doesn't it?"

"It does indeed!" said Francis. "The Dominicans are also known as Blackfriars because of their black capes. And the area of Blackfriars is where their medieval priory once stood."

"Blackfriars Bridge," I added. "That's where you cross the Thames, isn't it? We need to walk over Blackfriars Bridge."

"Of course!" Francis replied. But to what end?"

"I've no idea," said James. "A milestone, perhaps?"

CHAPTER 25

I ntrigued by the riddle, Eliza had agreed to accompany me the day I went to investigate Blackfriars. We met one morning in Water Lane, a narrow street behind Ludgate Hill train station.

"So where was the Dominicans' priory?" she asked.

"Somewhere in this location. We're standing beside Apothecaries' Hall." I pointed out a decorative arch within a brown-brick facade. "I recall Francis telling us the Society of Apothecaries moved into a section of the priory after it had been dissolved. Then the building was almost completely destroyed during the Great Fire of London but was later rebuilt."

"You've done well to remember the detail of Francis' conversation, Penelope. He knows an awful lot of things, doesn't he? I try my best to remain interested in it all – I *am* interested, in fact – but I simply struggle to remember it all."

"I'm sure he doesn't mind," I said. "No one else's brain seems to retain as much information as his. As we're next to the location where the priory once stood, it makes sense to walk down to the river and cross over the bridge."

A fresh breeze whipped at our hats as we followed the course of the railway line past the rumble of printing presses within *The Times* newspaper offices and across the wide thoroughfare of Queen Victoria Street. Blackfriars Bridge led us out over the river, where the wind tugged even harder at our hats and the trains clattered over the iron railway bridge which ran alongside us.

A broad vista opened up around us. The dome of St Paul's Cathedral soared up beyond the railway bridge, and ahead of us the southern bank of the river was lined with wharves and warehouses. Plumes of smoke rose up from the factory chimneys.

"Did you enjoy Francis' company during your trip to Derbyshire?" I asked my sister.

"Of course. He is very pleasant company indeed. I have always held Francis in high regard, as you know."

"Perhaps even higher now that he has been able to solve the puzzle of Father's disappearance."

"Naturally! Don't you feel the same way, Penelope? It's quite remarkable what he's been able to achieve."

"And to think that you travelled to Derbyshire together without a chaperone!" I smiled.

"There was no call for a chaperone."

"Might it not seem a little untoward for a married lady to travel such a great distance with an unmarried gentleman?"

"Well yes, I suppose it was rather irregular. But then it was rather an irregular situation. We had to visit Mother swiftly in the hope that she would learn nothing about Father from the newspapers, so we had little choice in the matter. What are you suggesting, Penelope?"

I smiled again.

"Oh, I see that you're joking with me."

"I'm the last person to pass judgement on the situation,

Ellie. I don't mind a bit, but it amuses me that neither of you questioned whether it would be appropriate to embark upon your journey together."

"There wasn't time to find another female companion. Besides, as a lady who is estranged from her husband and attempting to divorce him, I'm not the sort of woman society smiles upon, am I? I've received my fair share of judgement in recent months, and to be honest with you, Penelope, I can't say that I care all that much about it any more."

"That's the spirit!" I said.

Clouds of steam rose into the air from a steamboat passing beneath the bridge. As it did so, a brown-haired lady in a blue dress walked past us, holding on to her hat. She seemed strangely familiar. I stopped and turned to watch her retreating form.

"Do you know her?" asked my sister.

"She looked familiar. For a moment I couldn't place her, but I realise now that it was Mrs Worthers, whom I've encountered a couple of times in Piccadilly now."

"And who is she?"

"I don't know her well. She chased the women who committed the street robbery we witnessed, and she knows the jeweller I spoke to about the gangs, Mr Sowerby. That's all I know about her."

I turned around again and we resumed our walk across the bridge.

"I see," said Eliza. "Well, it isn't too uncommon to pass someone you recognise."

"No, I suppose it's not. There's just something about her that seems a little... I don't know."

"What?"

"Mysterious, I suppose."

"Sometimes I feel as though you want to find a story in

everything, Penelope. She's probably just another ordinary woman like you and me. Anyway," she said with a grin, "it's only six weeks until your wedding day now, is it not? I can't wait! It'll be such a wonderful day. Do you feel prepared?"

"I feel fairly well prepared for the day itself, and I'm certainly looking forward to it. I'm just not sure I've fully accustomed myself to how different life will be afterwards. I shall be leaving my home and my job behind. It feels like quite a wrench."

"I'm sure it does. Is there no opportunity at all to keep your current employment at the *Morning Express*?"

"I intend to broach the subject with Mr Sherman again. The decision ultimately rests with Mr Conway, and he always takes rather a traditional view of such matters."

"It would be a terrible shame if you had to leave. As your sister, I often feel your job puts you at unnecessary risk and you'd be better off doing something more befitting of a wife once you're married. But that said, I also know how much enjoyment your work gives you. And quite frankly, you wouldn't really be yourself if you had to stop doing it."

"You're right, Ellie. It wouldn't feel right at all. I'll do what I can to change their minds, but I fear the odds are stacked against me."

"If they insist upon it you could come and work for Mrs Sutherland and me at the London Women's Rights Society!"

"I suppose so." Important though Eliza and Mrs Sutherland's work was, I felt little excitement at such a prospect. Perhaps I just had to accept that certain sacrifices would have to be made in the pursuit of love.

"I can't say that you seem overly enthusiastic about the idea, Penelope."

"Oh, please don't take offence, Ellie." I turned toward her. "I'm sure that once James and I are married I would happily consider such a possibility. It's just that at the moment the idea seems..." I trailed off, unsure how to finish my sentence.

"I understand, Penelope. You have a lot to think about at the present time. But when you do feel ready to consider it, I'm sure you would take to Mrs Sutherland quite well. She can be a funny fish at times, but she's led such an interesting life."

"Why is she a funny fish?"

"She likes to do things a certain way and can be a little short with me when I disagree with her. Whenever there is a decision to make, she insists on discussing every little aspect of it. I prefer to just get things done rather than spend a lot of time talking about them. That said, she has some fascinating stories to tell. She was born an only child and was therefore the sole heir to her father's many businesses. He died when she was just sixteen years of age! She owns various factories and shops as well as a few residential properties. She's an extremely busy lady, as you can imagine."

"And what of her husband?"

"She was widowed at the age of twenty-two. Her story is a terribly sad one."

We reached the end of the bridge and the top of Blackfriars Road. To our left sat the brown-and-cream-brick Blackfriars Bridge Station. To our right was a row of shabby stores, along with two or three public houses.

"Now where?" asked Eliza. "We've crossed the river, but it doesn't look very salubrious around here. I can't remember the last time I travelled south of the river."

"Can you see a milestone anywhere?" I asked.

"No."

I retrieved my notebook from my carpet bag and began to write down everything we could see.

"Perhaps we're supposed to get on a train," suggested Eliza. "The site of the priory is beside a train station, and

here we are next to another train station. Is there any reference to a train in the riddle?"

"I don't think so."

"Let me take another look at it."

I found the riddle in my bag and passed it to her. She read
through it while I continued with my notes.

"'There's a friendly hostelry on every corner,'" read Eliza.
"Well, there's a hostelry on that corner there." She pointed to
a public house close by called The Crown. "Let's go inside."

She marched off toward it and I followed after her.

The publican stared at us as we entered The Crown. The
place smelled of stale beer and unwashed bodies. It wasn't
long before the drinkers noticed us and also began to stare.

"I can't imagine anyone from the Twelve Brides coming in
here," I muttered to Eliza. "There isn't another woman in
sight."

"Are yer lost?" asked the publican, removing his pipe from
his mouth.

"No, we're not," replied Eliza confidently. "Show him the
riddle, Penelope."

I felt far too wary of the publican to confess that I had it
in my possession. If he knew anything about the riddle there
was a very real danger that he would inform the gang of what
I was doing. I realised too late that Eliza and I should have
discussed what we intended to do in the public house before
we entered. I cursed myself for following her inside without
question.

"Penelope?" she said, noticing my hesitation.

"What riddle?" asked the publican, putting his pipe back
in his mouth.

"It's nothing," I said casually. "I think we've come to the
wrong place."

Eliza gave a laugh. "But this is a hostelry on a corner. Isn't that what we were looking for?"

"Let's discuss this outside, Ellie."

My sister gave me a puzzled look. I tried my best to give her a commanding stare to indicate that we could be putting ourselves in danger.

"We don't never get the likes of you in 'ere," a drinker with an unpleasant, squashed face piped up. He began to saunter over to us, tankard in hand. "Does yer 'usbands know you're 'ere?"

I didn't like the way he was looking us up and down.

"Yes, they do," retorted Eliza. "And my sister's husband is an inspector at Scotland Yard!"

I winced at the admission.

"I don't know no copper what'd let 'is missis go vistin' a place like this," said the publican. "I'd get meself back over the bridge if I was you."

"Have you ever heard of the Twelve Brides gang?" Eliza asked him.

I took Eliza's arm. "We need to leave, Ellie."

"Yeah, I've 'eard of 'em," replied the publican. "They keeps 'emselves north o' the river. Too scared to come dahn south. Knows they'd only get a punch on the nose for their trouble, they does. And worse'n that if they've chose to 'ang abaht any longer. Now why's two gen'lewomen like yerselves comin' in a place like this and askin' abaht gangs? Yer wanna be careful, yer do. Take my advice and 'op it back over the bridge while yer still can."

Eliza was ready to remonstrate, but I pulled her away and swiftly led her out of the establishment.

"So much for a friendly hostelry on every corner!" she fumed once we were out on the street. "Why didn't you show him the riddle, Penelope? Wasn't the reason we went in there to find out what he knows about it?"

"I'm not sure why we went in there, to be perfectly honest," I replied. "I should have thought it through more carefully. We can't just go around showing everyone a riddle we're not supposed to have. If that publican has anything to do with the Twelve Brides, he'll tell them what we're doing!"

"Ah, I see now. That explains why you behaved so strangely in there."

"I just wanted to leave."

"Right. I suppose I shouldn't have mentioned the Twelve Brides to him either."

"Not really."

"Well, it would have been helpful if you'd informed me of all this before we set foot in there!"

"Yes, it would, I'm sorry, Ellie."

"What an embarrassment."

I glanced back at the Crown and saw a face peering out through the window at us. "Let's get moving."

We walked back to the bridge and began to cross the river again.

"I'm sorry I haven't been much help on this little expedition," said my sister. "I don't see why you're going to so much trouble with this riddle, Penelope. There must be an easier way of tracking down the senior gang members. Couldn't you just leave it to James?"

"Sarah, that young gang member I met, gave it to me," I said. "I want to have a good go at solving it if I can."

"But the riddle doesn't even make sense. It told us to go into the hostelry on the corner, which is exactly what we did, and the bartender had no idea what we were talking about!"

"Unless he was pretending," I reasoned. "Perhaps he knew, but there was a special code word or something we needed to use to find out more."

"I don't fancy returning there with any sort of word," said Eliza. "Besides, he told us the Twelve Brides would be too scared to visit South London."

"That was probably just territorial talk," I replied. "But I can't pretend I'm in a hurry to return there myself."

CHAPTER 26

"Ah, a puzzle. Excellent!" said Edgar when I showed him the riddle. "It makes me think of Christmas. My father often has us all sit down to solve puzzles on Christmas Day."

"Does that mean you're an expert at solving them?" I asked hopefully.

"Not at all. And I can't say that I like the look of this one, if I'm honest. There's too much in it."

Frederick got up from his seat and peered over Edgar's shoulder. "The trick with these things is to study one phrase at a time," he said. "That way you don't get overwhelmed with ideas."

"Which phrase do you advise me to study first?" I asked him.

"The first line looks interesting. 'There's a friendly hostelry on every corner.'"

"I wonder why you like the look of that one, Potter!" commented Edgar with a laugh.

"It's quite true, though, isn't it?" said Frederick. "London does have a friendly hostelry on every corner."

"I wouldn't say they're all very friendly," replied Edgar. "Some are downright menacing, in fact. Have you ever been to a hostelry in the East End?"

"Once or twice."

"The ones down by the docks are particularly terrifying."

"Then why does the puzzle say they're friendly?"

"I don't know, Potter. You suggested we study one phrase at a time, but we don't appear to be getting anywhere with the first one."

"There's no need to address them in order. Perhaps there's an easier line to start us off. The Galtans sound familiar."

"Yes, they do," agreed Edgar. "They could be members of a prestigious family, perhaps."

"They might well be. Though I'm also beginning to think they could have been an ancient civilisation."

"Which is it?" I asked. "A family or an ancient civilisation?"

"Come to think of it, neither is correct," replied Frederick. "I'm sure I came across an area called the Galtans in the Lake District. I think it may be a range of hills."

I felt amused by this sudden change in theory. "Hills?"

"Yes, like the Quantocks."

"The Galtans are in the Lake District?"

"Yes, I think so," replied Frederick.

"The riddle says, 'A letter to the Galtans is widely read'," recited Edgar. "Why would someone send a letter to a range of hills?"

"I think it's more likely to be a community of people," I said.

"People who live in a place called Galta, perhaps?" asked Edgar. "Like Malta and the Maltans?"

"They're called *Maltese*," said Frederick.

"Speculating on the meaning of each individual phrase is taking up too much time," I said. "I think it'll be quicker if I go and look up some of these references in the reading room. I should be able to find out who the Galtans are if I do so."

"Hills, I tell you!" said Frederick.

"What's that, Potter?" asked Mr Sherman as he marched into the newsroom.

"The Galtan Hills, sir. You've heard of them, haven't you?"

"No, I can't say I have."

"I'm quite sure they're in the Lake District."

"I've holidayed in the Lake District on a number of occasions, Potter, and I've never come across the Galtan Hills. There are the Northern Fells, the Western Fells, the North Western Fells, the Central Fells, and so on. But no hills. They're all fells up there."

"Well the word '*hills*' isn't actually mentioned in the riddle," said Frederick. "Maybe it relates to the Galtan Fells?"

"Never heard of them," responded Mr Sherman. "What are you looking at there, Fish?"

I briefly explained the story behind the riddle.

Mr Sherman shook his head. "We don't have the time for nonsense riddles, Miss Green."

"But this one could lead us to the hideaway of the senior members of the Twelve Brides gang," I said.

"There must be a quicker way of finding them, and that's a job for the police, anyhow. I don't want you wasting all your time on this one, Miss Green."

"I'll make sure any effort I make to decipher it doesn't get in the way of my reporting work, sir."

"It had better not. I was expecting a few more words from you on Easter bonnet fashions for the weekend edition."

"I struggled to come up with anything more."

"We could really do with another hundred words. Surely you could list some other flowers that will be popular choices for Easter bonnets this year?"

"I shall try."

"I realise a lot has been happening with the discovery of your father, the return of Mr Edwards and the dreadful murders of those girls found in the river. However, our lady readers still need to know how to wear their Easter bonnets this year. It may sound trivial to you, but these matters are very important to some people."

"People who have nothing else going on in their lives," chuckled Edgar.

"Did I ask for your opinion, Fish?"

"No, sir."

"Then kindly remain quiet on the subject. A talented writer is able to turn his or her pen enthusiastically to any subject, regardless of its perceived importance in this world. I should add that a good writer is also able to do so in spite of any other matters that might be distracting him at the time. Please forget about riddles or matters of a personal nature, Miss Green, and take ten minutes or so to write a few more words about Easter bonnet flowers."

"Yes, sir, but before I begin I'd like a word with you in private, if I may."

"Come along, then," he replied, opening the newsroom door. "We can talk in my office, but you'd better make it quick."

"I've been wondering whether you'd found the opportunity to speak to Mr Conway again about me continuing my employment here after I am married," I said once we were seated in the editor's office.

I could tell from the way Mr Sherman scratched at his brow that this was not an easy topic for him. "I did, but unfortunately he still has rather fixed ideas on the matter."

"He insists that I must leave after the wedding?"

"I'm afraid so, Miss Green."

I felt my shoulders slump.

"If it helps at all," he added, "I'd let you stay if the decision were mine to make."

"Thank you, sir, but the fact remains that I'm to lose my employment, and I can't help feeling terribly disappointed about that. Are you certain he cannot be persuaded? Surely he listens to you as the editor of the newspaper?"

"He listens only when he agrees with me. He also listens to his wife a great deal about such matters, as I've previously mentioned. Sometimes it feels as though Mrs Conway is the real proprietor."

"And she doesn't want me to stay?"

"She does want you to stay, but not as a married woman. It would be considered quite inappropriate."

"Then there's nothing that can be done about it?"

"I'm afraid not."

"I suppose that settles it, then," I snapped, rising from my chair.

"Please try not to be upset, Miss Green. It's the natural course of things, as you must surely appreciate."

"It's rather difficult not to be upset, sir. How would you feel if your profession was suddenly taken away from you?"

He leaned forward and rested his elbows on his desk. "As you know, I did experience such an event, albeit briefly, and it was truly awful."

"You must feel relieved not to be a woman, sir."

"I can't say that I always feel pleased about being who I am, but you're certainly correct in that assertion."

I turned to walk toward the door.

"Miss Green!" he called after me. "If I can think of any solution, I'll do whatever I can to keep you."

"Thank you, sir." I had no idea what sort of solution he

could possibly come up with. "In the meantime, I shall assume that my last day working for this newspaper will be Friday the twenty-second of May."

Instead of looking for an omnibus as soon as I stepped out onto Fleet Street I decided to walk for a while. Reporters bustled past me, as did several printers in their ink-stained clothing and bookbinders in their aprons. Messenger boys weaved through the crowd, running with pages of copy to meet their deadlines.

I couldn't quite accept the fact that I would soon be leaving this place. I looked up at the large lettering on the newspaper offices: the *Daily News*, *The Daily Telegraph*, the *News of the World* and many more. I surveyed the telegraph wires strung across the street, carrying the latest despatches from across the globe. Whatever happened around the world, the inhabitants of this street were among the first to know about it. That's what had drawn me here eleven years earlier.

So much had changed since then. My father had been lost and found. My sister had been married and was now seeking a divorce. I had fallen in love and was to be married.

As I neared Ludgate Circus, the tall, tiered spire of St Bride's Church rose above the rooftops to my right. I crossed the road and paused at the entrance to St Bride's Avenue, a little walkway that led up to the church gates.

The Twelve Brides had named themselves after this church, but where was their hideaway? Surely it had to be in the vicinity.

The church appeared to have hidden itself amid a cluster of buildings, around which the streets and alleyways were barely wide enough for a cart to pass through. As I navigated my way through them, I understood how such a maze-like territory might appeal to a gang.

Yet I saw nobody there who looked as though they might

belong to one. I looked around for young women resembling Sarah in scruffy bonnets and shawls, figuring I could follow one of them to the gang's hideaway. Then I realised they would more likely be dressed as fine ladies at the present time, out thieving on the wealthier streets of the West End.

CHAPTER 27

I felt quite despondent as I worked in the reading room later that day. *Why couldn't Mr Sherman convince Mr Conway to let me stay?* There was no question of me putting a stop to my writing, so I reluctantly began to envisage a future of crafting genteel articles for dull periodicals. There would be little opportunity to travel around London the way I did now.

Much of my work would be done at my writing desk in the home James and I were to share. Our home life would no doubt provide me with a great sense of contentment, but I was concerned that I might grow bored. James' work would continue in much the same vein as before, and I already envied him the cases he would investigate while I sat at home writing about dinner party menus or excursions to the countryside.

In an attempt to put an end to my self-pity, I pulled the riddle out of my carpet bag and read through it again. A new wave of despondency washed over me as I recalled the futile walk Eliza and I had taken across Blackfriars Bridge, realising we must have misinterpreted the clues somehow. I wondered how on earth a gang member with a fairly low level of education could be expected to solve it.

Perhaps I was missing something obvious and the riddle alluded to subjects only a gang member would know. *But if that was the case, why hadn't Sarah picked up on any of the clues?*

"Good afternoon, Penny," came a whisper in my ear.

I jumped, caught off guard. I turned to see Francis standing next to me.

I grinned and whispered back, "This is just like old times!"

"Isn't it just?" He pushed his spectacles onto the bridge of his nose, glancing up at the galleries and the dome above our heads. "It's as if I never left!"

"Very little's changed here since you've been away," I said. "Which isn't terribly surprising, I suppose. You were only gone for six months, after all."

He gave a nod as he continued to look around appreciatively. "Only six months, but it feels like a lifetime."

"You couldn't resist visiting to remind yourself of your former workplace?"

"No indeed, but I've also come to see the head librarian. I'm interested to hear whether any vacancies have come up."

"Would you consider working here again?" I whispered excitedly. "That would be wonderful!" I noticed the dough-faced Mr Retchford approaching. "Look out," I whispered. "Here comes your replacement."

"Miss Green!" hissed Mr Retchford. "Yet again I find myself having to remind you not to talk inside the reading room!"

"Hello, Mr Retchford. This is Mr Francis Edwards," I replied with a smile. "Your predecessor."

The library clerk blinked a few times, then quietly cleared his throat, as if a little ashamed of his rudeness.

"Oh, I see. Mr Edwards, is it? Yes, I know the name, and

it's a pleasure to meet you. I began working here after you left for... Amazonia, wasn't it?"

"It was indeed. It's a pleasure to meet you, Mr Retchford. I'm off to meet with the head librarian now. It'll be interesting to hear how things have been ticking over here since I went away."

I returned to my work once they had both gone and, when I grew tired of it, I turned to the riddle once again. There appeared to be five main clues: the Order of Preachers, the Lapis Milliaris, the Galtans, the Earl of Pembroke and Hamlet. *Could each clue relate to a location?*

I began to write down the topics I could read up on while I was in the reading room. The Earl of Pembroke's residence was one of them, so I made a note to look the earl up in *Burke's Peerage*.

I paid a visit to the newspaper reading room and looked through the listings for any Shakespeare plays which had recently been performed in London. The most useful publication was a weekly periodical called *The London Stage*. From reading through its listings, I learned that *Macbeth* had been performed at the Olympic Theatre and *Richard III* had been performed at the Lyceum. However, I could find no reference to a recent performance of *Hamlet*. It occurred to me then that the riddle might have been written some time ago, which meant there was no knowing how recent the performance of *Hamlet* might have been.

Disheartened by this thought, I returned to the reading room and considered the mysterious Lapis Milliaris which Francis had believed to be a milestone. And not just any milestone; a *Roman* milestone. *What was the significance of that?* I called to mind the milestones I often saw at the side of the road, many of which were worn and grimy. Often the letters and numbers were barely discernible. But I couldn't recall seeing a Roman milestone. I decided to seek out a London guidebook.

I climbed the iron staircase to the galleries above and found the relevant section. *London in 1880* by Mr Herbert Fry caught my eye. I knew it to be a guide written for travellers who were unfamiliar with the capital. The subtitle was *'Illustrated with Bird's-Eye Views of the Principal Streets',* giving me another reason to select this particular book. If I couldn't find what I was looking for in the text, the illustrations would perhaps hold some clues.

I took the book back to my desk and began to leaf through it. I looked up the reference to Blackfriars but found no clues to enlighten me after the walk Eliza and I had taken over the bridge. I read on for a few more pages, which covered various other locations including the Old Bailey and St Paul's Cathedral. I reached Cannon Street Railway Station and was just about to turn to the table of contents when two words caught my eye at the bottom of the page: 'London Stone'.

I was immediately able to picture it, having often passed by the ancient block of stone encased in a cupola affixed to the front of St Swithin's church on Cannon Street. The book's author, Mr Fry, explained that the stone was Roman in origin and described it as a 'Milliarium': a central milestone from which all other milestones marked their distances in the City of London.

It had to be the Lapis Milliaris.

My heart began to pound with anticipation. I checked the clock on the wall and realised I had a little time available to visit the stone. I returned the book to its shelf, packed my papers away into my bag and stood to my feet.

Just as I did so, Francis reappeared.

"Have you finished here for the day?" he whispered.

"London Stone!" I hissed excitedly. "I think it could be the Lapis Milliaris from the riddle!"

His eyes widened. "What an interesting thought!"

"Shush!" scolded a man working close by.

Francis and I exchanged a glance, then strode out of the reading room without another word. Once we were outside, I told Francis what I had learned from the London guidebook.

"It sounds very likely to me that Lapis Milliaris and London Stone in Cannon Street are one and the same," he replied. "I can accompany you if you wish."

We hailed a cab on Great Russell Street.

"I hope we see something obvious while we're there," I said as we travelled down to Holborn. "Eliza and I made no progress during our visit to Blackfriars Bridge. We must have missed something, but I can't think what."

"Maybe it'll become evident once you've visited all the other places. Can you be sure that investigating this riddle is completely safe?"

"We'll be all right so long as we keep quiet about what we're doing."

"Only a prospective gang member should attempt it, isn't that right?"

"Yes, I suppose so. But no one knows we're trying to solve it, do they?"

"Sarah knows."

"Only because she asked for my help. She's not about to tell the other gang members what I'm doing, is she?"

"How can you be sure of that?"

"Because she'd find herself in a great deal of trouble if they discovered she'd given me the riddle!"

"I see." Francis sat back in his seat, appearing to accept this explanation. "Just so long as there's no danger involved."

"Nowhere near as much danger as you faced in Colombia."

He smiled. "To be honest with you, Penny, I never felt as though I was in great danger from the people there. The fever was the most perilous part, I suppose. For a time I wasn't sure whether I would recover from it."

"You must have been frightened."

"For brief moments I was, but when you're that unwell your mind is too muddled to realise how ill you really are. The days and nights drift into one another. I spent much of my time feeling quite disorientated. There wasn't much conscious thought on my part. I felt as though I was merely existing, and that my fate lay in the hands of a superior being."

"Thank goodness the outcome was a happy one."

"Yes indeed. It was a bit of luck, really. Had I not recovered it would have been a good while longer for your father to be found!" He laughed.

"How did he seem to you?"

He turned to me, his brow slightly furrowed. "What do you mean?"

"Did he seem troubled or was he content? Is he really happy out there, do you think?"

Francis looked ahead at the horse pulling our cab. "He seemed fairly content. There was something rather restless and distracted about him, but perhaps he's always been like that."

"Not really. Can you tell me more?"

"He struggled to sit still for long periods, and he was quite fidgety. He also made a lot of jokes, and I'm sorry to say that very few of them were particularly funny."

"Jokes?" I stated in surprise.

He gave me a bemused glance. "Yes. Do you recall him telling jokes?"

"Not at all! Are you quite sure you found the right man?"

"Perfectly sure," he replied. "You saw the photograph yourself, did you not?"

"Yes, of course. Although he looks quite different now, it is unmistakably him. I suppose all those years in the jungle have taken their toll on his mind. The environment out there is so different, I don't suppose we could expect him to be the same man today. I imagine it's equivalent to being at sea, as you pointed out once before. Some people completely lose their minds at sea."

"They can do."

"At least it sounds as though he's happy, even if he does seem rather restless and is suddenly prone to telling terrible jokes."

"He appeared to adore his family. Oh dear, I am sorry. I spoke without thinking. That was rather tactless of me, I do apologise."

"There's no need to apologise, Francis. The facts are as they are, and there's very little we can do about them. I appreciate you being so honest with us. You could have lied about his circumstances to save our feelings, but I'm exceedingly grateful you didn't."

"I felt you and your family deserved to hear an honest account."

We exchanged a smile.

"You've been sorely missed in the reading room," I said. "Mr Retchford is hardly an adequate replacement. He's incredibly rude and unhelpful."

"I noticed."

"I remember you being particularly helpful, Francis."

"Was I?"

"You know you were! You helped me find that interesting map of Colombia and a wide range of books describing the places my father had visited. It was ever so useful."

"I'm pleased it was."

"In fact, you were helpful with a whole range of things now I come to think of it. Do you remember when you chased after that woman who had been following us in Russell Square?"

We both laughed.

"Yes, I do remember. I found myself in terrible trouble for restraining her once I'd caught up with her in the mews."

"The people standing nearby had no idea what a trouble-maker she was. I remember being extremely impressed by how quickly you could run."

"Oh well," he gave a bashful smile. "I won the hundred-yard dash on a few occasions during my youth, and I suppose one's body simply recalls how to do these things when the need arises."

We held each other's gaze for a moment, and I suddenly remembered the affection he had once held for me. I looked away, feeling an unexpected warmth in my face. I had always been fond of Francis... just not quite fond enough to marry him.

"Eliza told me she enjoyed your company during the trip to Derbyshire," I commented.

"Did she? Well, that's good to hear. Your sister is a very pleasant lady indeed."

"Did you enjoy her company?" I asked with a smile.

Despite his sun-darkened skin I noticed some colour had risen into his cheeks.

"Of course I did," he replied. "Eliza is very good company indeed. Are we at Cannon Street yet?"

He peered past the horse in what I felt sure was a delib-erate attempt to put an end to the conversation.

CHAPTER 28

Our cab stopped opposite Cannon Street Hotel, a stone edifice with two spires which fronted a train station. Francis and I climbed out of the cab and found the baroque-styled St Swithin's church close by.

"It's a beautiful place, isn't it?" he said, pausing to admire the church. "It was designed by Sir Christopher Wren." Its three tall arched windows were topped with stone embellishments, and a great clock was supported over our heads by a carved stone arm. Below the central arched window sat a small stone alcove, within which lay London Stone.

"Here it is," I said. "The ancient milestone. According to Herbert Fry, it once stood on the opposite side of the road, where Cannon Street train station is now."

"Herbert Fry?"

"The chap who wrote the guidebook I was telling you about. He also said the stone receives a mention in Shakespeare's *Henry VI*. Jack Cade, the play's rebel leader, strikes London Stone with his staff and then sits upon it, proclaiming himself Lord Mortimer and declaring that nothing but claret wine will run in the conduit for the first year of his reign."

Francis gave an appreciative nod. "A great tale, and one that I believe is based on fact. It's a shame he didn't achieve his promise of running the Great Conduit with wine. He was killed a week later."

"Where does this leave us in terms of solving the riddle?" I asked, glancing around. I took out my notebook and wrote down everything I could see around me. "Cannon Street Hotel is the most prominent building. And there is also the train station there. When Eliza and I crossed Blackfriars Bridge we found ourselves standing opposite another train station. I'm beginning to wonder if the stations might be a clue."

"What else did you see at Blackfriars?"

"We visited a horrid public house, immediately wishing we hadn't because it was rather intimidating. There's a line in the riddle, if you remember, that says, 'There's a friendly hostelry on every corner'."

"There just happens to be a hostelry opposite us now."

"So there does." I wrote down its name: The Three Feathers.

"And there's another one behind us," said Francis.

We both turned to look, and I wrote down the name of this smaller establishment: The King's Arms.

"The problem we have is that London is home to countless public houses," continued Francis. "You can walk along the street and find one at every twenty paces. That's often a good thing, of course, but less so when you're trying to solve a riddle like this one."

"I wonder if any members of the Twelve Brides frequent the King's Arms," I said. "Shall we take a quick look inside?"

The interior of the public house was small and dingy. A

few faces turned in our direction, but I saw no other women inside.

"Perhaps the men in there have something to do with the Twelve Brides," I suggested to Francis once we were outside on the street again.

"Maybe, but I wasn't tempted to ask them, were you?"

I laughed. "No! Shall we try The Three Feathers?"

This next public house was much the same as The King's Arms, and we soon left feeling a deep sense of disappointment. Francis accompanied me on my fifteen-minute walk to the *Morning Express* offices on Fleet Street.

"Another unsatisfactory outing," I said. "I can see some similarities between the two locations, given that both are close to train stations and public houses. Then again, most places in London are close to a public house, as we've already discussed."

"Public houses are mentioned in the riddle, whereas I don't recall seeing any reference to a railway station," said Francis.

"You're right, there isn't one. The answer must therefore lie with the public houses, mustn't it? I don't see where that gets us, though. There's nothing about the public houses we've visited so far to suggest a way the riddle can be solved. I'm beginning to think one would have to be part of a gang to solve the riddle. Perhaps there's a code word they use in each of the public houses."

"And perhaps the riddle supplies the code word."

"Perhaps it does, though I can't see how. In fact, I really cannot comprehend this riddle at all."

"I think we're on the right track with London Stone," said Francis. "I think that must be the Lapis Milliaris."

"Perhaps we're supposed to go into one of the public houses and use the code words 'London Stone'?"

"Perhaps. I wouldn't want to try it right now though, would you?"

"No, it's a little too risky. Perhaps we need to solve more of the riddle first, though I don't know how. At the moment it seems like an impossibility."

We paused our conversation as we passed the imposing southern section of St Paul's Cathedral. Its great arched windows and columns made me feel rather small. I could see that Sir Christopher Wren had used the same carved stone decoration on St Swithin's church. I recalled a book my father had once owned which contained etchings of London's famous buildings, and the picture of St Paul's had always enthralled me.

"What were the rest of the tribe Father lives with like?" I asked. "Were they friendly?"

"I didn't see them. I only met his... common-law wife and his children. They occupy a small area of jungle, which they've made their own. They built their own house there and your father maintains the jungle around them. He grows food and has cultivated a good variety of orchids. He says it's most rewarding to see orchids in their natural environment. It really is quite a beautiful place up on the hillside."

"Does he have anything to do with the tribespeople who first captured him?"

"When he and his common-law wife fell in love there was a fair amount of disapproval; so much so that they decided to elope together one night."

"Gosh, really?"

"Yes, and that was how they left the tribe. He told me that his, er... lady friend found being separated from them terribly difficult at first. Her tribe – her family – was all she had ever known. But peace was made with the tribe after the birth of their first son, and they now live close by. They're still treated as outsiders because the tribespeople have struggled to accept a European as one of their own. But there is peace, and that has been of great reassurance to your father. Oh, and I meant to say that one other thing has occurred to me about him."

"What is it?"

"He told me he suffers from headaches and has done since his fall down the ravine."

"Oh dear. I don't suppose there are many physicians nearby!"

"Some of the natives possess a little medical knowledge. Their own form of medical knowledge, I should add, which has been passed on through the generations. But when I mentioned his telling of jokes you felt it seemed rather unlike him."

"Yes, he was never much of a joke-teller."

"That got me thinking. Do you recall the case of Phineas Gage?"

"The American railroad worker who survived a dreadful accident?"

"Yes. As I remember it, an iron bar passed through his head while he was blasting rock. It was a miracle the chap survived, in fact. Do you recall the reports afterwards claiming his personality was quite changed?"

"Yes, I remember."

"He became an object of curiosity, didn't he? And for many years after his death the doctors were intrigued by his injuries and the effects they had on him."

"Is this of some relevance to my father?" I asked.

"A little, I suppose. I was wondering whether the fall down the ravine had caused a similar injury to your father's brain. Not as significant as Gage's, of course, but enough to have caused some damage and perhaps an alteration to his personality."

"You think my father's personality could have been changed by his fall?"

"Not only that, but also his judgement. It might help to explain the decision he made to abandon his family."

CHAPTER 29

"Her name is Margaret Brown," said Sergeant Bradshaw.

James and I stood with him in the parade room at Thames Police Station in Wapping.

"Her mother has been calling in at all the police stations and hospitals for the past three weeks in the hope of discovering any news of her daughter," the sergeant continued. "Now we know her identity, the inquest into her death can be resumed."

"What do you know about her so far?" I asked.

She was twenty years old and sold fruit in Covent Garden. She lived with her mother and siblings in White Horse Yard, just off Drury Lane."

"Did her mother know she was in the Twelve Brides gang?"

"No. She wasn't aware that her daughter was a member of that gang or any other. Nor do we have any evidence that she was, aside from what that other young woman Sarah has told you, Miss Green. The girl claims to have known both victims, is that right?"

"Yes."

"It would be extremely helpful if she agreed to speak to us. Perhaps you could persuade her to make a deposition at the inquest into Miss Brown's death."

"I can certainly try when I see her again. *If* I see her again," I stressed. "I don't know where to find her and, so far, she has refused to speak to the authorities."

"Then the girl must be arrested," replied Sergeant Bradshaw.

"On what grounds?"

"For her refusal to cooperate. We need her to talk, Miss Green."

"I agree," added James. "The riddle she passed on to us is of little use as things stand."

"Riddle?" queried the sergeant.

James quickly filled him in.

"It could lead us to Rosie Gold," I added.

"It could," replied James. "But Inspector Paget is already making good progress on that front, he told me yesterday that his men have discovered she'll be attending a party at the Mondragon Hotel in Fitzrovia this Friday. He's planning to arrest her there."

"That's wonderful news!" I commented.

"In the meantime, we need to gather as much information about her as we can," continued James. "That's why we're so keen to speak to this Sarah."

"She knows nothing about Rosie Gold. I've already asked her."

"She may be lying about that," responded Sergeant Bradshaw.

"She may be lying about a lot of things," added James. "We only have her word for the fact that Miss Miller and Miss Brown were murdered by the Twelve Brides in the first place."

"As soon as Paget has Miss Gold in custody, we'll be able to find out for sure," said Sergeant Bradshaw. "In the meantime, if this Sarah girl calls on you again, Miss Green, you must summon the police as a matter of urgency."

"I don't think I'll be able to persuade Sarah to speak with the police," I said to James as we left the station and walked along Wapping High Street. An odour that reminded me of rotten eggs lingered in the air as the low tide exposed the mudbanks of the river.

"I agree," he replied. "We'll have to spring a surprise on her."

"That doesn't seem fair," I replied. "Besides, it would require some sort of deception on my part."

"You appear to be placing a great deal of trust in her. How do you know it's not misplaced?"

"It's not trust, exactly," I replied, "but I believe what Sarah told me about the riddle. Her manner and her words seem genuine and I feel that it would be most unreasonable to surprise her with an unexpected visit from the police. And I can't even see how it could be done given that I have no idea when I'll see her next."

"If she visits you at home or at your office, you can excuse yourself for a brief moment and instruct Mrs Garnett or one of your colleagues to send me a telegram."

"I think that would make Sarah instantly suspicious."

"I'm sure you can come up with a convincing explanation to excuse yourself for just a brief moment."

"But she was adamant that she didn't want to speak to the police."

"Of course she was! The girl no doubt has a murky past. But we can forget about any minor misdemeanours if she's willing to help us. She's said herself that she'd like to see the murderer of those two girls brought to justice, and the very best way for her to help is to speak to us rather than insisting that someone solve that foolish riddle of hers."

"How do you know it's foolish? It was obviously written for a reason. In fact, Francis and I have made some progress with it." I told James about our journey to London Stone as we crossed the swing bridge where the street boy had snatched my bag.

"Perhaps it is the correct location," he said, "but what are you expected to do with that information?"

"Francis and I decided it must be something to do with the public houses," I replied. "I'm wondering whether a code word of some sort is needed when a person enquires within them."

"And supposing you knew the code word, what would they say to you in response?"

"Perhaps they'd tell us how to find Rosie Gold."

"It's possible, I suppose, though it seems Inspector Paget is already quite close to doing so."

"What puzzles me most is the number of locations we'll need to identify from the riddle. It seems to me that we're supposed to visit all of them."

"How many are there likely to be?"

"I think I've identified five clues and that could mean five locations. Five public houses, possibly."

"It could take a while to find them," he replied with a sigh.

"Francis has proved helpful so far."

"He has little else to do with his time at the moment. Don't forget that I can still be of help even if I am busy. I solved the Blackfriars clue, didn't I?"

"Yes, James, you did."

Although he had been largely dismissive of the riddle, I sensed he was also sorely tempted to have a go at solving it, especially when it came to pitting his wits against those of Francis Edwards.

We paused beside a large warehouse with the words 'Watson's Wharf' painted on its side, and James removed his notebook from his pocket.

"Tell me the names of the public houses you've visited, and I'll make some enquiries. If it transpires that any of these establishments have known criminal connections, we could question the publicans further."

I pulled my notebook from my carpet bag and read the names aloud to him. "The Crown on Blackfriars Road, just south of the bridge. The King's Arms on Cannon Street, opposite the station. And the Three Feathers, right next to the station."

"Why did you choose these particular public houses?"

"They're the closest ones to the suggested location. And each is on a corner, which is how the riddle describes them."

"Do you have the riddle with you?"

"I always have the riddle with me." I smiled as I searched for it in my bag before handing it over.

"'There's a friendly hostelry on every corner,'" he read. "'Call at the one with our best-known mourner.' What does that second part mean?" He ran a hand over his chin.

"It suggests we don't need to call in at all the hostelries; only at the one with the 'best-known mourner', whoever that might be."

"You've written down one from your visit to Blackfriars Bridge and two in the vicinity of London Stone."

"Yes. We didn't know which public house near London Stone was the right one. If there is a right one, that is. It could be that the public houses have nothing to do with it after all."

"I think there may be something in what you've said," said James. "Hostelries are mentioned in the riddle and there seems to be no doubt that we need to visit one of them if we're to solve it."

I peered over at the riddle in his hand, willing a new idea to spring out at us from its familiar words.

"Royal!" said James eventually.

"Royal rewards?" I said. "In the last line?"

"Yes. The word 'royal' is interesting. Look at the names of the public houses you've visited. Two of them have royal connections: The Crown and The King's Arms."

"You're right, James!"

"It may be nothing more than coincidence. Let's not read too much into it just yet."

"But if we can work out the other locations and visit them, we could look out for another public house with a royal-sounding name!"

"It's just an idea, The Three Feathers might also have some relevance for all I know."

"Feathers and crown?"

"One crown, three feathers? Perhaps we need a pub name with two of something. It may be a sequence. Then four of something, five of something and so on."

"The riddle doesn't allude to that, but it does mention the word royal."

The names of various public houses with royal names ran through my head.

"Prince..." I said. "Queen... Oh, just a moment!"

"What?"

"The Queen, our best-known mourner!" I grinned.

"Yes! That could be it, couldn't it?"

"Prince Albert died in 1861, didn't he?"

"I think so.

"And she's been in mourning ever since then."

"Twenty-four years."

"Surely she has to be our best-known mourner! I think we need to find a public house that bears the Queen's name."

"And that's the one we must call at, according to the riddle."

I pondered this for a moment. "I hope we're right. Do you think we're right, James?"

"I can't think of any other explanation at the moment, but it's important that we keep our minds open."

"There's a possibility that the train stations may also be relevant, as well as public houses with numbered names, such as the Three Feathers. We must try to keep track of those ideas, too. I'm worried we might be placing too much hope in public houses with royal names."

"We'll need to identify the other locations to be certain."

"We will indeed. But where are they?" I looked down at the riddle again. "The letter to the Galtans part completely baffles me. But the Earl of Pembroke's home and the place where Hamlet once trod the boards should be easier to solve. I shall continue with my research. Francis is likely to have some other good ideas."

"I think we managed quite well without him just now," said James with a smile.

He handed me the riddle and I tucked it back inside my carpet bag.

"Francis mentioned something quite interesting when we visited London Stone," I said as we continued along Wapping High Street. "He wondered whether my father's fall into the ravine may have caused some damage to his brain."

"I shouldn't be surprised. I imagine it caused great damage to most of his body."

"We know it did because he broke a leg, an arm and several ribs. But Francis suggested he may be suffering a form of brain disease from the injury to his head."

James gave an interested nod. "It's possible, isn't it?"

"Francis mentioned the case of Phineas Gage, the American railroad worker whose character changed after a metal rod passed through his head."

James gave a laugh. "That's rather a different scenario from falling down a ravine!"

"It is, yes," I replied impatiently. "However, the similarity lies in the possible damage done. If Father suffered an injury which affected his brain it might help to explain his odd behaviour. Francis told me Father suffers from headaches and enjoys telling jokes. I don't recall him ever being a joke-teller. Perhaps his personality was altered by the fall."

James gave this some thought. "I must admit I didn't take the suggestion enormously seriously when you first suggested it, Penny. But now you've explained it I can see how that could perhaps be why your Father has behaved so abominably toward you all."

"Although I feel very sad that he has possibly suffered such a serious injury to his brain, it could go some way to explaining his behaviour. It would provide some sort of reason."

"He can't go using it as an excuse, though."

"But what if he was unable to help himself? Perhaps he isn't as accountable for his actions as we assumed if his brain has been affected."

"It's a difficult one to comprehend."

"I intend to speak to a doctor about my theory," I said. "Hopefully an expert can tell me if it's even possible."

CHAPTER 30

E dgar Fish swiftly hid something beneath a pile of papers on his desk as I entered the newsroom. Miss Welton, who stood next to him, had clearly been looking at something over his shoulder.

"Good morning, Miss Green!" Edgar chirped.

"What are you hiding?"

He pushed his lower lip out in apparent puzzlement. "What do you mean?"

"You hid something on your desk when I walked into the room," I said.

"I don't think I did—"

"I'm not a complete fool, Edgar," I interrupted. "Why would you need to hide something from me?"

He sighed, realising there was little point in pretending any longer.

"Is it a secret?" I asked.

"No, it's nothing secret," he replied with a resigned air as he pulled a newspaper out from beneath the pile of papers.

I saw that it was a copy of *The Holborn Gazette*.

"What have they written about my father now?" I asked.

"How did you know it was about your father, Miss Green?"

"Because that's the only reason I can think of to explain why you would hide it."

"All right then, you've obviously got me all worked out."

"That's hardly difficult!" Frederick piped up.

"I would strongly advise against you reading it, Miss Green," said Miss Welton.

"I've better things to do with my time than read that inferior publication." I sat down at my desk. "Will you please tell me what the article said?"

"I have some typewriting to do," said Miss Welton, making a swift exit.

"I'm not sure it's a good idea to tell you, Miss Green," said Edgar.

My stony stare prompted a swift response from Frederick. "I think you'll have to tell Miss Green, Fish. She won't stand for it otherwise."

"No, I won't," I replied, staring Edgar directly in the eye.

"Oh, all right. But please don't be angry with me, Miss Green. I wasn't the one who wrote it."

"I have no doubt my good friend Tom Clifford did."

"You're quite right."

"What did he say?"

"He emphasised the surprise everyone felt after your father was found to be leading a double life."

"And no doubt he has sensationalised the tale."

"Yes, he has sensationalised it quite a bit, there's no doubt about that."

"In his defence, it does make for a rather good story, doesn't it?" I said.

Edgar raised his eyebrows. "That's extremely accommodating of you, Miss Green."

"I expected some of the publications to make the most of

it. Hopefully they'll grow tired of the story before long and then it will all be forgotten about."

"How very magnanimous of you," said Edgar.

"I feel as though I've been presented with a choice of either magnanimity or anger," I replied. "And I feel compelled to choose the former."

"I'm impressed," he replied. "I'm not convinced I'd manage it in the same situation."

"That's the fairer sex for you," added Frederick. "Always full of grit and determination."

A slam of the newsroom door announced the arrival of Mr Sherman, who was perusing a piece of paper.

"Here you are, Miss Green. I've a nice light piece for the ladies' column this week. Three hundred ladies have been asked to give their favourite Christian names, and the results are here. The most popular is Mary, followed by Anna and then Elizabeth."

"Where does Penelope feature on the list?" I asked.

"I can't see it at all, I'm afraid. Nevertheless, I think it would be quite entertaining to include the results, don't you think?" He handed me the piece of paper.

"Yes. Thank you, sir."

"What's the latest on the two girls found in the river?"

I told him what we had learned of the second girl, Margaret Brown.

"That's good progress. Now all they need to do is find the culprit. Make sure you keep track of the story."

"I intend to, sir. Until the twenty-second of May, at least."

He gave an uncomfortable smile.

"Sir, I was wondering whether I could speak with your brother," I ventured.

"Why's that, Miss Green?"

"In his capacity as a physician, I should add."

Mr Sherman's twin brother had agreed to give his expert

medical opinion in the Bermondsey poisoner case I had worked on.

"I should like to find out whether a man's personality could be affected by an injury to his head," I added.

Mr Sherman considered this. "I'm sure we've reported on one or two instances where that has proved to be the case."

"I'd like to hear the view of a medical professional, if at all possible. Do you think he'd be willing to speak with me?"

"I'll gladly ask him, Miss Green."

I was pleasantly surprised to find Sarah waiting for me at the steps of Mrs Garnett's house when I returned that evening. I hoped she was beginning to place some trust in me and would be willing to tell me more about the Twelve Brides.

"Evenin', Miss Green!"

I cautiously returned her smile, mindful of the fact that I would have to ask Mrs Garnett to telegram James while Sarah was in the house. My heart thudded heavily at the thought.

"I suppose you're here to find out how I've been getting on with the riddle," I said.

"Yeah."

I invited her inside and we climbed the stairs up to my room together. Tiger was sitting outside my window waiting to be let in but, catching sight of the stranger in my room, she strolled away across the rooftops.

"Yer cat's scared again," commented Sarah.

"Please don't take it personally; she's like that with everyone. Have a seat here at my desk. Can I get you a drink?"

"No, I'm fine."

I lit my little stove and placed the kettle on it to boil some water for a cup of tea.

She perched stiffly on the chair at my writing desk, then

glanced down at my papers. "Look at all that writin'! I can't write fer toffee, me."

"Has anyone ever taught you?"

"Yeah, I've 'ad some lessons, but I'm no good at writin'."

"What do you enjoy doing?"

"I like the music 'all." Her face brightened. "I go down the Oxford."

"The Oxford Music Hall?" I clarified. I was familiar with the large venue on Oxford Street, though I'd never been inside it.

"Yeah."

"Which are your favourite acts there?"

"Lillie Barrett. I like the songs she sings. Peculiar Alice is funny an' all. I like the acrobats and them high wire acts. Makes me 'ead spin when I look up at 'em!"

"Is that your favourite thing to do in the evenings?"

"Yeah, with a stop-off at the pastry shop on Avery Row, too. They got the best fruit tarts of anywhere."

Sarah seemed to realise she was giving away too much about herself and her lips tightened, as if she wished to stop herself talking.

"I've made a little progress with the riddle," I said.

I told her about my visits to Blackfriars Bridge and London Stone, as well as the theory James and I had about the royal public house names.

She smiled. "I dunno 'ow yer done it, but it sounds good ter me!"

"Do the locations mean anything to you?" I asked her. "Have you heard of any gang members visiting those places?"

Sarah shook her head. "I 'aven't 'eard nothin' about 'em. It's all news ter me."

"Do you know if any of the gang members frequent particular public houses?"

She shrugged. "Nope."

"Are there any you visit regularly?"

"Wheatsheaf. I bin in there a few times, but not often, like."

I tried to conceal my disappointment that the name of the public house she'd mentioned had no royal associations.

"The police have learned the name of the second girl," I said, sitting down on my bed. "Margaret Brown. Have you heard of her?"

"That's 'er name, is it? I only ever known 'er face."

"The police are really keen to talk to you about Margaret and Josephine."

"I don't know nothin' about neither of 'em! And besides, I ain't talkin' to no coppers. I've told yer that."

"I understand there may be reasons why you might prefer not to speak to them, but they're willing to ignore any criminal behaviour which may have occurred in the past... not that I'm suggesting any such thing has occurred, but if it had—"

"'Ave you been talkin' to 'em about me?" Her eyes narrowed.

"They know you gave me the riddle. That's why they'd like to speak to you."

"I ain't got nothin' ter say to 'em."

"They need all the help they can get, Sarah. They're eager to arrest whoever murdered Josephine and Margaret. After all, the perpetrator could easily do the same thing to someone else."

"I gave yer the riddle and that's all I'm doin'." She pursed her lips, seemingly resolute.

I got up from my bed. "I've just remembered that I needed to tell my landlady something," I said. "I shan't be a minute, and when I return I'll be able to tell you more about Rosie Gold if you're interested."

Sarah's eyes brightened. "Yeah, course I'm interested!"

"I'll be as quick as I can."

I hurried downstairs, praying Sarah would remain where she was. I found my landlady mending stockings in her parlour.

"Mrs Garnett, I wonder if I could ask a favour of you. I've received another visit from Sarah. She's up in my room as we speak."

"That young ruffian who came here the other evening?"

"She's not all that bad, but it's a matter of urgency that Inspector Blakely be informed. I wonder if you wouldn't mind paying a quick visit to the police station around the corner and asking them to telegram Scotland Yard to summon him here."

Mrs Garnett put down her sewing and jumped to her feet. "Is she causing trouble?"

"No, not at all, but it's very important that James speaks to her. I can't persuade her to do so voluntarily, so we'll need to take her by surprise, as it were."

She grabbed her shawl from the back of the chair and hurriedly tied it around her shoulders. "Don't you worry, Miss Green, I shall have him summoned at once!"

"Thank you, Mrs Garnett."

"And you be careful now." She looked at me with wide, concerned eyes. "Any trouble at all and you get out onto the street, hollering as loud as you can."

"I'm sure it won't come to that."

"You never know with these girls." She wagged a finger at me.

I returned to my room and was relieved to find that Sarah was still there. She was smiling at Tiger, who was cautiously peering in through the window. All I had to do now was detain her here until James arrived.

I sat down on my bed again.

"Would you like to hear what I've learned about Rosie Gold?" I asked.

Perhaps my manner was a little too forced and cheery because Sarah's expression appeared as guarded as Tiger's.

"Yeah," she replied.

"They've discovered that she frequents the Mondragon Hotel, and apparently she's to attend a party there this Friday. If they manage to arrest her, the murderer of Josephine and Margaret will finally be behind bars."

Sarah gave a faint smile. "Be good if they can get 'er. But they need ter get the rest of 'em an' all."

"What do you mean by 'the rest of them'?"

"It ain't just 'er, is it? There's more of 'em. That's what the riddle's for. It'll help yer get ter all of 'em."

"Do you know any of their names?"

"Nope." She shifted impatiently in the chair. "But just gettin' Rosie on 'er own won't be no good."

"Well, it would be a start at least," I replied. "Hopefully the rest will be soon rounded up too. Perhaps even Miss Danby."

Sarah smiled in response to this. "Where d'yer reckon yer'll go next?"

"What for?"

"The riddle. What yer gonna do next?"

"There are three more references I need to look up. The Earl of Pembroke, Hamlet and the Galtans," I replied. "The line, 'Hamlet no longer treads the boards' might refer to a theatre, so I think I'll need to visit some of the theatres in the West End and find out which have recently performed the play. It might not be a theatre in the West End, of course, but as there are plenty of theatres in the area it makes sense to start there. I'll have to continue my research on the Earl of Pembroke and the Galtans at the library."

"And yer goin' to them theatres tomorrah?"

"I might enquire at the offices of *The London Stage* first. It's a periodical that reports on the theatre world, and the offices are on Drury Lane. Perhaps you'd like to join me?"

"I wouldn't be no 'elp."

"Why not? You might know more than you realise, and then you'll have a chance of solving some of the riddle yourself."

Sarah gave a laugh as she got to her feet. "It don't seem likely."

I felt rather alarmed as she appeared to be readying herself to leave. I knew it would take about twenty minutes for James to get here by cab from Scotland Yard. I needed to detain her for at least another fifteen minutes.

"Perhaps we could look at the riddle together for a moment," I suggested.

"I gotta go."

She made her way toward the door and I knew that if I made any further effort to detain her, she would start to grow suspicious.

"Perhaps I'll see you tomorrow, then," I suggested as she opened the door. "I'll be in Drury Lane at ten o'clock."

She gave me a smile and then was gone.

CHAPTER 31

"I did all I could to keep her here," I told James fifteen minutes later.

He stood in the hallway, bowler hat in hand. "Do you think she knew you'd called for me?"

"I don't see how she could have done."

He gave a long sigh.

"I told her I'll be going to the offices of *The London Stage* in Drury Lane tomorrow," I continued. "I asked her to join me there."

"And she said yes?"

"She gave no answer either way."

"It's fairly unlikely, then."

"She's interested in having the riddle solved, so her curiosity just might get the better of her. I told her I'd be there at ten o'clock."

"I can arrange to be there with some men in plain clothes at that time. They won't make themselves obvious, so you can go about your business as usual. That way she hopefully won't suspect anything if she does turn up."

"And what will you do? Will you arrest her?"

"We'll try speaking to her nicely first, and ideally she'll agree to help without us having to resort to drastic measures." He took his notebook out of his pocket. "Give me a good description of her, Penny, so we know exactly who we're looking for."

◈

I ambled along Drury Lane at the allotted time the following day, hoping beyond hope that Sarah would join me. A light drizzle had started to fall, and various street hawkers tried to sell me watercress and playbills as I passed. A number of dirty-faced children congregated at the end of the narrow streets and passageways. I glanced at the street names, trying to decipher the lettering among the dirt.

When I reached White Horse Yard I paused, wiped the rain from my spectacles and looked up the narrow street, which was crowded with tumbledown buildings. This was where Margaret Brown had lived with her family. The poverty-stricken district was only a short distance from the rich pickings of the West End, so it was really no surprise that some of the inhabitants had turned to shoplifting and even street robbery in an attempt to improve their lot.

I continued on, wondering where James and his men had positioned themselves. Two labourers in shabby woollen suits and flat caps strolled toward me. One was smoking a clay pipe.

Were they really labourers or police officers in plain clothes?

I reached the offices of *The London Stage* and paused, waiting to see whether Sarah would join me. A clock above the nearby ironmonger's shop showed the time to be five minutes after ten o'clock. I turned to walk the length of Drury Lane again, looking out for her all the while.

By the time the clock showed a quarter after ten I

decided I could wait no longer and stepped inside. I felt disappointed Sarah had decided not to join me, but also a slight sense of relief that she hadn't done so. A confrontation with James would have been difficult to endure, and it would almost certainly have meant the end of our brief acquaintance. I still maintained the belief that keeping myself on good terms with Sarah would pay dividends in the long term.

Inside *The London Stage* office I met with Mr Harris, a gentleman with neatly trimmed whiskers who wore a velvet jacket and a silk cravat. He showed me into a room with numerous framed theatre posters on the walls.

"And how can I be of help to the *Morning Express*?" he asked, gesturing toward a chair by the fireplace, then sitting directly opposite me.

"I'm wondering whether there have been any particularly notable performances of *Hamlet* in recent years," I said. "Can you recall any?"

"What do you mean by notable?"

"I'm not really sure. Perhaps the performance was particularly well received or the role of Hamlet was played by a well-known actor."

He steepled his fingers and puzzled over this for a moment. "Well, there have been a fair few. I hope you don't mind me saying so, Miss Green, but your request seems rather an obscure one."

"It does, doesn't it?"

"May I ask the reason behind it?"

"Certainly. I'm seeking the answers to an unusual riddle, you see."

"Oh?"

I opened my notebook and took out the now crumpled

piece of paper. "This riddle purportedly leads to the secret headquarters of a local gang."

His eyebrows raised with interest. "Does it indeed? May I read it?"

"Of course."

He read through it, then gave a sigh. "None of it makes any sense to me, but I see the Hamlet reference now."

"Does it mean anything to you?"

"Nothing at all."

"'Hamlet no longer treads the boards,'" I stated. "Was a performance of *Hamlet* ever cut short unexpectedly?"

"Not that I remember."

"Have any of the theatres decided to stop performing Shakespeare plays?"

"Not that I'm aware of."

"Has an actor who was famous for playing Hamlet recently died?"

"There's Samuel Phelps, I suppose. He died about six or seven years ago."

"Perhaps that's it. Do you know where he's buried?"

"I don't, I'm afraid. I believe he was living out in the direction of Essex when he died."

"Do you know where he lived prior to that?"

"Islington, I think. He managed Sadler's Wells for a number of years, if that's any help."

"Then perhaps the riddle relates to Sadler's Wells Theatre."

He gave a shrug. "Perhaps you're right. I'm no good with riddles, I'm afraid. It could be anything, really, couldn't it?"

"Mr Phelps played Hamlet, managed Sadler's Wells and is no longer with us," I said. "Therefore he no longer treads the boards. It must be Sadler's Wells, mustn't it?" I began to feel a little more hopeful.

"It sounds quite possible. However, Phelps didn't just play

Hamlet; he put on hundreds of Shakespeare productions at Sadler's Wells. His portrayal of King Lear was particularly acclaimed, as was his portrayal of Macbeth."

"Then why would Hamlet be specifically mentioned?"

He shrugged again. "Perhaps the reference has nothing to do with Sadler's Wells after all."

"Is there a theatre where only Shakespeare plays are performed?"

"There's the Shakespeare Memorial Theatre in Stratford-upon-Avon."

"And Sadler's Wells Theatre... That's in Clerkenwell, isn't it?"

"That's right, Miss Green."

I thanked Mr Harris for his time and stepped back out onto Drury Lane.

It seemed to make sense to visit Sadler's Wells Theatre in order to look for a public house nearby with a royal name. I glanced around in the hope that I might see Sarah, but there was no sign of her. I couldn't catch sight of James either. *Were he and his men still in the area?*

I crossed the road and hailed a cab to Clerkenwell. Just as we turned into Great Queen Street, I saw a familiar figure standing on the pavement. I opened the hatch in the roof and requested the driver to stop.

"Sarah!" I called out.

She jumped, then smiled when she saw me.

"There yer are, Miss Green. I've bin lookin' for yer."

"I'm heading over to Sadler's Wells Theatre. I think it may be another location from the riddle!"

"Do yer?"

"Would you like to come with me?"

She gave a nod, so I asked the driver to unlock the door

for her.

I told Sarah about my conversation with Mr Harris as we travelled. "We should hopefully see a public house nearby with a royal-sounding name," I added.

I suspected James would be annoyed to have missed her for a second time. She must have gone looking for me in Drury Lane while I was busy speaking to Mr Harris.

"Some bloke tried speakin' ter me while I was lookin' round for yer."

I felt my heart skip a beat. "Really?"

"Yeah, summat weren't right about 'im. 'E was with another bloke an' all. One asked fer me name but the other didn't say nothin'."

I suspected she had been approached by two police constables.

"Did you tell him your name?" I asked.

"Yeah. Said I was Millie, I did."

The cab stopped outside Sadler's Wells Theatre fifteen minutes later. I paid the fare, climbed out and immediately looked around for the nearest public house. The street we had alighted on, Rosebery Avenue, was wide and lined with trees. Across the road stood a line of townhouses and a small park. A little further down the road from where we stood was a reservoir and waterworks. The immediate area was quiet and pleasant, making it noticeably different from the noise and bustle around Blackfriars Bridge and London Stone.

The drizzle had turned to steady rain, so I opened my umbrella.

"Have you ever been here before?" I asked Sarah.

"Nope. Can't say I 'ave."

We walked on past the theatre and the townhouses toward a road junction. My hopes were raised when I saw a large red-brick public house across the road but sank again when I saw that it was called The Rising Sun. I made a note of this in my notebook anyway and we continued along a rain-soaked street lined with smart four-storey terraced houses on either side. Once I began to feel as though we had ventured too far from the theatre we turned left and walked back toward the start of our walk.

"I haven't seen any other public houses," I said to Sarah. "Only The Rising Sun."

"It don't sound like a royal name ter me."

"No, it doesn't. Perhaps we were mistaken about the royal names. Perhaps we're mistaken about the names of the public houses having any sort of relevance at all."

Our circular route brought us back to the theatre. I paused in front of the building and looked up at its large, pitched roof. The entrance had a wide, columned porch, beneath which we sheltered from the rain for a short while.

"We've had a good look around and I'm struggling to see anything that might be of relevance to the riddle," I said, pulling the piece of paper out of my bag one more time and looking at it. "'Hamlet no longer treads the boards,'" I said again in the hope that the answer would suddenly be revealed to me.

I glanced around at our wet surroundings, and at the rain dripping off the front of the porch. A ball of frustration began to expand in my chest. This seemed to have been the most fruitless visit of all.

"I don't know what the answer here is supposed to be," I said, pushing the riddle back into my bag, aware that it was becoming so crumpled that I would soon need to copy it out again.

I glanced over at Sarah, who stood watching the rain. She

said nothing in response. Perhaps it was unreasonable of me, but I felt a snap of irritation that she had no ideas to share. I was so used to the lively conversation I frequently shared with James, Eliza and Francis that I perhaps had unrealistic expectations of this girl with her limited education.

"I suppose we should take a cab back," I said.

"I'm sorry, Miss Green."

"Whatever for?"

"I ain't been much 'elp, 'ave I? There weren't no point me comin' 'ere with yer."

Sarah spoke as if she had somehow read my mind, making me feel ashamed of my unspoken irritability.

"There's no need to apologise, Sarah. And besides, perhaps this is simply the wrong location. Or perhaps it's the right location but the clue is something other than a public house. To be quite honest, I feel as though my patience is beginning to run out. It would make matters much easier if you could just tell the police everything you know about the gang."

"But I don't know nothin'. I've told yer!"

"You could tell them where to find Miss Danby, for a start."

"What, and get meself murdered fer me trouble?"

"No one need ever know you spoke to them."

"They'd find out some'ow. Them types always do."

CHAPTER 32

In the reading room that afternoon I worked on an article about the number of births and deaths registered in London the previous week. Once I had grown tired of it, I looked up the Earl of Pembroke in *Burke's Peerage* and made a note of everything which seemed relevant. Then I read through these notes and sighed. Even if I managed to identify a location related to this part of the riddle, I was likely to be met with the same disappointment I'd faced at Sadler's Wells Theatre.

"Penny!" came a whisper at my shoulder.

It was James. I returned his smile, then hurriedly packed away my papers so we could talk outside.

"Sarah eventually turned up," I said as we stood on the steps of the British Museum. The rain had stopped and gentle rays of sunshine were making their way through the clouds. "I saw her on the street after I'd left *The London Stage* offices and was in a cab travelling toward Sadler's Wells Theatre. She came with me, in fact."

"At least she showed up. We spotted three or four girls

matching her description," he said, "but none admitted to being called Sarah."

I told James she had been approached by two men but had told them her name was Millie.

He shook his head and tutted. "We nearly had her, then. Had we seen her speaking to you we could have been certain. It was rather clever of her to reply with another name. I'll speak to the constables who approached Millie, as she called herself, and hopefully they'll be able to spot her again in future. Did she reveal anything more about herself during your visit to Sadler's Wells?"

"Not really."

I told James about the disappointing visit, then added, "I don't think it can have been the right location. It didn't feel right, at least. It was rather too leafy and green, and too far away from the centre of London."

"Are you sure the riddle is worth all this time you're spending on it?"

"I was sure we'd made some progress the other day when we realised there was a royal connection between the public house names."

"But how can you be sure we're right?"

"I can't be completely sure, but it seemed to make sense. And if we stumble upon a public house with the Queen's name upon it, I shall feel certain that we're correct."

"And if we don't?"

"Then there must be another connection."

"How much longer do you intend to work on this? I'd much rather we questioned Sarah to find out what she knows."

"I don't think she knows very much at all."

'That's what she wants you to believe, but someone will have recruited her to the gang. She must know some of the other members, and who knows what else they've told her?"

"We can't force Sarah to talk, James."

"There are ways and means."

"She's had a difficult life. You mustn't treat her harshly in any way."

"I'm not suggesting for a minute that we would, but there are certain negotiation techniques we can employ."

"I'll let you know when she visits me next."

"She'll probably slip through the net again, knowing her!"

"She told me she sometimes goes to the Oxford Musical Hall and also to a pastry shop on Avery Row. Perhaps your men could try looking out for her there."

"It's worth a try, but I'm beginning to feel as though she's leading us a merry dance."

The sun had broken away from the clouds and was beginning to warm the steps we were standing upon.

"Meanwhile I've encountered someone else who's keen to help," James added.

"Who might that be?"

"The lady who chased the three girls after the street robbery on Piccadilly. Do you remember her?"

"Mrs Worthers?"

"That's right."

"I've encountered her a couple of times, most recently on Blackfriars Bridge. I'm not sure what she was doing there."

"Crossing the river, perhaps?" James smiled.

"Very amusing! I was surprised to see her there, that's all."

"She's proven to be a useful witness of a few more robberies in the Piccadilly area."

"Does she just stand around waiting for them to happen?"

"It almost seems that way! From what I understand, she lives locally and is rather concerned about crime levels in the area. She's been able to give us good descriptions of the women involved, and Inspector Paget has already made a couple of arrests. If she continues to help us and Paget manages to arrest Rosie Gold, we may not need to speak to Sarah at all."

"I feel sure we're about to make progress with this, James. Either you'll manage to speak to Sarah or we'll have the riddle solved. I've just looked up the Earl of Pembroke in *Burke's Peerage*. I'm assuming the riddle refers to the current earl."

"Why so?"

"Because there have been hordes of them over the years. The title is currently in its tenth iteration, having been revived in 1551. The current Earl of Pembroke is the thirteenth."

"And where is the family seat?"

"Wilton House in Wiltshire."

"Do you intend to travel to Wiltshire?"

"I hope that won't be necessary. There must be a London location to find."

"The earl's London home, perhaps. Have you found out where that is yet?"

"Not yet. 'The Earl of Pembroke rests his head', the riddle says. That suggests a place where he sleeps, doesn't it? Perhaps he has a favourite hotel in London."

"Or perhaps it means a final resting place. Perhaps the riddle refers to a deceased Earl of Pembroke."

"But which one?"

"His father, perhaps? Where is he buried?"

"I wrote it down." I took out my notebook and leafed through my jottings. "Père Lachaise Cemetery in Paris."

"That's even further away than Wiltshire! Does the title of 'earl' have anything to do with Pembroke in Wales?"

"The original title did. About seven hundred years ago the family seat was Pembroke Castle."

"Which is nowhere near London either."

"Perhaps this initiation ritual involves a lot of travelling about."

"But it's for a gang of London-based thieves. It can't be that complicated."

"In which case it must refer to the Earl of Pembroke's London home."

"Or his favourite hotel." James shook his head. "Penny, I think you need to forget about this riddle for now. It's too much of a distraction, and we can't even be certain that it'll lead us to anything useful."

I closed my notebook and put it back in my bag. "I don't want to give up hope just yet," I said.

"I'm not suggesting you should, but you probably need to make a judgement on how much time you plan to devote to it."

"I'll forget about it for now, shall I?"

James laughed. "I'm not suggesting you completely forget about it. Just try not to let it take up too much of your time."

"I'll change the subject, then, at least. Eliza and I are to visit Dr Sherman tomorrow to discuss the possible impact of Father's head injury."

"Are you indeed? It'll be interesting to hear what the physician has to say on the matter."

"If the injury had any bearing on his behaviour it will help me feel a little better about the whole situation."

CHAPTER 33

Eliza and I met at Ludgate Hill Station, this time our destination was Clapham Station.

"It's Dr Henry Sherman, is it?" she asked as we waited on the draughty platform.

"Yes, my editor's twin brother," I replied. "Hopefully he can tell us a little more about the possible effects of an injury to the head."

"I do hope so. Poor Father. I'm beginning to wonder whether I've been rather unkind about him."

"You haven't, Ellie, you were understandably upset."

"But he can't help it if his injury caused him to abandon his family, can he?"

"We can't be sure that's what happened yet," I replied. "That's why I want to speak to Dr Sherman."

"What sort of doctor is he?"

"He's a medical registrar at St George's Hospital, but I don't know what his specialism is."

As the train trundled through south London, Eliza told me she and Francis had visited Hyde Park together, taking turns to ride her bicycle there.

"Without a chaperone again?" I asked with mock scorn.

"We don't require one. It's not as though we're courting!"

"But we've already discussed this, Ellie. A married lady fraternising with a bachelor cannot be considered entirely respectable."

She laughed. "You're a fine one to talk, Penelope!"

"Did you and Francis enjoy your bicycle ride?"

"Yes. It's purely because he's thinking of purchasing a bicycle himself, you see. Nothing more than that."

I pictured the two of them enjoying the spring sunshine in Hyde Park together and smiled.

"What does that expression mean, Penelope?"

"I think you hold some affection for Francis, Ellie."

"Of course I do! But not in the romantic sense; merely because he's a thoroughly decent fellow who has gone to great lengths to help our family. Not only is he brave and generous, but he's also a very interesting chap. He's enormously clever, too."

"He is indeed."

"I do wish you'd stop smiling at me in that odd way."

"You deserve some happiness, Ellie," I said.

"What's that supposed to mean?"

"Having wasted years of your life with that miserable husband of yours, you deserve an opportunity to spend some time with a gentleman who is good company and enjoys yours."

"I think you're reading too much into things, Penelope. It's not that I *deserve* to spend time with Francis, but more that I *enjoy* seeing him. I'm looking forward to having more bicycle rides with him."

"It would be fine by me if you wished to admit that your affection was romantic in nature," I said. "He's a thoroughly decent man, as you say, and would no doubt care for you a great deal."

"I'm a married woman, Penelope!"

"A married woman who happens to be estranged from her husband."

"I won't hear another word about it! Now, you may be interested to learn that the head librarian has offered Francis new employment."

"That's wonderful! He must be very pleased about that."

"He is."

Eliza smiled and I noticed there was a slight flush to her face.

"He's been extremely supportive of the work Mrs Sutherland and I have been doing for the London Women's Rights Society," she continued. "He's even offered to attend our inaugural meeting. You haven't forgotten about it, have you?"

"No, I haven't."

"Good."

"Remind me of the date again."

"You had forgotten, hadn't you? It's on the twenty-second of April."

Dr Sherman lived in a curved row of smart townhouses, appropriately named Crescent Grove, which was just across the street from Clapham Common. His housekeeper showed us into the drawing room where he joined us a short while later.

I had last seen him while investigating the Bermondsey poisoner case. He looked remarkably similar to his brother, with the same thick black moustache and his hair parted to one side. He greeted us warmly and bade us take a seat on a settee upholstered in a smart brocade. The print of a ruined abbey above the fireplace caught my eye, its dark, broken walls silhouetted against a hazy sky.

"The Ruins of Holyrood Chapel," said Dr Sherman,

noticing my glance. "In Edinburgh. I feel quite an attachment to the city where I studied medicine."

"I've heard it's ever so beautiful," commented Eliza.

"Parts of it are breathtaking, though it's a city not without its problems. Like London, I suppose."

I tried to accustom myself once again to conversing with a man who looked just like my editor but whose mannerisms were so different. He was more animated in his speech and his voice had a softer tone to it.

A maid brought in a tray of tea.

"My brother said you'd like to speak to me about injuries of the brain," he said. "It's not a subject I'm a great expert on, I'm afraid."

"But you must know more than the average layperson," I replied.

He gave a laugh. "Oh, I should hope so. I believe the case you wish to discuss concerns your father. I've read about him being found in South America, by the way. You must be overjoyed."

"We're overjoyed that he's alive. It was the best news we could ever have hoped to receive. We are, however, a little concerned about the state of his health."

"I must say at this point that, without being able to examine a patient directly, I'm unable to suggest any clear diagnosis."

"We realise that, but there's an idea we should like to discuss with you if possible."

I told Dr Sherman about my father's fall down the ravine and how we suspected he might have suffered an injury to his head.

"Could the injury have caused a form of brain disease?" I asked. "Might it have impaired his judgement?"

"It sounds like a valid concern, if I may say so," he replied. "And from your description it would seem your father is not quite as you remember him. That will be due, in the most part, to him having lived in a jungle environment for the past ten years, of course. But the complaint of headaches is an interesting one."

"Have you come across this sort of thing before?" I asked.

He smoothed a finger over his moustache as he gave this question some thought. "There was a murder trial in Liverpool about four years ago," he replied. "The defendant was Arthur Watson, a man who had suffered a severe injury to his head five years previously. He was on trial for the murder of his thirteen-month-old daughter."

"Oh, how awful!" exclaimed Eliza.

"The crime was truly barbaric. However, the deliberations during the trial revolved around how accountable the man was for his actions. It was reported that after the accident the pupil in one of his eyes was larger than in the other. He had suffered fits and attacks of paralysis, and his manner was excitable and restless, which he claimed had left him unable to work. Unfortunately, he was also given to the habit of drinking, and this affected him a great deal more because of his medical condition. His doctor strongly advised him to stop. Advice he ignored, I might add. There was a great deal of debate among the medical experts at the trial over whether the head injury had caused him to suffer some form of brain disease or not."

"What conclusion did they reach?'

"The physicians were never able to agree, I'm afraid. Some said the accident had indeed affected his brain, while others said there was no evidence of it."

"And what did the jury decide?"

"They found him guilty of his daughter's murder, and the judge ruled that he had known he was committing a terrible crime."

"And that there was no excuse for his actions, presumably," added Eliza.

"Exactly."

"Does that mean our father is completely responsible for his actions and any supposed brain disease caused by his fall cannot be the cause?" she asked.

"Without being able to medically examine your father, Mrs Billington-Grieg, it's quite impossible to say. There is no doubt that Arthur Watson's head injury caused a change in his health, so the same may well be the case for your father. In the case of Mr Watson, it was decided that his crime was too heinous for his medical condition to excuse it."

"At least Father hasn't committed a murder," I said. "Father's deeds hardly seem dreadful at all when we consider what Mr Watson did!"

"Indeed," agreed Eliza. "But to what extent might his actions have been influenced by a possible injury to his head?"

"I'm afraid that's something you'll have to form an opinion on yourselves," said Dr Sherman.

"But you think there may be a possibility that a head injury could lead to brain disease, and therefore to actions that are inconsiderate or out of character?"

"That is certainly a possibility."

"I suppose he may have some sort of excuse for his behaviour, in that case," said Eliza.

"I don't like to think of it as an excuse," I said. "I think the word '*explanation*' describes it more accurately."

"I see. Then we have an *explanation* for his behaviour."

"A *partial* explanation, perhaps," said Dr Sherman. "But please don't accept my words as a diagnosis. I'd need to examine your father properly in order to provide a more informed opinion. Does he have any plans to return to England?"

"Not that we know of," my sister replied bitterly.

CHAPTER 34

Weigh out four pounds of flour and sift into a pan. Stir in a quart of milk and water, then add a pint of milk, in which an ounce of salt and one and three-fourth ounces of yeast has been dissolved. Place a cloth over the pan and leave for three-quarters of an hour.

"Good morning, Penny," came a whisper at my shoulder.

I turned and smiled when I saw Francis standing there.

He peered down at my page. "Are you writing up some interesting news?"

"If only," I replied. "It's a recipe for Vienna bread to appear in the next ladies' column. Congratulations on your return to the reading room, by the way!"

"Thank you." He grinned. "A return to the ordinary routine is certainly welcome. How are you progressing with the riddle?"

I was about to reply when I noticed Mr Retchford glaring at us.

Francis followed my gaze. "I'll be taking a break shortly," he whispered. "Shall we talk outside then?"

I gave a nod.

Francis and I stood on the steps of the British Museum and I told him about the royal connection in the names of the public houses, then about my journey to Clerkenwell and how it appeared to have yielded nothing.

"The Earl of Pembroke has been bothering me," I added.

"Has he indeed? How very inconsiderate of him."

I laughed. "I'm quite tired of reading about his lineage. However, I found some time to do a little more research this morning before I had to get on with my Vienna bread recipe, and I think I may have identified a possible new location."

"That sounds promising! Where?"

"The line in the riddle reads, 'the Earl of Pembroke rests his head', which suggests he is either asleep or dead."

"That sounds reasonable."

"I decided to consider deceased earls first because I couldn't begin to work out where the current earl might like to sleep."

"A matter that is presumably the man's own business and no one else's."

"Indeed. So I studied all the earls in order, looking for one who might stand out."

"And is there one?"

"Yes, there is. I read a little more about him and found he was described as one of the greatest knights who ever lived."

"Really?"

"Yes. He was the first earl of the second creation of the Pembroke title in 1199. His name was William Marshal and he served five English kings. Of greatest interest to us, however, is his burial place."

"Ah yes, I know him now! And I recall that he is buried in the church built by the Knights Templar. Temple Church, isn't it?"

"That's right. Conveniently, it's just a stone's throw from the *Morning Express* offices! I've been reading all about it in Mr Fry's guide to London."

"That sounds promising."

"I hope so. And even if it's a wasted journey at least I won't have to travel far to get to work."

I noticed a familiar figure in a bowler hat turning into the courtyard in front of us.

"That looks like James," I said happily.

"I think you may be right. Perhaps he'll visit Temple Church with you if he has the time."

"James is growing tired of the riddle," I said. "He'd rather arrest the girl who gave it to me than persevere with it."

"That's because he's a police officer and prefers to get his job done quickly and efficiently," said Francis. "This riddle is taking quite a while to solve, after all."

James greeted us both with a smile as he climbed the steps.

"It sounds as though Penny has solved another line of the riddle," replied Francis.

"I don't know for sure that I have," I added. "It's just an idea."

"Let's hear it, then," said James.

I told him about my latest research.

"There could be something in that," he said with an appreciative nod once I had finished.

"It's conveniently close to my work," I said. "I'll visit the church on my way back to the *Morning Express* offices. What brings you here, James?"

"Rosie Gold has been apprehended."

"That's excellent news!"

"It should be, but it's not. She's in St Thomas's Hospital at the present time. She attended the Mondragon Hotel as Inspector Paget and his men anticipated but, before they had a chance to apprehend her, she was attacked."

"Goodness, that's awful!" I exclaimed. "Is she badly injured?"

"Yes, quite seriously. The nurses at St Thomas's refused to let us speak to her. It seems we weren't the only people who were tipped off about her being at The Mondragon."

"Has the culprit been apprehended?"

"Not yet. It's possible she knew her attacker and will be able to give us a description, but until we're able to speak to her we'll just have to continue with the investigation as best we can."

"I suppose we should be pleased we finally know where she is."

"Yes, I suppose there's that."

"Do you think a member of the Twelve Brides might have harmed her?"

He gave a shrug. "Either that or someone from a rival gang, such as the Bolsover Gang or the Portman Mob."

"At least you can keep her in custody once she's well enough to be detained," I said. "Perhaps there will be no need to solve the riddle after all."

"Even so, it still needs to be unpicked," said Francis. "I can't bear the thought of it remaining unsolved."

"You're more than welcome to take it on, Francis," said James with a smile.

"I'm quite tempted to, and now that I'm employed in the reading room again I have all the knowledge I need at my disposal. What have you learned about the Galtans? They're the most puzzling of all in the riddle, aren't they? I've never heard of them."

"My research has turned up nothing," I replied. "It would

be extremely helpful if you could find out something about them, Francis."

"There was something about a letter, wasn't there?"

"Yes. 'A letter to the Galtans is widely read,'" I recited.

"Do you know the riddle off by heart now, Penny?" he asked.

"I'm afraid so."

"Leave the Galtans with me for now. I can read up on them during any quieter moments we have at this fine institution." He nodded in the direction of the building behind us. "Let me know how you get on with Temple Church, won't you?"

"We will," I replied. "Oh, and I'm looking forward to hearing more stories of bicycle rides in Hyde Park."

Francis' face coloured. "Eliza mentioned that, did she?"

"Of course." I grinned.

"I'm thinking of buying one, you see, so I thought it prudent to ask your sister if she'd allow me to have a ride on hers just to test it out."

"What an excellent idea," I replied.

CHAPTER 35

James had offered to accompany me to Temple Church, so we travelled by cab to Fleet Street.

"It's excellent news that Rosie Gold has been arrested, or at least it will be when she recovers."

"*If* she recovers."

"Oh dear, are her injuries that serious?"

"She was attacked by three women, one of whom had a knife, and if it hadn't been for the swift actions of the hotel staff she could have been killed."

"I wonder who might have wished to harm her so viciously."

"Paget is doing what he can to find out, but I think it's most likely to be a rival gang. The women fled before any of his men could get hold of them."

"Have you seen her in person yet?"

"No, not yet. The nurses won't allow us anywhere near her."

"I wonder what she looks like."

"According to Inspector Paget, she changes her appearance quite regularly."

"I wonder if Mrs Worthers and Rosie Gold are one and the same."

James turned to me. "Do you think that might be possible?"

"It might be. It would explain why she took such an interest in the street robberies, wouldn't it? Perhaps she wasn't helping you, as she claimed, but misleading you instead."

"That's an interesting thought."

"You'll find out soon enough once you're able to speak to Rosie Gold. Or when you find that Mrs Worthers is mysteriously no longer around."

We disembarked from the cab on Fleet Street.

"Temple Church is located within the Inner Temple," I said.

"One of the four inns of court," added James. "Home of the barristers, some of whom are extremely accomplished at their craft and others less so. While I think about it, I learned some news today that will please you. Have you read the family announcements in the *Morning Express* today?"

"Not yet."

"When you have the chance to do so, you'll be interested to see that an engagement between Charlotte Jenkins and some poor chap from the Pinner area has been announced."

"And you're quite sure it's *the* Charlotte Jenkins?"

"Yes, her father's name and address is listed."

"Well, that is good news, is it not? Hopefully she'll forget all about you now."

I felt relieved that James' former fiancée had found someone else to marry. Not only did it mean that she would bother us no more, but it also assuaged some guilt I felt at having played a part in putting an end to their engagement.

We entered the Inner Temple through an old stone archway on Fleet Street. The archway was set beneath an ancient building that was now home to a hairdresser's shop. The sign, placed up high, read: 'Formerly the Palace of Henry VIII and Cardinal Wolsey'.

The noise of Fleet Street was replaced by a calmer, more collegiate atmosphere as we walked. Two gentlemen in black barrister gowns and long white collars passed by. A narrow lane led us up to a church with a low, round tower, which was quite encroached upon by the surrounding buildings of the Inner Temple. The church's cream stonework and Romanesque arched windows contrasted with the dark brick and uniform squares of the buildings around it.

"This place dates back to the twelfth century," I said as we walked around the church to its entrance. "It was built by the Knights Templar as their English headquarters."

James glanced around. "This area must have looked very different back then," he commented. "When did the lawyers move in?"

"At about the same time, from what I've read. The earliest ones were legal advisers to the Knights Templar."

James smiled. "You're starting to sound almost as knowledgeable about these matters as Francis."

"I've been reading almost as much as he does lately."

We stepped into the quiet interior of the church, where the vaulted ceiling of the chancel rose high above our heads. It was decorated with an intricate design of red, blue and gold.

"Herbert Fry mentioned some carved stone effigies on the ground," I said.

"Who is Herbert Fry?"

"He wrote a guidebook to London in 1880, which is proving extremely useful for my research. I think we should visit the tower section. It's the oldest part of the church."

We walked along the nave until we reached a number of stone figurines lying among the marble pillars.

"These look just about life-sized," said James. Each man appeared to be a knight dressed in chainmail and holding a sword and shield.

"I think they must be," I replied, counting them. "There are nine in total. Now, which one is William Marshal?" Some of the effigies were labelled with names, while others had no label at all.

"There's a Gilbert Marshal here," I said, pausing beside one of them. "I think he was another Earl of Pembroke."

"Here," said James, standing before one of the effigies. "This one says William Marshal." I joined him and we examined the recumbent knight together.

"He's been here an extremely long time," I commented. "Almost seven hundred years."

"And you think William Marshal is the one the riddle refers to, do you?"

"I can't be completely sure, but there are two other earls of Pembroke here as well... descendants of his." I glanced around at the other knights. "So we have three earls here altogether. I'm sure this has to be the right place."

"What do we do now?"

"I think we should look for the nearest public house."

"There isn't likely to be one close by, is there? We're standing in the middle of a church."

"I realise that, but there must be one somewhere. I'm sure the lawyers would be rather put out if they didn't have a local drinking hole to frequent."

"Then I suppose we'd better get looking for one."

I took one last glance around the round tower we were standing inside. The vaulted ceiling rose high above our heads and the daylight filtered through the stained-glass windows in varying streams of colour. I removed my glove and felt the cold of the heavy marble pillar next to me.

"It's so peaceful in here," I said. "It almost seems a shame to go back outside."

"It certainly feels like a haven of some sort," said James. "It's quite astonishing to think it's been here for so long. There's something rather fascinating about the Knights Templar, isn't there?"

"I hope this is the correct location," I said as we turned to leave.

"But if not, it was still a nice place to visit."

We stepped out of the church and began our search for a public house. James stopped a gentleman dressed in a black gown and asked where the nearest one might be.

"There are a great number on Fleet Street. It depends what sort of establishment you're after. I tend to avoid the ones that are popular with the ink-scribblers."

James gave a wry smile in response to this comment. "There's no public house within the Inner Temple itself, then?" he asked.

"No, but I can recommend The Golden Lion on Temple Lane. It's much quieter than some of those noisy establishments on the main street."

"That wasn't a great deal of help," I said quietly as the barrister went on his way.

"I suppose we should return to Fleet Street," said James. "That's where all the public houses are."

"I can't recall seeing any there with a royal title."

"Are you familiar with all the public houses on Fleet Street?"

"The only one I've ever visited is Ye Olde Cheshire Cheese."

"Perhaps there are one or two you regularly pass without giving them any thought. Shall we take a look? One of the public houses has to be named after 'our best-known mourner', don't you think?"

"Yes, but I don't recall ever seeing a public house around here with 'queen' in its name."

We walked back along Inner Temple Lane until the noise and bustle of Fleet Street assaulted our senses once again. We turned right and I pointed across the road to a site where a couple of buildings had recently been pulled down.

"The Cock Tavern used to stand there," I said. "The Bank of England intends to erect a building there for its business with the law courts. It's a shame the old pub was demolished, it was rather famous."

"I've heard of it," said James, "though it doesn't have the right name for the purposes of our riddle, does it?" We walked on a short distance and came across a public house called The White Horse.

"This isn't right," I said. "I think we've strayed too far from Temple Church now. We should retrace our steps."

"I agree. However, I can't help but feel that this accursed riddle is sending us on a wild goose chase. Perhaps Temple Church is the wrong location again. Or perhaps we're simply wasting an inordinate amount of our time on this." We began to walk back in the direction from which we had come.

"All we need to do now is arrest Sarah," continued James. "Together with Rosie Gold the pair should be able to give us some extremely useful information. We need to speak to *people*; that's the way to piece all this together. Not following some convoluted, nonsensical riddle."

While James had been talking, something of interest had caught my eye. I stopped.

"Well, look at that," I said, pointing straight ahead.

"Oh!" James replied with a nod. "Well done, Penny."

"And to think we didn't even look at it properly before we turned into Inner Temple Lane!"

Just beyond the entrance to the lane stood a public house. The sign hanging outside proclaimed it to be The Prince of Wales.

"There you have it!" I gave James a broad grin. "That's the third public house with a royal name. That has to be the connection, doesn't it? If we're looking for five public houses then we just need another two with royal names: one that's associated with the Hamlet clue and the other with the Galtans."

"Whoever they might be."

I took out my notebook and wrote down the name of the public house. "We're getting closer."

James and I parted ways on Fleet Street. He headed back toward Scotland Yard while I walked the short distance to my office. Waiting outside it was a familiar figure in a worn bonnet and shawl.

"Sarah!" I exclaimed.

I glanced behind me to see whether James was still within sight, but he had disappeared into the crowd.

"Thought I'd come down to yer office to see 'ow yer gettin' on."

I suspected she had seen me with James and kept her distance until I was alone.

"Did you see Inspector Blakely just now?" I asked.

"I din't see no one. I don't want ter speak to no coppers, anyways."

"Have you heard about the attack on Rosie Gold?"

"Yeah, I've 'eard it alright."

"Do you think the attacker meant to kill her?"

She shrugged. "I dunno."

"Who did you hear the news from?"

"Miss Danby." She shrugged again.

"The police will arrest Rosie Gold once she has recovered

a little more, which means they'll have the person responsible for the murders of Josephine and Margaret in custody."

"Yeah, but they gotta prove it now, ain't they? She'll 'ave a trial, but she won't never 'ave got 'er own 'ands dirty. She'll 'ave ordered someone else ter do it. 'Ow d'yer go about provin' that?"

"I don't know. I suppose that's a matter for the police. They're working extremely hard on the case, Sarah, but it would really help if you could speak—"

"I ain't doin' it. I keep tellin' yer!"

"I see. Well, you'll be pleased to hear that Inspector Blakely and I have just identified The Prince of Wales as the third public house in the riddle," I said. "That's three hostelries with royal names now."

"That's good news, that is. Any idea about them other ones?"

"Not yet, but I shall keep working on it. With the help of a few other people, of course."

This appeared to be all Sarah wanted to hear. She bid me good day and was gone.

CHAPTER 36

I took my seat for the inaugural meeting of the London Women's Rights Society in the Craven Lecture Hall; a draughty venue hidden away on Foubert's Place, close to Regent's Street. A number of well-dressed ladies took their seats around me, and at the front of the room Eliza was chatting animatedly to Mrs Sutherland. Both were modestly dressed: Eliza in her divided skirt and matching jacket, and Mrs Sutherland with her neat, plain hair and simple dress. Some of the other ladies around me appeared dressed for the occasion, however, with feathers in their hats, furs around their shoulders and frilled trimmings encircling their necklines and cuffs.

Although I supported the causes of these groups, I had attended a number of similar meetings before and often found the discussions rather tedious.

As I glanced around me, I was struck by a familiar face: with her brown hair and freckled complexion there was no mistaking Mrs Worthers at the end of the row. I bit my lip as I pondered this. *Why did she keep turning up?* With Rosie Gold now in hospital, I realised she couldn't be the infamous gang leader. *But might she still have something to do with the Twelve Brides?*

I decided a conversation with her might be informative, so I got up and squeezed past the knees of the ladies sitting between us as politely as possible.

"Oh, Miss Green!" She seemed surprised by my approach and got to her feet. "How nice to see you here." She adjusted the brim of her burgundy hat. I wondered how she had remembered my name, but reminded myself that I had also remembered hers.

I greeted her with a smile, then said, "Inspector Blakely tells me you've witnessed several more robberies on Piccadilly."

"Oh, I have. Dreadful, it is. These girls just keep on getting away with it."

"Well, it seems you've provided some useful witness accounts. I know he's very grateful for them."

"Oh, is he?" She seemed a little bashful on hearing this. "I'm just pleased I could be of some help. The police have a difficult job to do. They're quite outnumbered, aren't they? These gangs seem to grow their numbers rather easily."

"I suppose it's quite easy to persuade girls who are living in poverty to join them if they can promise money and protection."

"But the girls must surely realise the risks of being caught. Not that the police seem capable of catching them very often."

"The robberies should stop once the ringleaders have been apprehended," I said.

"They'll no doubt be replaced by another gang," she replied.

I gave a nod of agreement. "The ultimate solution is to tackle the reasons why people join gangs in the first place."

"They are many and varied," she added. "It could take us a lifetime to solve, couldn't it?"

I found myself warming to Mrs Worthers a little.

"How did you hear about the London Women's Rights Society?" I asked her.

"I was already a member of the North London Women's Rights Society and, when Mrs Sutherland told us about this new organisation, I was more than keen to support it. Mrs Billington-Grieg seems an interesting lady. I like the fact that she prefers rational dress to corsets and bustles. I hear she founded the West London Women's Society."

"Yes, she did."

"Do you know her?"

"She's my sister."

Mrs Worthers smiled broadly. "Well, I didn't know that! You must be very proud."

I glanced over to where Eliza stood chatting with Mrs Sutherland. "I am, actually. Despite our differences she's always been a good sister to me."

I bid Mrs Worthers farewell and returned to my seat. I was reading through the agenda when I felt someone slip into the chair next to me. I looked up to offer a cordial greeting.

"Francis!" I exclaimed. "I think you may be the only gentleman here."

"I like to support such excellent causes."

"That's very noble of you. I'm sure Eliza will be extremely grateful for your attendance." I glanced down at the copy of the agenda in my hand. "We could be in for rather a long evening. There are all sorts of people to be voted onto the committee, and the terms of the new organisation need to be agreed." I had readied myself with my notebook in anticipation.

"How did you get on at Temple Church?" he asked.

"Very well, thank you. We found another public house with a royal name!"

"Excellent! That does seem to be the connection, then. Hopefully we won't have much more to do before we can solve the rest of it. I've done a bit of work on the Galtans but I really haven't been able to find anything at all. I'm beginning to wonder whether it's a spelling mistake. There was another error in the riddle, wasn't there?"

"Yes, 'Pembroke' was missing an 'r'."

"I wonder whether 'Galtans' might also be a misspelling. It's unusual to find so little information on any given subject. And if you're going to find out about something, the British Library is surely the place to do it!"

"It's possible that line was copied down incorrectly," I said. "But I wonder what it should be if that's the case."

"I'll carry on looking into it and consider a few alternatives. What was the other location?"

"My failed journey to Sadler's Wells. I think it must have been the wrong theatre. I asked Mr Harris at *The London Stage* if there was a theatre that only performed Shakespeare plays and he told me about the Shakespeare Memorial Theatre in Stratford-upon-Avon. It couldn't be that far away, could it?"

"All the other locations appear to be in the centre of London."

"They do, don't they?"

The audience fell silent as Mrs Sutherland rose to speak. She thanked everyone for their attendance and spoke with a clear, authoritative voice, commanding the attention of the room.

"I'm sure I'm not the only one who was disappointed to read Mr Philip Vernon Smith's recent opinion piece in the *National Review*," she continued. "A number of you are no doubt acquainted with his words, but for those who aren't I shall paraphrase them here, giving them as little weight as possible. His main objection to universal suffrage is based upon the fact that women outnumber men in this country. According to Mr Smith, this could result in the transfer of the government of this country to the fairer sex. Can you imagine anything more frightful, ladies?" She paused until the laughter had died down. "Yes, it seems Mr Smith is extremely afraid of being governed by women. He is also fearful that the pursuance of women's suffrage will lead to a battle between the sexes!" More laughter ensued. "He also states that women could never sit in parliament because to admit them into the violent conflict of political life would be as unnatural as sending women into battle as members of the army or navy. His solution, therefore, is to prevent women from sitting in parliament by passing a special law."

This statement whipped the audience around me into a suitable frenzy, with proclamations of outrage widely shared. Once everyone had been given their say and the room had quietened again, Mrs Sutherland continued with her speech. Although pertinent and impassioned, it lasted longer than I had ideally hoped, and I found myself having to stifle a few yawns.

It came as a welcome relief when Eliza began to speak. She introduced the women who wished to join the committee and requested the approval of the audience via a show of hands. The vote went in their favour and a discussion regarding the remit of the new organisation began.

I made notes as I listened but my thoughts drifted back to Rosie Gold. I hoped she was making a swift recovery; less for her sake and more for the sake of Inspector Paget and Sergeant Bradshaw's investigation. *How had those poor girls ended up in the river?* I could only hope that Rosie Gold had the answers. *If she didn't, who could possibly be behind the murders? And who was responsible for the attack on Rosie herself?*

The debate taking place around me continued. I glanced up at Francis and noticed that, despite his profession of enthusiasm, the expression on his face appeared a little weary.

My interest was piqued again when Eliza was voted in as chairwoman. It was wonderful to witness her broad smile. I could see how much the moment meant to her, and I also noticed a lingering glance between her and Francis.

"She has done extraordinarily well," he said to me as we stood and applauded. "Your sister really is quite special, isn't she?"

"I certainly think so," I replied. "She can be quite infuriating at times, but that makes her all the more special, I suppose."

The lady who had been voted in as treasurer stood to her feet and read aloud from a piece of paper in her hand: "The new organisation need not struggle to get up and running, for it has received a loan of five hundred pounds from Mrs Sutherland, and I should also add that no interest will be due on the repayments. We are very lucky indeed to have such a generous benefactor."

There was a loud round of applause, following which Mrs Sutherland rose to her feet once again.

"Thank you for your gratitude," she said, "but it really isn't necessary. I believe in making financial gifts to all the causes I support. However, the London Society for Women's Rights is a cause that is particularly close to my heart." Her speech continued for a while longer and, although I was trying to make notes my eyelids began to feel heavy. I pressed the sharp nib of the pencil into my fingertips to keep myself awake.

I felt relieved to get up from my seat and stretch out my legs once the meeting had drawn to a close.

"Returning to the subject of the riddle, I've been giving it some further thought," said Francis. "I was obviously paying attention to the proceedings here, but something also occurred to me about the riddle." He took his spectacles off and gave them a polish.

"You're enjoying trying to solve it, aren't you?" I commented.

"I am!" He grinned. "With regard to the *Hamlet* clue, I'm wondering if the location is specific to the play itself or whether it refers to Shakespeare in general."

Eliza joined us. "Are the two of you talking about that riddle again?" She gave a sigh.

As Francis and I were congratulating her on the evening's event, Mrs Sutherland then came over to speak to her, allowing us to return to the riddle.

"Hmm, 'Hamlet no longer treads the boards'," I mused. "I think it either means the play has ended or the theatre has closed. The problem is, we don't know exactly when. It could be a recent event or it may have happened quite some time ago."

"Perhaps even in Shakespeare's time," suggested Francis, replacing his spectacles.

"Didn't he have his own theatre company?"

"Yes, he did. I think it was called the King's Men."

"This sounds interesting," said Mrs Sutherland, breaking off from her conversation with Eliza. "Do you enjoy Shakespeare?"

"Yes," Francis and I chorused.

"We were trying to remember the name of his theatre company," I said. "We think it was the King's Men."

"Yes, that rings a bell," she replied. "I think they were the Lord Chamberlain's Men when Elizabeth was queen, then changed the name to the King's Men under James I."

"Fascinating!" said Eliza. "I didn't realise you had a head for history, Mrs Sutherland!"

"I don't really, but I do enjoy a bit of Shakespeare."

"We're trying to remember whether they had a playhouse or were merely a travelling company," said Francis.

"They had a few," replied Mrs Sutherland. "The first was called The Theatre. Hardly original, is it? After that there was the Curtain Theatre and then the Globe. None of them stand any longer, of course. The Theatre eventually moved across the river and became the Globe."

"Which was closed during the English Civil War," said Francis. "I know that much."

"This is all very interesting, but it has nothing to do with why we're here this evening," said Eliza.

Mrs Sutherland gave a laugh. "I suppose it's nice to change the subject now and then."

The conversation returned to the evening's main discussion points and, as Eliza and Mrs Sutherland talked, Francis and I managed to extricate ourselves.

"The Globe!" I whispered excitedly. "That could be it, couldn't it?"

"The Globe is long gone," he replied. "The Puritans demolished it more than two hundred years ago when they forbade anyone to enjoy themselves."

"But it's the most famous of Shakespeare's theatres, is it not? The line 'Hamlet no longer treads the boards' suggests the theatre is gone."

Francis gave a laugh. "Good luck to anyone who tries to find it again. From what I've read, its foundations lie beneath one of the breweries in Southwark."

"Do you know which?"

"Barclays Brewery, I think. That's the best-known one there."

"That could be the location the riddle is referring to!"

"But there's nothing to see there, Penny... just a brewery. From what I recall there isn't much of interest in the area at all. It's close to the riverside, where there are various wharves, stores and a number of factories."

As he spoke, I noticed Mrs Worthers glancing in my direction. As I met her gaze she turned away again.

"I think it's worth a visit all the same," I said distractedly.

"Are you all right, Penny?"

"I'm fine, just a little tired. And rather baffled by a few things, too."

CHAPTER 37

It was a warm, hazy morning as Eliza and I travelled by cab to the northern end of Southwark Bridge and then walked across the river to the south side. Beyond the cranes and warehouses of the southern bank wharves lay the golden-brown sprawl of the Barclays Brewery buildings. A heavy malt smell filled our noses as we reached the end of the bridge. We continued down Southwark Bridge Road, passing a pair of large gates which led into the brewery.

"I don't suppose we're allowed to wander in there," I said.

"I wouldn't have thought so," replied Eliza.

"Perhaps we should walk a little further and then decide whether we need to venture inside the brewery itself."

We turned left into Castle Street and began to traverse the perimeter of the brewery walls. We passed a number of gates and passageways leading into the brewery and, before long, we reached the main entrance where carts laden with caskets passed through the large gateway. I asked a man where we might find the site of the old Globe Theatre.

He pointed in through the gates. "They say it's under the porter store'ouse."

"Is there nothing to see of it now?"

He gave a laugh. "Not likely! It's long gone."

I thanked him and we continued on our way, turning left into Park Street. Here the brewery buildings loomed on either side of us, connected by iron walkways that ran high above our heads.

Eliza paused and looked around. "Shakespeare's theatre once stood here? In the middle of a brewery?"

"Apparently so."

"It seems such a shame that the site has been built over without any thought, and now it's lost forever. It's rather sad, don't you think?"

"It is indeed."

As we walked on, we could see the end of Southwark Bridge crossing the road we were on.

"We're almost back where we started," commented Eliza. "This is beginning to feel as hopeless as that time we walked across Blackfriars Bridge."

"But that wasn't hopeless in the end, Eliza. We came across The Crown that day, remember? Another public house with a royal name."

"We hardly received a royal welcome in there!"

"It's the name that matters. All we need to find here is another public house with a royal name. Perhaps one that's named after the Queen, 'our best-known mourner'."

Eliza stopped suddenly. "Well I never!" She exclaimed. "How astonishing!"

Shortly before the end of the bridge was a narrow lane that led off to the right. On the corner of it sat a public house.

"The Royal Oak, that's it!" said Eliza. "We've found it, Penelope!"

I pulled my notebook out of my carpet bag and wrote down the name.

"Perfect!" I replied. "That's the fourth one now. The Crown, The King's Arms, The Prince of Wales and The Royal Oak."

"You were right all along!" she said.

"I can't claim to have solved this particular clue; that was more Francis' doing. Come to think of it, we really have Mrs Sutherland to thank! She overheard us discussing Shakespeare's theatres and mentioned the Globe."

"Quite a bit of perseverance is required with this riddle, isn't it?" said Eliza. "We've been walking around the boundary of a brewery gradually convincing ourselves that nothing will come of it. If only we'd taken the steps down from the bridge just there, we'd have found it much sooner!"

"We weren't to know," I replied. "I think we only have one more public house to find now."

"It's quite fun, really, isn't it?" said my sister. "It's a shame the origins of it are so awful, what with its connection to an unpleasant gang and the suchlike. I think more riddles like this should be devised purely for fun. If there wasn't a tragic reason behind our solving it, I'd be quite enjoying myself now!"

⚜

"Was my brother able to be of any help, Miss Green?" asked Mr Sherman when I arrived back in the newsroom.

"He was indeed. Thank you, sir."

"I'm pleased to hear it. What was his verdict?"

"He told us it was impossible to be certain of anything without examining my father in person, and he stated that he cannot be considered an expert when it comes to head injuries."

"That sounds just like him. He's always keen to stress a note of caution before he gives an opinion on anything. I think it's quite common among physicians; it absolves them of a certain measure of responsibility."

"That wasn't the impression he gave, sir. Dr Sherman was able to describe to us the case of a man who had suffered an injury to the head and then he explained the subsequent debate on whether it had caused brain disease or not."

"I see. Well if the conversation was of assistance, I'm pleased to hear it, Miss Green."

"Yes, it was helpful, thank you. I feel sure there must be some explanation for my father's behaviour, which would make the matter a little easier for me to accept. I simply cannot imagine that he willingly abandoned his family. It's far easier to believe that the uncharacteristic decision he made was caused by a form of brain disease."

"I'd argue that Mr Green wasn't using his brain at all," Edgar piped up.

"Quiet, Fish!" scolded my editor, who seemed keen to protect my feelings. "It sounds like a highly plausible explanation to me, Miss Green. On another note, I must say that I liked your report on the new London Women's Rights Society. I shall include it in the ladies' column."

"Couldn't it appear elsewhere in the paper, sir? How about under notes of the day? Or general news, at the very least? It should be of interest to gentlemen as well as to ladies."

Edgar gave a cynical snort. "Are you sure of that, Miss Green? I can't imagine many chaps showing an interest in it."

"It's certainly relevant to our lady readers," said Mr Sherman, "and we don't want them missing out on the news, which is why I felt it should appear in the ladies' column. It will probably be the only section of the newspaper many ladies read. If I include it there they'll go on to read your excellent recipe for Vienna bread, which I also liked very much. In fact, there's room for one more recipe if you could work on that. I think syrup scones would prove rather popular."

"I must confess that I've never actually made syrup scones."

"Perhaps you have another recipe you prefer?"

"I'm not a great cook at all, sir. My landlady cooks most of my meals."

"I see, well our readers needn't know that you've never made syrup scones. Do you have time to research a recipe today?"

"I should imagine so, sir," I replied with a sigh. The thought of writing out the recipe gave me little excitement. "Am I right in thinking that this new society for women's rights carries the same level of importance as recipes for bread and scones in the eyes of the *Morning Express*?"

"Of course not, Miss Green!" He scowled. "The report on the London Women's Rights Society will sit at the very top of the column. You know that's how we arrange the layout. The most important stories are always at the top."

"But it's not important enough to be included under notes of the day?"

"There's rather a lot of news to report at the moment. I'm afraid it would be completely buried under notes of the day. And under general news too, for that matter."

"Who will write the ladies' column when I'm gone, sir?"

Mr Sherman scratched at his temple. "Good question, Miss Green. The suggestion at the present time is that Mrs Conway may do it herself."

"The proprietor's wife?" I asked incredulously. "What writing experience does she have?"

"I must confess that her experience is minimal, but I'm told she has a lot of good ideas."

"It sounds as though the ladies' column will be in excel-lent hands, then," I replied with an insincere smile.

CHAPTER 38

"I've been told I must leave my job because I'm to become a married woman," I stated, "and yet the new writer of the ladies' column is also a married woman!"

"She's married to the proprietor, though," said James. "That's the difference."

"It's complete hypocrisy," I fumed, "and she has no writing experience whatsoever! Being replaced is one matter, but being replaced by someone who isn't even a writer... That newspaper will regret it soon enough."

"I'm sure they will," agreed Eliza.

James and I were sitting in her dining room along with Francis.

"Besides all that, the London Women's Rights Society is deemed no more important than syrup scones!" I added.

"Says who?" my sister queried.

I told her about the decision Mr Sherman had made. "Perhaps it's best that I'm leaving after all," I added. "If I were to stay any longer, I'd find myself constantly frustrated by the odd decisions Mr Sherman and Mr Conway seem increasingly determined to make."

"But Mr Sherman has no desire for you to leave," said James. "He's been forced to let you go because of Mr Conway."

"And because of *Mrs* Conway, who has probably spotted an opportunity to fulfil her own writing aspirations. Perhaps she's been looking for the first excuse to be rid of me all this time."

"I'm sure that's not the case," said Francis.

"Well I'm sure that it is!" I snapped.

James and Francis exchanged a glance that suggested there was no use in trying to argue with me.

"Have you heard Francis' theory on the Galtans, Penelope?" asked my sister, changing the subject.

"No." I was instantly interested. "What is it?"

Francis cleared his throat. "I've been puzzling about this for a long time now. In fact, I've found myself lying awake a few nights just thinking about it. I haven't found a single reference anywhere to the Galtans. I wondered whether it was a geographical area or a group of people. Then I began to think about the letter and wondered why it might be widely read. That suggested to me that a lot of people must have read it, so perhaps it was posted in a prominent position somewhere or even published.

"As we discussed previously, there was also a chance that this version of the riddle had been copied down incorrectly. Perhaps an error had been made. After all, the person who wrote it down managed to copy down 'Lapis Milliaris' but misspelled 'Pembroke'. So I thought 'Galtans' might also have been misspelled."

"But what else could it be?" I asked.

"There are all sorts of possibilities, and I wrote down a great number of them. Galthans, Gallans, Garlans, that sort of thing, but none of them made any sense to me."

"Did you come up with anything that did make sense?"

"Yes. I believe it should be 'Galatians'."

"Isn't that a book in the Bible?" asked James.

"Yes, it is. The ninth book in the New Testament, in fact. Its proper title is 'the Epistle to the Galatians'."

"And an epistle is a letter," I said.

"Exactly."

"And it's part of the Bible, which means it has been widely read!"

"Indeed."

"But how do we find the location we need from that? Might there be a clue somewhere in the book of Galatians?"

"I've read through it a few times but nothing has leapt out at me so far."

"I must see a copy myself," I said. "Where might I find a Bible?"

"There's one in George's study," said Eliza. "Well, I suppose it's *my* study now."

I stood to my feet, ready to fetch it.

"You're welcome to read through it, as I have done, Penny," said Francis, "but you may still find yourself at a loss as to what to think."

I sat back down and gave this some thought. "The Epistle to the Galatians is a letter," I mused. "Do we know who wrote it?"

"My knowledge of the Bible isn't particularly vast, but I believe Galatians is one of the Pauline Epistles," replied Francis.

"What does that mean?"

"The epistles written by Paul."

"Paul the Apostle?"

"Yes."

"Saint Paul?"

"Yes."

I smiled as the meaning of this suddenly dawned on me. "St Paul's Cathedral!" I exclaimed.

"Of course," said James. "It must be! Well done, Francis for working out the Galatians. We knew you'd come in useful before long."

"Francis has always been extremely useful!" protested Eliza.

"I realise that," replied James. "It was my attempt at a joke. And well done, Penny. It has to be St Paul's Cathedral."

"I can't think what else it could be," said Francis.

"I must reluctantly admit that this riddle may turn out to be quite important to the investigation after all," continued James. "Rosie Gold's health is no better and the police are still forbidden to talk to her. Despite the work Paget and his men have carried out we're no closer to uncovering the ins and outs of her gang. I wonder whether someone might have been tipped off that night."

"The night she was attacked?" I asked.

"Yes. I wonder whether someone knew the police were planning to arrest Rosie and got to her first. The attack may have been a genuine attempt on her life. Perhaps someone didn't want her speaking to the police."

I recalled mentioning the plan to arrest Rosie Gold to Sarah while I was attempting to detain her at my home. *Surely she wouldn't have passed this information on to anyone?* I felt an uncomfortable shift in my stomach.

"Wasn't it a rival gang?" I asked.

"It may have been," replied James. "Or perhaps it was someone from the same gang who wanted to silence her. We simply don't know at this stage, unfortunately."

"Has Mrs Worthers offered any information on the matter?"

"No, why should she?"

"She's been a helpful witness to the street robberies on a number of occasions, hasn't she?"

"Yes, but I shouldn't think she would have been a witness to the attack on Rosie Gold."

"And we know now that she's not Rosie Gold because she was present at the inaugural meeting of the London Women's Rights Society, which took place after the attack."

"Was she indeed?" James raised an eyebrow.

"She certainly gets about."

"She does seem to," he replied. "If she pays us another visit, I'll see if I can obtain any more information about her."

"If she's up to no good, you probably won't get much out of her."

"No, but in the meantime there's St Paul's Cathedral to visit. The final location! Or so I hope."

CHAPTER 39

I found Sarah waiting on the street outside the *Morning Express* offices as I left the following day.

"You've timed your visit extremely well," I said after we had greeted one another. "I'm off to visit the final location now. Would you like to join me?"

She nodded, and we began to walk together in the direction of St Paul's Cathedral.

"Last one, eh?" she asked.

"Yes." I grinned as I explained that the Shakespeare clue related to the site of the Globe theatre and not Sadler's Wells. "I'm hoping we can find a public house with a royal name close to the cathedral now," I continued.

"What's the names yer've got so far?"

"The Crown, The King's Arms, The Prince of Wales and The Royal Oak."

"I see what yer mean," she replied. "All o' them names sound royal."

"We're just missing the Queen now. I do hope we'll be able to find her at St Paul's."

The great dome of the cathedral rose up ahead of us as we

crossed the road at the busy junction of Ludgate Circus and passed beneath a railway bridge. It was only a short walk up Ludgate Hill from there.

"I understand Rosie Gold is far from recovered," I said.

"Yeah, they're sayin' she's in a bad way."

"Have you heard who was behind the attack?"

"Nope."

"I wonder whether there have been any rumours among the gang members about who might have carried it out."

"Can't say as I've spoken to none of 'em for a good while."

"Do you remember me telling you that the police were planning to arrest her at the Mondragon Hotel?"

"Yeah, I 'member yer sayin' summat about it."

"Did you tell anyone else?"

"Nope. Who would I of told?"

"I don't know. You might have mentioned it to someone in passing, and then that person might have told someone else in turn. Before long, whoever meant Rosie harm could have found out where she would be that night. It might have been someone from a rival gang."

Sarah shook her head. "I din't tell no one."

"Or perhaps Rosie's attacker was someone from within the gang... someone who was afraid of her being arrested and speaking to the police. Have you heard any rumours along those lines?"

"I told yer, I dunno nothin' about it."

"And you told no one of the plan to arrest Rosie?"

"Nope."

I couldn't be sure whether Sarah was telling the truth, but I felt utterly foolish for ever mentioning the police's plan to arrest Rosie Gold at the hotel. It would have given her plenty of time to tell someone about it had she'd wished to. However the word had spread, it seemed certain that Rosie hadn't been party to it but questioning Sarah any further seemed futile. I had harboured a vain hope that I could somehow gain her confidence and that she would eventually tell me more about the Twelve Brides, but I realised I had made no progress at all on that front.

"What will you do once the riddle is solved?" I asked her.

"I'll help yer find 'em."

"Find whom?"

"The people who's murdered Josephine an' Margaret. I'll find 'em and then yer can tell yer police friend."

"But Rosie Gold has already been arrested. Wasn't she behind the murders?"

"It won't be just 'er, though. There'll 'ave bin others be'ind it an' all. I wanna find the ones who's really done it. Rosie'll only've given 'em the orders."

"How can you be sure who was really behind the deaths? How will you find them?"

"They'll be at the 'ideaway I told yer about. If yer can get all the people in there, yer got yer murderers."

We reached St Paul's Cathedral and stood before its enormous facade. A wide row of steps led up to a large portico, where one row of columns had been set upon another. Rising up on either side were two clock towers topped with decorative little arches and statuary. Despite having passed the cathedral countless times I remained in awe of its sheer size and dominance.

I glanced around us, searching for a public house with a royal-sounding name.

"It must be named after the Queen," I said. "'Call at the one with our best-known mourner', the riddle says. That means we have to visit a public house with the Queen's name on. Oh, I do hope it's here somewhere." A heavy sensation began to weigh on my shoulders.

What if I'd been completely mistaken about St Paul's?

"I can't see anything here that might be relevant," I said.

"I do hope we're on the right track this time. This is the very last part of the riddle we need to solve."

"St Paul's is real big," she replied. "Why don't we 'ave a walk round it?"

"You're right, we should."

We began to walk along the north side of the cathedral, craning our necks to see the famous dome as it loomed into view.

"I'm still astonished as to how they managed to go about constructing such a beautiful building," I said.

"Looks old ter me," replied Sarah.

"Yes, it was built about two hundred years ago. Or *re*built, I should say. There has been a cathedral on this site for a very long time, but the previous one was destroyed during the Great Fire of London."

I examined the buildings opposite the cathedral but saw no public houses there. We continued our walk past the churchyard until we reached the junction with Cheapside, where Sir Robert Peel's statue overlooked the traffic. I glanced up at the buildings across the road and saw a public house standing directly opposite.

The Queen's Head.

My heart gave a leap.

"It's just as we thought!" I exclaimed, gripping Sarah's arm excitedly. "Do you see it there? The Queen's Head! We knew it had to be named after the Queen. I don't know which queen, mind you. It can't be the current one, because it's only named after her head. Perhaps one of the wives Henry VIII beheaded? But that doesn't matter, anyway. It's the queen we were searching for!"

I checked the road for a gap in the traffic and began to cross over.

"'Call at the one with our best-known mourner'," I said. "I suppose that means we should go in and speak to them. But what do we say? Do you think we should show them the riddle?"

Sarah seemed rather subdued considering we had just solved the final part of the puzzle.

We reached the pavement outside The Queen's Head and I turned to face her. She looked up at the sign for a moment, as though she wanted to say something but was unable to find the words.

"Would you prefer not to go inside?" I asked. "I won't mind if you'd rather wait out here. I can speak to them about the riddle alone and see where that gets me." I peered in through the grimy leaded windows. "I can't see much in there."

I couldn't understand why Sarah suddenly appeared to be struck dumb.

"Are you all right?" I asked.

There was no response.

I walked toward the door and Sarah walked closely beside me, positioning herself between me and the public house. Her unusual behaviour was beginning to unnerve me.

"What's wrong?" I asked.

Again, there was no reply. I saw that she wasn't looking at me; rather her eyes were fixed on the junction with Cheapside.

Had she seen a fellow gang member? Were we in trouble?

I followed her gaze but saw no one of note that she might have had cause to look at. A number of people passed us briskly on the path, and the road was busy with horses and carriages. I wondered whether this decisive moment was testing her nerve a little.

I decided to walk past her and enter the public house. As I turned to do so, I was met with a force that sent me flying sideways toward the road. The movement felt as though it were happening at a slowed-down pace, as if I almost had time to ask what was happening.

My mouth tried to form the question, but at the same time a cry rang out. My eyes locked on Sarah's as I fell back, and I saw that her face had hardened into a passive stare, her arms and hands stretched out toward me.

It was then – in that moment which seemed to last an eternity – that I realised she had pushed me. Indignation was swiftly followed by fear as I felt the road drawing nearer and the dark form of a horse looming above me.

I instinctively squeezed my eyes shut and found myself engulfed in darkness.

CHAPTER 40

"Penelope?" My sister's voice sounded distant.

My head felt thick and heavy. A bright white light sent a sharp pain into my head as I opened my eyes. A whitewashed ceiling and a gaslight fitting gradually came into focus.

"Penelope?" Eliza's voice echoed in my ears. "She's waking up!"

It hurt to move my head but when I did so, I saw my sister's face to my right. Her large brown eyes were fixed on mine, and she smiled as I met her gaze. I felt her hand grip my upper arm.

"Can you hear me?" she asked.

I tried to reply in the affirmative but no sound came out. My lips felt cracked and dry when I attempted to move them.

"She can hear me!"

I wanted to ask her to quieten her voice but was unable to speak. I managed to frown a little.

"What's the matter, Penelope? I expect you need water." Eliza's face turned away. "Nurse? She's awake! She needs water!"

My ears filled with a high ringing sound and I closed my eyes again. Fatigue overwhelmed me as I tried to take a deep breath and, as I did so, a sharp pain shot through my chest. I heard someone cry out, then realised it must have been me.

"Penelope?" came Eliza's concerned voice.

I wanted to ask what had happened to me but the light was too bright for me to open my eyes and trying to put the words together was too much of a struggle. I desperately needed to sleep.

I heard another voice, one I didn't recognise. "I'll give her some more morphine."

I felt fingers on my lips and then my mouth was filled with a sweet syrup. I choked as it reached the back of my throat, sending another shot of pain through my chest.

"Try to swallow it, Miss Green," said the soothing voice.

More syrup was poured into my mouth and I did as I had been told.

"You're going to be all right, Penelope," said my sister.

I felt her hand on my shoulder, which provided a small amount of comfort. "You're going to be all right."

Her voice faded away as my body filled with warmth. Then I felt as though I were beginning to float, my body slowly lifting up into the beams of the whitewashed ceiling above me. I gently rose and fell, as if traversing the crests of gentle waves. Only I didn't feel as though I were out on the sea, but somewhere high up in the clouds.

CHAPTER 41

Eventually, I returned home from St Bartholomew's Hospital. James and Eliza carried me up the stairs to my room and Mrs Garnett brought up some food supplies.

"You need to get your strength back as soon as possible, Miss Green," she said. "I've made you a fruit cake, and this here is a game pie. You'll need a good pint of porter every morning and evening, too. I'll fetch it from The Red Lion each day."

"I don't need two pints of porter every day," I remonstrated as Eliza tucked me into bed and wrapped a blanket around me for good measure.

Mrs Garnett had heated the mattress with a bed warmer.

"Yes, you do," argued my landlady.

I sighed, quite fed up with being unable to do anything for myself and having to follow everyone else's orders.

James moved the chair from my writing desk and seated himself beside the bed.

"I'm so glad we finally have you home again, Penny," he said softly, holding my hand.

"So am I, James." I gazed into his blue eyes and squeezed his hand.

"I'm sure you'll make a swift recovery now."

"I'll have to," I replied. "I need to be better in time for our wedding! How far away is it now?"

"Two weeks," he said, "but we can delay it if we need to. You must be fully recovered before we are married."

"I will be."

"You're still very weak," said Eliza.

"Only because I've been forced to lie in bed for so long. If they'd let me get up and walk around the hospital, I'd have been a lot stronger by now."

"You've had a great shock as well as suffering a number of injuries," said my sister.

I groaned at this, tired of people assuming my nerves had somehow been damaged in the accident.

"I've kept all the newspapers, Miss Green," said Mrs Garnett. "You'll want to read them, no doubt. You made quite the news story for a good few days!"

"I'm sure Penelope has no wish to be reminded of it," said my sister. "That's why we kept the newspapers away from her at the hospital."

"Which you know I wasn't happy about!" I remonstrated. "Now I can finally read all about it."

"But you need to concentrate on getting better," said Eliza. "Reading about it will simply replay it all in your mind and set your recovery back."

"While I'm grateful for all your help, Ellie, you've been far too protective of me. I need to know everything. Now is the time for all the questions I have to be answered. First and foremost, has Sarah been arrested?"

James and Eliza exchanged a glance which suggested they were looking to one another for advice on what to say.

"Tell me the truth," I protested. "I need to know!"

"You need to get better first," Eliza reiterated.

"I shan't get any better while my mind is consumed with what has happened. You must stop keeping these things from me. It's not fair!"

"We're only thinking of your health."

"I can look after myself!" I retorted. "Tell me everything you know or I shall get angrier and angrier about it. I'm sure you'd agree that anger wouldn't be particularly good for my health."

"I'll read the newspaper report to you, Miss Green," said Mrs Garnett.

Eliza gave her a sharp glance.

"She won't be happy unless she hears it," my landlady added. "You know your sister well enough by now, Mrs Billington-Grieg. She has a lively mind and she won't rest until she knows all there is to know. Your average woman would prefer to lie in bed for several weeks and give no thought to such things, but not our active Miss Green, I'm afraid."

"You're right, Mrs Garnett," said James.

"I don't want Penelope getting herself upset," said Eliza.

"I'm *already* upset!" I bellowed.

"Here goes, then," said Mrs Garnett. She held a copy of the *Morning Express* up in front of her and cleared her throat. "The headline reads: 'Miraculous escape as lady is saved by her corset'." Did you hear that, Miss Green? A miracle, it was!"

She turned back to the newspaper. "'A thirty-five-year-old lady reporter had an extremely lucky escape on Tuesday when she fell beneath the wheels of a brewery dray cart. Miss Green, a reporter for this very newspaper, was pushed into the road by a young woman, who immediately ran away. The incident took place at the junction of St Paul's Churchyard and Cheapside yesterday at approximately five o'clock in the evening. Fortunately, the quick actions of the horse allowed the animal to step over Miss Green. However, two of the cart's wheels passed directly over her mid-section. Horrified witnesses felt sure the lady must be quite dead, for she lay in the road after the cart had passed over her and gave no response to those who rushed to her aid.

"'The driver of the cart, Mr Patrick Jones, was described as being in a distressed state immediately after the event, but he soon recovered his wits sufficiently to help lift the injured lady onto the cart and swiftly proceed with her to St Bartholomew's Hospital, which happened to be close by. A number of onlookers gave chase to the young woman who had pushed Miss Green, but unfortunately she evaded capture.

"'Dr Michael McKinsey from St Bartholomew's Hospital spoke to our reporter yesterday. He said: "There is little doubt that Miss Green was saved by the bone-work in her corset. She has suffered some broken ribs, but the effects of the wheels passing over her would otherwise have been far worse. In fact, the incident would most likely have proved fatal."

"'Dr McKinsey stated that further injuries suffered by Miss Green included a fracture to her arm, along with several cuts and extensive bruising to her face. He added that the patient is expected to make a full recovery.

"'Miss Green is engaged to marry Inspector James Blakely of Scotland Yard. The inspector told our reporter that police officers across London are now on high alert for any sighting of the woman, believed to be called Sarah, who pushed Miss Green beneath the wheels of the dray cart. Witnesses have described her as being between five feet two and five feet four inches tall. She was wearing a cream bonnet, a brown woollen shawl and a dark brown skirt at the time of the incident. The woman has fair hair and was described as having a sunken-cheeked appearance. Inspector Blakely urged anyone who may have seen 'Sarah' or knows of her whereabouts to visit a local police station at their earliest convenience.'"

Mrs Garnett folded up the newspaper and I thanked her for reading the article to me.

"This is why every woman should wear a corset," she added, giving my sister a pointed look. "It's another reason why I've no patience with this so-called *rational* dress movement. Corsets are not only important for a lady's silhouette; they save lives too!"

After making this declaration, Mrs Garnett left the room to make some tea.

"It's the second time it's saved my life, in actual fact," I said. "The boning in my corset once stopped a bullet, too!"

Eliza gave a wry smile. Almost a year had passed since she'd stopped wearing a corset.

"Is there any news on Sarah?" I asked. "The article Mrs Garnett kindly read out must have been written a while ago."

"We think we have news on her whereabouts, but we can't be sure quite yet," said James.

"What does that mean?"

"I mean to say that the body of a woman matching Sarah's description was found last week."

CHAPTER 42

"Where? What do you mean? I don't understand. Is she dead?"

James responded with a solemn nod. "She was found in Arundel Place; a small street leading off Coventry Street between Leicester Square and Piccadilly Circus."

"Was she murdered?"

"She had been shot."

"Oh, good grief! The poor girl!"

"She tried to kill you!" exclaimed Eliza.

"But there must have been a reason for it."

"I'm sure she did have a reason, but that hardly justifies her actions," replied James.

"Did someone wreak revenge on her for what she did to me?" I asked.

"We don't know that, either," said James. "But we do know that Rosie Gold, who is now well enough to answer our questions, claims never to have come across her before. In fact, we've been unable to find anybody who knows her. Not a single friend or family member has come forward."

"How awful," I said. "She seems to have been entirely alone in the world."

"We also know that she returned to The Queen's Head the day after she'd pushed you into the road. The publican there told us so. Apparently, she spoke to him about the riddle, but he claimed that he knew nothing about it."

"But he must know something."

"If he does, he's choosing not to tell the police."

"It seems as though she waited until she had the names of all the public houses referred to in the riddle, then decided to get me out of the way in an attempt to solve the final part herself."

"It certainly seems that way."

"But we don't know whether she solved it or not, do we?"

"The publican at The Queen's Head says he was unable to tell her anything."

"Do we know what she said to him?"

"She told him the names of all the other public houses from the riddle, but he maintains that he had no idea what she was talking about."

"Does that mean the riddle is completely meaningless? I thought it would lead to the gang's hideaway as soon as it was solved. I thought Sarah wanted to help us! I still can't understand why she tried to kill me."

"It seems as though her motivation was not as we first thought," said James.

"What was her true motivation?"

"Sarah wanted the riddle solved, there's no doubt about that. She needed someone to solve it for her, Penny, and that's where you came in. Then once she had everything she needed, Sarah decided you had to be disposed of. The decision may not have been hers, however. She may have been ordered to do it."

"By whom?"

"We can't be sure exactly but when the police surgeon examined Sarah's body, he found a tattoo on her inner forearm. It was a small tattoo and only visible when her sleeve was rolled up."

"What did it depict?"

"We believe it to be the insignia of the Bolsover Gang."

"But Sarah was a member of the Twelve Brides."

"That's what she told you."

"So she lied."

Despite all her falsehoods and her attempt to have me killed, I didn't feel any anger towards Sarah. Perhaps it was because she was dead, or perhaps because I sensed she had been ordered to do what she'd done.

"I wonder if she was given no choice in the matter," I said.

"What do you mean?" asked Eliza.

"Perhaps Sarah was ordered to murder me, so she had no choice."

"Of course she had a choice!" James said scornfully. "If she was being intimidated by members of the Bolsover Gang she could have run away. Better still, she could have reported their activities to the police."

"She had no one to blame but herself," said Eliza.

"But she had such a difficult upbringing—"

"Maybe she did," interrupted Eliza, "or maybe that's what she wanted you to think so you'd feel sorry for her. And even if it were true, a difficult upbringing doesn't give her the right to join a gang, thieve, steal, lie or attempt to murder someone! Plenty of people have difficult upbringings and manage to create an honest life for themselves. Don't pity her, Penelope."

I thought back to the time when I had first encountered Sarah. I'd assumed she was a good person because she'd stopped a boy from stealing my bag. I wondered now whether the incident had been staged in order to win my trust.

"Someone must have told her to seek me out," I said. "I suppose someone in the Bolsover Gang knew of me, but how?"

"They needed someone with intelligence and an enquiring mind," said James. "You no doubt came to their attention because you've reported on so many important cases. You've built a reputation as a skilled and compassionate news reporter. And they most likely chose you because you're a lady. They probably reasoned that a woman was more likely than a man to have sympathy for a street urchin like Sarah."

"And they weren't wrong," I replied, feeling a little bitter. "I was too trusting of her. I've been so stupid."

"Not at all," reassured James.

"You warned me about her but I didn't listen."

"You never listen, Penelope," said my sister sourly.

"That seems rather uncalled for, Eliza," said James.

"She's right," I added. "I should listen to other people's advice more."

"Now isn't the time to be ruing any decisions you've made," said James. "This isn't finished yet."

"It should be as far as Penelope's concerned," said Eliza. "The finishing off must be done by the police."

"We still don't know who murdered Josephine and Margaret," I said. "And the riddle isn't completely solved."

"It's not your job, Penelope," said my sister. "You've done enough."

"I'll have no job at all in two weeks' time!" I retorted. "I want to see this resolved. It could be the last chance I have!"

"It's too dangerous," replied my sister. "Please tell her, James, that this must stop. She has a wedding to recover for."

"Sarah was tasked with encouraging me to solve the riddle," I said, "but she pushed me under the wheels of that cart a little too soon. There was something more that needed to be done. Perhaps that's why she was shot. She failed to find the hideaway of the Twelve Brides, so she was punished. Do you think it's possible that anyone in the Twelve Brides knows what she was trying to do?"

"That's difficult to say," said James, "but there has been no official word that the attempt on your life was anything to do with the riddle."

"Then we're safe to continue solving it?"

"I'm not sure 'safe' is the correct word."

"It's completely *un*safe!" exclaimed Eliza.

"But there's a chance, isn't there?" I said. "A chance that we can solve the very last part of the riddle?"

Eliza walked over to my bedside. "You look very tired, Penelope. You need to rest." She repositioned my pillow and tucked the blanket around me again. "How's the pain?"

"The same as ever," I replied. "Anyway, what are we going to do next?"

CHAPTER 43

T he following few days felt interminable. I was confined to my room with Mrs Garnett keeping a close eye on me. Whenever she caught me out of bed, she would order me back in and command me to lie down. I was so tired of staring at the cracked plaster ceiling. Tiger kept me company, often sleeping next to me, but she soon leapt off the bed and hid whenever Mrs Garnett put in an appearance.

I had little appetite, but I didn't want to appear rude by turning down the food my landlady brought me. She kept her word about the two pints of porter each day, which she insisted would build up my strength. Any attempts I made to argue only caused upset and, although I did not enjoy being waited on, I had little choice but to endure it for the time being. I read books to while away the time, but Mrs Garnett chided me if ever I tried to sit down at my typewriter to write.

I felt stronger day by day and the pain in my ribs and left arm grew a little duller. On cloudless days, the morning sun's rays shone into my room and, even though I was confined indoors, I noticed the increasing strength of the sun as spring progressed.

Soon realising I would have to stay in bed most of the time, I propped myself up on the pillows and made copious notes in my notebook. The incompleteness of the riddle was deeply unsatisfying to me. Sarah had tried to solve it by approaching the publican at The Queen's Head, but apparently she had made no further progress with it.

Could it be possible that the publican knew nothing about it, or was that just a story he was telling the police to cover his tracks?

I felt sure that someone in at least one of the public houses must know something of the riddle, but maybe they were only prepared to divulge it to the right person. I thought back to the discussion Francis and I had shared about a possible code word and wondered whether the code word was concealed within the riddle somehow.

I was quite convinced Sarah had called in at the correct public house. The second line of the riddle, 'Call at the one with our best-known mourner', suggested a public house with something to do with a queen in its name. But the last line – 'What can you poach for Royal rewards?' – surely contained the final clue.

I wrote down the names of the five public houses and spent hours creating anagrams out of them. As there were so many letters to use, some of the anagrams I came up with were quite impressive. But given that so many anagrams could be created from the five names, how would someone who was trying to solve the riddle know which was the correct one? I was convinced the riddle had to be more prescriptive than this. It had to contain some sort of guidance.

I was busy working on the riddle one evening when James came to visit. Mrs Garnett insisted on the door to my room remaining open, despite the fact that James and I were engaged to be married. I had become accustomed to obeying her every instruction, so I made no attempt to argue with her.

"You're resting well, I see!" said James with a grin as he surveyed the reams of notes I had written.

"I am indeed. I find this sort of thing very restful," I replied. "Besides, I have to keep my mind occupied or I'll completely lose my patience. The last line of this riddle has to mean something. It's the part we haven't properly solved yet. Sarah walked into The Queen's Head without paying any heed to this section, I think. I'm sure a code word must be needed."

"'What can you poach for royal rewards?'," read James. "We know about the royal connection, but what does 'poach' mean? Something to steal, remove or take away, I assume."

"Steal, I think. The word poach suggests it must be done secretly. You wouldn't want to be seen doing it."

"But what would you steal? And what would the rewards be?"

"Presumably the reward is whatever one would receive in exchange for solving the riddle."

"What does this mean?" asked James, pointing to a line of letters I had written out.

"It's the first letters of each pub name. 'TC' is The Crown, 'TRO' is The Royal Oak, and so on. It doesn't mean anything, though. I've rearranged all the letters and haven't been able to make any sense of them."

"The letter T features a lot. Why don't we remove it? It stands for 'the' in each case."

I wrote the remaining letters down, leaving us with ROQHCKAPOW.

"It still doesn't make a lot of sense, does it?" said James, his brow furrowed.

"Just a moment," I said. "I can see the word 'poach' in there!"

James peered at it more closely. "Yes, the letters that make up 'poach' are there all right! Which words do they stand for?"

I wrote them down. "'P' is for prince, 'O' is for oak, 'A' is for arms, 'C' is for crown and 'H' is for head."

A grin spread across James' face. "One word from each public house's name!

"Do you think 'poach' could be the code word?"

"I'm not sure the code word would be included in the riddle. I think all five code words would have to be used. In the correct order, of course."

"Do you think we could go inside The Queen's Head and say 'prince, oak, arms, crown, head' to someone there?" I asked.

"I suppose it's worth a try. It's the final piece of the riddle, which Sarah didn't hang about to solve."

"What do you suppose will happen when we give them the secret words?"

"I imagine they'll either give us short shrift or we'll receive a new piece of information. I'll go and speak to them tonight."

"But you've already spoken to the publican, James, and he denied all knowledge of the riddle."

"It might work if I use the five words."

"They know you're a police officer!" I laughed but instantly felt a pain in my side. "They're not likely to tell you anything even if you give them the correct words."

"Then I can use my powers of arrest. I'm fed up with all this nonsense, to be honest with you. It seems the riddle has been solved and you almost lost your life in the process. I've a good mind to raid all five public houses and arrest the publicans within each of them."

"And where will that get us, exactly? It won't help us find the people who murdered Josephine and Margaret. We can use this opportunity to find out more about the gang. If the publican at The Queen's Head accepts the code words, surely we'll be able to find out more about these people. Has Rosie Gold mentioned anything about the riddle?"

"She has denied all knowledge of it."

I sighed. "I suppose we shouldn't be too surprised about that. What did she have to say about Josephine and Margaret? I assume she also denies having anything to do with their deaths."

"You're quite correct there."

"Then we only have the riddle to go on."

"I'm sure Rosie Gold will talk before long."

"But we don't know how long that'll take. In the meantime, it makes sense for someone to be granted access to the Twelve Brides' secret hideaway using the code words."

James gave me a calm stare. "You're not considering yourself for the role, are you?"

"Of course I am! I can go to The Queen's Head and pretend to be a gang member."

James gave a groan. "It's too dangerous, Penny."

"Who else is there?"

"I've already told you I intend to do it myself."

"You'll be met with a wall of silence. Even if you arrest them, they'll stay quiet."

"And you think they'll speak to you, do you?"

"I could disguise myself in some way."

James laughed. "With false mustachios?"

"There's no need to laugh at the idea! I've dressed in scruffy clothing plenty of times before. I've also pretended to be a maid in the past. I could pretend to be a gang member who just happens to have solved the riddle."

"And what happens if it works and you encounter the other gang members in their hideaway?"

"You could be waiting close by in case of any trouble. In fact, it would make sense to have some officers in plain clothes inside the public house, wouldn't it?"

"Yes, I suppose that would be helpful. I'll have to speak to the City of London Police and explain what we're planning to do, as The Queen's Head falls within their jurisdiction. Hopefully they'll be willing to spare a few constables to assist us."

He paused and rubbed at his brow.

"What's the matter?"

"I really can't allow you to do this, Penny. You're still recovering from a recent attempt on your life. Our wedding is just nine days away and I'm not even certain you'll be well enough for that. I think we need to speak to Reverend Crosbie—"

"Nonsense!" I interrupted. "I'm quite all right. Spending any more time within these four walls will be far more detrimental to my health than my getting out and solving the last piece of this puzzle. I want to do this, James," I implored. "I *have* to do it. Once it's done my work will be finished, we'll be married and an entirely new chapter will begin. This is the last opportunity I have to solve the riddle once and for all."

James held my gaze, then smiled. "It sounds as though your mind is quite made up."

"It is indeed. Now, let's work on finalising our plan."

CHAPTER 44

Eliza visited me the following morning. Her eyes were bright and lively, and there was more colour than usual in her cheeks.

"You look well, Ellie," I commented.

"Thank you, Penelope, I'm feeling extremely well." She didn't sit on my bed, but instead paced the floor. "It looks as though you have your strength back."

"Yes, I'm quite recovered now. And James and I have solved the final part of the riddle!"

"Really?" Her reply was lacklustre.

"We've managed to work out the five code words. I'm preparing a visit to The Queen's Head to see what happens when I impart them to the publican there."

"You're not to go back there, Penelope!"

"I have to finish this."

"No, you don't! Leave James and his colleagues to see it through. I cannot believe he's agreed to let you do such a thing!"

"He'll be accompanying me, Ellie, along with a team of plain-clothed policemen."

"That makes me feel a little better, I suppose, but you're still putting yourself at risk, Penelope. I really don't think it's wise given that you're only just recovering from your injuries after someone attempted to kill you!"

"But I couldn't possibly give up on it now! Not after all the weeks of work I've put into it."

"Please let James take care of it, Penelope."

"He'll be there to help me, but I want to be involved. I need to find out the meaning behind the riddle. I want to do this myself."

"Despite the fact you'll be putting your life at risk again?"

"There won't be any risk; not with James and his police colleagues there with me."

Eliza gave a sigh. "If James couldn't talk you out of this foolish idea, I don't suppose I have any chance of doing so."

"Everything will be fine, Ellie. Aside from all this, there seems to be something rather restless about you today. What's happened? I feel sure you came here to tell me something."

"How very observant of you, Penelope. I did, yes. It's good news on the one hand, but also a little shameful, I'm afraid." Her face reddened.

"I don't understand. In what way is it shameful?"

"I shall explain presently."

She seated herself on my bed and fidgeted with one of her cuffs as she spoke. "I've received papers from George's solicitor stating that he wishes to petition for a divorce after all."

"That's wonderful news, Ellie! You've been hoping for such a thing to occur for almost a year now."

"Yes, that's the good news. Now there is some hope of our divorce being agreed. It's far easier for the husband to divorce his wife than the other way around."

"What has brought about this change of heart in George?"

Eliza cleared her throat. "That's where it becomes a little shameful. The whole situation has been rather exaggerated, you understand. However, I must say that I'm not about to disagree with the reason stated, even if it has been considerably conflated."

"What on earth do you mean, Ellie? What reason is he citing?"

"It's... well, it's... it's adultery."

"You've committed adultery?" I felt my jaw drop.

"Of course not! You know I would never do such a thing! However, it has been construed by George's solicitor – most likely because I have been spending rather a lot of time with him lately – that Francis and I are more than mere acquaintances. I don't know how George even knows about it or reached such a conclusion, but I suppose it cannot be considered entirely appropriate for a married lady to spend so much of her time with a bachelor."

"Goodness, this is a surprise. A divorce is what you want, of course, but to achieve it in this way could be rather troublesome."

"It'll do little for my reputation, that's for sure. What will the ladies at the London Women's Rights Society make of it all? And what will Mrs Sutherland think? She may withdraw her generous funding as a result."

"They need never know of it."

"They'll find out before long; you know how news travels, particularly if there is any hint of a scandal in it. And besides, everyone will hear the details when the case is heard in the divorce courts. I've a good mind to deny it all."

"Why would you do such a thing?"

"To salvage my reputation."

"But you want nothing more than to obtain a divorce from George, isn't that right?"

"Yes, it is."

"And this may be your only chance of securing one. I think your reputation would be saved if you told everyone you had been forced to leave your husband because of his criminal associations. You couldn't possibly have stayed married to him after finding that out."

"No, I realise that."

"You left your husband for an extremely valid reason, and then you struck up a close friendship with a kind and decent man who had found your missing father in South America."

"Yes."

"What's wrong with that? I think anyone who casts aspersions on your reputation once that has been explained to them isn't worth knowing anyhow."

"Thank you, Penelope, you're quite right. I'm just worried about being misrepresented. The adultery charge suggests I have behaved inappropriately with Francis, and I really haven't. We're nothing more than good friends."

"I know that, Ellie, though I believe the pair of you hold a little affection for each other."

"Of course we do. We're close friends, as I say."

"Perhaps you'll be a little more than that one day if you can get this divorce case over and done with."

"I don't think Francis would consider me as a potential wife, Penelope."

"Why ever not?"

"I shall be a divorcee! I'm quite sure his parents would have something to say about it if we were to become engaged."

"They'd be utter fools if they weren't prepared to be understanding of the situation. Would they rather you'd remained married to a crook?"

"I don't suppose they'd care, just so long as I had nothing to do with their son!"

"You can't possibly know what Francis' family would

think, Ellie. And besides, it shouldn't matter. All that matters at the present time is that you're able to proceed with the divorce you'd hoped for. And if Francis proposes marriage after that... well, that would be wonderful."

Eliza's face darkened to a deeper red. "I'm quite sure he never will. Anyway, it wouldn't be proper to leap from one marriage straight into another."

"You could become his common-law wife instead."

"That's quite enough! I intend to concentrate on the divorce for the time being while I work out how best to manage the situation."

"Have you told Francis about George's petition for divorce?"

"Not yet, but I shall."

"I imagine he'll be rather pleased."

"Enough, Penelope!"

CHAPTER 45

I watched from across the street as three police constables in plain clothes sauntered into The Queen's Head. About five minutes later James and another officer followed them in, they were dressed in rough woollen suits, heavy boots, collarless shirts and flat caps. James also wore a false beard to prevent the publican from recognising him. Despite my nerves, I couldn't help but laugh a little at the sight of him.

This was the first time I had returned to the location since Sarah had pushed me into the road. I found myself carefully watching the people and traffic around me. I knew that it was very unlikely to happen again, but my heart pounded nevertheless. As I glanced over at the door to the public house, I recalled the moment when Sarah's behaviour had suddenly changed. We had been conversing quite normally up to that point and I felt a shiver as I remembered how the odd change had come over her. I hoped never to experience anything like that again.

I waited a while longer, calmed myself with a deep breath and then crossed the road. I reassured myself that, with

James and several police officers inside, no harm would come to me.

A cart trundled along the road and I watched as the heavy feet of the horse and the large wheels passed me by. Despite experiencing a few residual aches and pains on occasion, it was difficult to believe that I had been pushed beneath such a cart. I found it quite astonishing that I was still alive.

I pushed against the door to The Queen's Head and stepped inside. I was dressed in simple clothing with an old bonnet and shawl. I had decided to leave my carpet bag at home, though I felt rather lost without it.

Tobacco smoke and lively chatter filled the bar. The smell of beer reminded me of the pints of porter Mrs Garnett had forced me to drink during my recuperation. A few heads turned in my direction as the men noticed an unaccompanied woman had stepped inside.

I avoided looking at James and his men as I approached the bar, where a man holding a grubby cloth fixed me with a cool stare.

How was I to introduce the five words? Was he even the correct person to recite them to?

I reminded myself that my clothes were shabby so I would need to adapt my accent and tone of voice to fit my attire. I cleared my throat.

The man at the bar opened his mouth slightly but said nothing, as if he were waiting for me to speak. I stepped closer to the bar, knowing that what I was about to say was not supposed to be overheard.

"Prince," I said quietly. "Oak."

"What's that?" he asked, leaning in toward me.

I moved a little closer.

"Prince," I said again. "Oak, arms, crown, 'ead."

His eyes narrowed and he took a step back. Then he glanced quickly to his left and strode off in that direction.

As he hadn't questioned, or appeared confused by, what I'd just said, I took this to mean that I should follow him. I walked along the bar then paused to watch as he stepped out from behind it and made his way over to a dingy area in the far corner. My stomach flipped with anticipation and worry. Although I felt relieved to have said the correct words in the right order, I was concerned about what I had let myself in for by doing so.

I gave a quick glance over my shoulder to see whether James was watching. Sure enough, he was. I didn't want to risk anyone spotting our momentary exchange, so I turned back and hurried to catch up with the man, who was busy unlocking a black door.

He pulled it open and gestured for me to step through it. On a little shelf just inside the door sat three lanterns and a box of matches. I peeked into the corridor beyond and saw that it was in complete darkness.

I looked back at the man. *Did he intend to enter the corridor with me?* It didn't appear so, given that his hand was still resting on the door handle as if he were about to close it again. He nodded at the lanterns, and I realised I was expected to light one. I chose the one with the largest candle remaining and, as soon as the wick was lit, he gave me a nod, closed the door and locked it again.

My heart pounded in my throat. *Would the locked door prevent me from re-entering the bar area if I needed to?*

I turned and examined the passageway in front of me. The brickwork was exposed and there were bare floorboards beneath my feet. I took only a few steps before arriving at another brick wall. I turned and scanned the area with my lantern. I appeared to be locked inside a large cupboard. *Was this some sort of trap?*

I raised my lantern, holding it high as I looked all around me. There appeared to be no other way out than the door I had just come through, which had been promptly locked. I couldn't imagine the publican taking kindly to me knocking and asking to be let out again. With no other door visible I looked down at the floor and saw the only way out.

I was standing on top of a trapdoor.

A small iron ring was attached to one side. I bent down and pulled it up to reveal nothing but complete darkness beneath me. As I lowered my lantern, I saw a set of narrow stone steps leading down into the void. It seemed the riddle had led me to an underground tunnel. *Where would it take me?*

I looked down at the steps warily, not relishing the idea of climbing down them. But when I considered all the work we had put into solving the riddle, I knew it would be cowardly to turn back now. I wished I could fetch James and ask him to accompany me; however, that would certainly have raised the publican's suspicions.

Holding the trapdoor up with one hand I descended the first few steps. With my other hand holding the lantern I moved slowly, taking care not to slip. Eventually I was low enough to bring the trapdoor down over my head. I felt a pang of nausea as it closed above me. The air below felt cold and dank.

I climbed down a few more steps and saw that I didn't have to descend much further. Ahead of me was a roughly paved tunnel with brick walls forming an arch. The tunnel was barely wide enough for two people to pass one another in, and anyone taller than me would have had to lower their head and walk with a stoop. I tentatively began to creep along it with my lantern held out in front of me. I could hear the echoing sound of dripping water from somewhere. As the light of the lantern shone on the damp brick walls, I wondered who had built these tunnels. Perhaps they had been constructed to provide access to London's new sewerage system around twenty years previously. I wondered how often these tunnels were used. This was presumably how the gang moved around London undetected.

A movement up ahead caught my eye. Startled, I froze where I was and held my breath, not daring to move. Another movement followed and I realised I was looking at the retreating form of a rat. I gave a shudder, sincerely hoping any other rats would run away before I reached them.

I had to remind myself to keep breathing, not least because it helped me remain calm. I must have been walking for five minutes or so by this time and I felt my steps becoming a little quicker as I grew impatient for some sort of resolution to my walk. The tunnel was mainly straight with just a slight bend here and there.

What would I say if I happened to meet someone down here? I decided I should introduce myself as Amelia.

Then I felt sure I could hear the sound of water once again. It wasn't a dripping sound this time, but moving water, as if there happened to be an underground stream nearby. The sound grew louder as I walked, and before long it completely filled my ears. An unpleasant odour also reached my nose.

The lantern light picked out a dark archway ahead of me and, when I reached it, I saw a small slipway leading down into gushing brown water from right to left. I could only imagine that it ran down to the Thames. *Was I expected to walk through it?*

Looking around with my lantern I realised the tunnel I was following turned sharply to my right, appearing to run parallel with the underground stream. A stream which, judging by the stench, would more be accurately described as a sewer. I turned right and moved swiftly along the tunnel, hoping to leave the stink of the water behind me. Although it receded a little, the smell continued to hang heavily in the air.

A flight of stone steps came into view and I paused at the

foot of them, looking above my head for a trapdoor, but I couldn't see one. Instead, the tunnel turned left at the top of the steps. I wondered whether it was a bridge over the sewer. I walked up the steps, turned left, and sure enough found another flight of steps leading down again. I continued along the tunnel, which began to widen a little.

An even greater sense of impatience stirred within me as I wondered when I would ever reach the end of the tunnel. I felt a desperate need to be out of the damp, stinking air, and away from the rats, which scurried off ahead of me every few minutes.

All of a sudden, a figure stepped out in front of me and I had to silence the cry that leapt into my mouth.

I instinctively took a few steps back and gasped for air, desperately trying to calm my heartbeat, which was thudding almost audibly in my aching chest.

CHAPTER 46

A young woman holding a lantern stood before me. Her pale face and scruffy shawl made me think of Sarah.

"Hello?" I ventured nervously.

"Follow me," she replied.

The girl turned right into what appeared to be a doorway in the wall of the tunnel. I followed and turned, as she had, into another short tunnel that led to another flight of steps.

The skirts of the young woman had almost disappeared from view at the top of the steps. As I followed, I wondered what I was about to face. I could think of no reason for the girl to have been waiting in the tunnel other than that she was expecting me. She hadn't seemed particularly surprised by my appearance, nor had she bothered to ask who I was or what I was doing here.

The steps brought us to the foot of a stairwell which was lit with a gas lamp. From what I could see, we appeared to be standing in the basement of a building. Was this the head-quarters of the Twelve Brides? The girl extinguished our lanterns and closed a trapdoor over the steps we had just ascended from the tunnel. I observed the girl in the flickering gaslight. She had pock-marked skin and looked no older than twenty, but she was much taller and broader than me.

There were countless questions I wished to ask, but I decided to remain silent for the time being. There was a risk that I would reveal my true identity and I didn't want to volunteer any information that could put me in danger.

The staircase rose up to our right and turned a corner above my head. The walls were wood-panelled and I wondered whether we were now inside another public house. The girl proceeded up the wooden staircase and I followed closely. I listened intently for any sound that might tell me where we were, but heard nothing. There were no voices from any other rooms or noises from the streets close by.

The staircase curved round onto a small landing with three doors. The girl pushed one of them open and showed me into a room with a large sash window.

"Wait in here," she commanded.

"Where are we?" I asked.

She gave no reply and the door was swiftly closed behind me. Six carved wooden chairs had been arranged around a well-polished table. The fire was as yet unlit but had been neatly laid. I walked over to the window, which overlooked a busy thoroughfare. As I peered out, I could see that I was at least two storeys above street level. The building I found myself in was positioned beside a busy set of crossroads with two distinctive stone obelisks in the centre. Opposite me, a building that appeared to be six or seven storeys high was emblazoned with the words: 'Cook's Tours to All Parts of the World.'

I felt a warm sensation of familiarity wash over me. I knew exactly where I was. I was looking down on Ludgate Circus, and I could see right down Fleet Street, almost as far as the *Morning Express* offices. Just to the left of Fleet Street rose the distinctive tower of St Bride's Church. I felt sure I could remember seeing a public house on this corner of the junction, and that it was called The King Lud.

As I leaned on the windowsill it began to vibrate with a deep rumbling sound. I felt momentarily alarmed before realising the railway line into Ludgate Hill Station was just behind the building. As I peered to my left, I could see a train crossing the railway bridge over Ludgate Hill; the very same bridge Sarah and I had walked beneath the day she had tried to kill me. I realised the tunnel I had walked along followed the route of Ludgate Hill from St Paul's to Ludgate Circus.

I surveyed the room and the closed door again, wondering what would happen next. I hadn't heard the girl lock the door, and I considered whether I should try to leave the room and take a look around. I decided it would be best to follow the orders I had been given and wait where I was. I had no desire to antagonise anyone.

I sat down on one of the chairs and considered the girl's response upon finding me in the tunnel. She had seemed prepared for my arrival. I wondered whether the publican from The Queen's Head had sent word that I was on my way. I surmised there had been just enough time for an urgent telegram to be sent from The Queen's Head to the King Lud. Alternatively, a running messenger could have made the journey along Ludgate Hill more swiftly than I had navigated my way beneath it.

There was a clock on the Cook's Tours building, and I watched a full hour pass as I came and went from the window.

Did anyone intend to visit me? Was being shut up in this room part of an initiation process? Were they waiting for me to make the next move?

I opened the door a couple of times and peered out onto the quiet landing but saw no one there. The other occupants of the building were like ghosts. I had heard light footsteps on the stairs and on the floorboards of the room above me, but nothing more.

I wondered what James was doing at this moment. *Were he and his colleagues still waiting for me to emerge from behind the door at The Queen's Head?*

I felt a snap of impatience as the clock passed the hour mark. Up to this point, I had bided my time and calmly waited but I wondered how much longer I would be detained.

I decided it was time to leave the room in search of someone I could speak to. I had only made it halfway across the room when the door opened and two women walked in: the young woman who had accompanied me and an equally tall and broad companion.

"Hello," I said with false confidence.

Neither woman acknowledged me.

I was considering how I might go about striking up a conversation when a third person stepped into the room. This lady was much smaller in stature. Her brown hair was parted in the centre and neatly fastened at the nape of her neck. Her dark dress was clean and simple.

Standing before me was Mrs Sutherland.

CHAPTER 47

To my surprise, she gave me a broad smile.

"Miss Green!" she said. "How nice to see you again."

Could this all be a strange coincidence? Or did Mrs Sutherland know about the riddle and the tunnel?

Countless questions ran through my head, but I decided to see how she would conduct herself before I posed any of them.

"Please," she said, gesturing toward the chair closest to me, "do take a seat."

She sat down at the table, but her two companions remained standing. They took up their positions on either side of the door, as if they were guarding it.

"I must apologise for keeping you waiting," she continued. "I've just travelled here from Kensington. Have you been offered a drink yet?"

"No, I haven't," I replied, feeling rather confused.

Mrs Sutherland was conducting herself as if we had previously arranged to meet. She hadn't questioned how I had come to find my way here or even commented on the style of my dress. I felt rather foolish wearing my shabby bonnet and shawl now.

"Could you call for some tea, please, Maria?" she called over her shoulder.

The woman I had met in the tunnel glanced over at me, then stepped outside.

Having initially felt disarmed by the appearance of Mrs Sutherland, the significance of her arrival was beginning to dawn on me. The riddle had led me to her. Sarah had said the riddle would lead to the gang's headquarters.

Had Sarah been correct or was Mrs Sutherland here purely by chance and entirely innocent of any crime?

Her pleasant manner suggested the latter.

"I haven't seen you since your terrible accident, Miss Green," she said. "I hope you're feeling quite recovered now."

"I am, thank you. It's just as well, given that I had to make such a long journey through the tunnel."

I mentioned the tunnel to gauge her reaction but she didn't acknowledge it.

"It was quite awful," she said. "I don't know what that girl was thinking."

"Did you know her?" I asked.

"Not at all." She gave a regretful smile.

"Someone has killed her," I replied. "Do you know who?"

"No, I don't."

"She told me she was a member of the Twelve Brides Gang," I said, "but it turned out she was part of the Bolsover Gang. She bore their tattoo. She was using me to help her find out more about the Twelve Brides."

We were interrupted by a maid carrying a tea tray, who was followed in by Maria.

Mrs Sutherland appeared to take no interest at all in what I had just said.

"How do you take your tea, Miss Green?" she asked,

arranging two tea cups, a small jug of milk and the sugar bowl on the table.

"Just a little milk, thank you," I replied.

My curiosity got the better of me as she poured out the tea.

"Why are you here?" I asked.

She passed me a steaming cup and saucer.

"I own The King Lud."

"I had no idea."

"I see no reason why you would."

I wondered why she was giving so little away. *Was she expecting me to question her?*

"Do you use the tunnel to access the building?" I asked.

"Only when I have to. It's rather damp and odorous, isn't it?"

I picked up the silver teaspoon from my saucer and stirred the tea as I thought.

"I must confess that I feel quite confused, Mrs Sutherland," I said.

"I'm sorry to hear it, Miss Green."

I detected a slightly mocking tone in her voice.

"I had to solve a riddle to get here," I continued. "It took quite a bit of time and I almost lost my life working on it. I eventually managed it, and now I find myself here in a room within your public house. Sarah assured me the riddle would lead to the secret headquarters of the Twelve Brides gang. Is that where I am now?"

She gave an amused smile and added a sprinkle of sugar to her tea. "The word '*gang*' is rather undignified, don't you find?"

"Do you have any connection to the street robbers on Piccadilly?"

"Not personally, no."

"Do they work for you?"

"A lot of people work for me, Miss Green."

"There are legitimate businesses and then there are criminal ones, Mrs Sutherland."

Her expression darkened. "What are you implying?"

"The riddle has led me here, to where the Twelve Brides gang supposedly meets. Poor Josephine Miller and Margaret Brown were members of this gang. They were brutally murdered and thrown into the river."

"I hope you're not suggesting I had anything to do with that, Miss Green." She sat back in her chair and regarded me sullenly.

"I'm merely telling you what I've discovered so far. The path I followed to find out who was behind those murders has led me to you, Mrs Sutherland. Now perhaps I'm mistaken—"

"Yes, you are," she interrupted before taking a sip from her cup.

"In that case, can you explain to me what is happening? You are one of the very last people I expected to discover here, yet you didn't seem at all surprised when you entered the room and saw me. Did you know what I was doing all along?"

"Of course I did." She sat forward with her hands resting on the table, her fingers interlinked. "I helped you with one of the clues, if you remember."

"Yes, I do remember."

I recalled my conversation with Francis at the inaugural meeting of the London Women's Rights Society. She had overheard it and mentioned the Globe Theatre to us.

"Did you write the riddle?" I asked.

"I couldn't possibly say," she replied, "but I think you enjoyed working on it, didn't you? It certainly kept you out of trouble for a while."

"What do you mean by that?"

"Only that it kept you occupied."

I felt a pang of shame on finding that I had allowed myself to be manipulated so easily. "But why was it written? Why lead people here?"

"It was written for the benefit of the Bolsover Gang."

"It was passed to them on purpose?"

"In a roundabout way, I suppose, through a series of messengers, along with a rumour that there was a hideaway and money to be found."

"Sarah didn't mention any money to me. I suppose she decided to keep that part quiet. So you mean to say that the riddle was a trap?"

"Which they almost fell for... and you fell for completely, Miss Green!"

"But why lure me into a trap?"

"You weren't the intended target. The riddle was obviously too complicated for the Bolsovers, so they recruited you to help them."

"They didn't recruit me!"

"Yes, they did. You just weren't aware of it."

"Sarah told me she wanted to help me find out who had murdered Josephine and Margaret."

"She just told you what you wanted to hear, didn't she? The Bolsover Gang knew all about Miss Green the reporter with her strong sense of justice." Her voice had taken on a mocking tone again. "They knew you would do anything you possibly could to right the wrongs of this city, is that not so? Sarah played you like a fiddle."

"I hope you haven't involved my sister in any of your criminal activities, Mrs Sutherland."

"What makes you think I've done anything of a criminal nature?"

"The gang rivalry, the secret tunnel—"

She gave a hollow laugh. "The tunnel has been here far longer than you or me, Miss Green."

"But why all the secrecy?"

"You're making the assumption that secrecy and criminality go hand in hand."

"Do they not?"

"Not necessarily."

"But your connection to the Twelve Brides... surely you can't deny that?"

"Let me explain how my businesses work, Miss Green. I took them over from my parents after they lost their lives in an accident. Suffice to say I inherited a few properties as well, this public house being one of them. It's in the very heart of London, and I'm sure you'd agree it's a good location for a company headquarters. You work very close by yourself, don't you?"

"What would you have done to Sarah if she'd managed to find her way here?"

"It would simply have led to some fresh negotiations with her superiors."

"Would you have killed her, Mrs Sutherland?"

"What an impertinent question."

"Would you?"

"She could have been extremely useful to me. It's a shame she died."

"And what of Rosie Gold?"

"What of her?"

"Did you plan the attack on her?"

She laughed. "You really must think me a dreadful sort judging by the accusations you're throwing at me, Miss Green."

"It wasn't an accusation. It was a question."

"It's a shame Rosie's reign has come to an end. She was the perfect dogsbody."

"You simply allowed people to believe she was the one in charge?"

"Of course. It meant I could be left alone to get on with what I need to do."

"Which is?"

"Running my businesses, Miss Green."

"Why is the gang known as the Twelve Brides?" I asked.

"There were twelve founding members, though eleven of them are no longer alive."

"Was Rosie Gold one of them?"

"Goodness me, no."

"Then you are the remaining one?"

"Perhaps."

"I'll assume the answer is yes. Can you tell me what happened to Josephine Miller and Margaret Brown?"

"They died."

"They were murdered – we know that much – but why?"

She sighed and poured herself some more tea. "Would you like another cup?"

"No, thank you. Why were Josephine and Margaret killed?"

"I don't involve myself in disputes between those who are lower down the ranks, Miss Green, but I'm told they were both trouble-makers."

"That's no excuse for having them murdered."

She smiled and took a sip of tea. "You really don't understand the way these things operate, Miss Green. An organisation depends on every one of its workers. They must adhere to certain rules and regulations... to a code of conduct, if you like. Anyone who breaks the code puts their colleagues in danger."

"How so?"

"They threaten the very existence of the organisation.

Not only must a definitive end be put to their behaviour, but their punishment must serve as a warning to others."

"You freely admit that you murdered Josephine and Margaret?"

She smiled again. "I admit to nothing, Miss Green. Do I look like the sort of person who would murder two young women?"

"No doubt you have plenty of associates to do that sort of thing on your behalf."

"I would certainly never involve myself in such matters."

"Then the two girls were killed at your behest. Did you order Rosie Gold to murder them?"

"The people working within this organisation know what's expected of them. I couldn't pass comment on anything specific in relation to Josephine or Margaret because I'm a busy lady, Miss Green. I trust my subordinates to deal with these matters."

I felt a snap of anger. "But what about the London Women's Rights Society? And the Hanwell Schools' Fair? You merely associate yourself with these causes in order to draw a veil of respectability over yourself, I assume."

"I'm already respectable, Miss Green."

I laughed. "You run a gang! Your girls rob people on the street and steal from shops. And then they are brutally murdered if they step out of line!"

"I donate significant sums of my income to worthy causes and support those who are committed to making positive changes in our society. Your sister is a fine example."

"You leave my sister out of this!"

"You're the one who introduced us, Miss Green."

I took a deep breath and tried not to allow myself to become any more riled by this woman. "And what of the people your girls rob?"

"Rich people indulging themselves by spending excessive

amounts of money in London's finest boutiques? I never imagined your sympathies would lie with them, Miss Green."

"My sympathies lie with the poor girls you recruit."

"The way they make a living is their choice, Miss Green. They earn better money than they would working in service or in a factory."

"You're encouraging them to become criminals and putting their lives in danger. You may tell yourself you're robbing from the rich and giving to the poor, but you can never justify exploiting these poor girls. Nor could you ever justify committing murder."

Mrs Sutherland sat back in her chair and regarded me coolly. "How nice it must be to live in a world in which good and evil are so clearly defined, Miss Green. I envy you and the pleasant, law-abiding family you grew up in."

"You know nothing of my family."

"I know a little." She gave a weak smile, which quickly faded again. "More than you know about mine, perhaps. My parents were murdered when I was sixteen years of age. My father did whatever he had to in order to survive, and he was good at it, too. He was well-respected, and he always rewarded loyalty. He also had difficult decisions to make, and he had to be tough. His opponents needed to be dealt with before they had a chance to deal with him. He lost out in the end, but he died knowing I was provided for. What other choice did I have than to build on the foundations he had put in place and paid for with his life? I know no other world, Miss Green."

"But all the deceit..." I began.

A sudden banging from downstairs startled us both. Mrs Sutherland rose from her chair in alarm and glanced over at her two assistants.

"It appears we have visitors. It's time for you to leave, Miss Green. Maria, Beth, show her out."

CHAPTER 48

"Who might those visitors be?" I asked as Maria and Beth escorted me out of the room. There was no reply from either. Mrs Sutherland walked briskly along the corridor and out of sight.

Perhaps they were from the Bolsover Gang, or maybe it was the police. Either way, the visitors appeared to have taken Mrs Sutherland by surprise.

I prayed the police were on the scene as we walked back down the staircase I had climbed earlier. I had anticipated being led through a passageway to the bar downstairs, but instead we returned to the trapdoor.

"I don't want to go through the tunnel again," I said. "Isn't there another way out?"

"'Fraid not," replied Maria brusquely.

"Too dangerous," added Beth. "You 'eard Mrs Sutherland. We got visitors."

The two women had positioned themselves in such a way that the only exit was through the trapdoor. I was intimidated by their height and presence.

"Where are you planning on taking me?"

"We're showin' you out, just as Mrs Sutherland told us," Beth replied.

"But where to?"

"Yer'll find out soon enough," said Maria. "Now let's not 'ang about, else there'll be trouble."

She calmly removed a sheathed knife from a concealed pocket in her skirts. I felt my feet root to the floor as a cold nausea gripped me.

"Do as we tell yer, Miss Green, and there'll be no need fer us to use it," she said, bending to lift the trapdoor.

"C'mon Miss Green," said Beth, nudging me in the back.

"How long is the walk?" My voice sounded tremulous. I didn't want them to know how frightened I was but I struggled to conceal it.

"Not long."

Beth lit a lantern and climbed down the steps. Maria gestured for me to follow and, seeing no alternative, I did so. Maria closed the trapdoor behind us and we made our way inside the tunnel. Instead of walking in the direction from which I had come, which led beneath Ludgate Hill, we entered the next part of the tunnel, which by my estimation would take us in the direction of Fleet Street.

"Where does this tunnel lead?" I asked.

"Yer'll find out soon enough," answered Maria.

The vague replies to my questions only served to increase my anxiety.

"Why not leave me here?" I asked them. "I can find my way back to The Queen's Head."

Beth gave an empty laugh. I was about to remonstrate but realised it would be unwise to argue within such a confined space beneath the streets of London. I couldn't take my mind off the knife in Maria's possession. *Was she only holding it to ensure that I was compliant, or did she intend to use it?* I thought of how Josephine and Margaret's throats had been cut and my stomach gave a sickening turn.

After a few minutes, I heard the rush of water again and the tunnel turned sharply to the left. The same unpleasant odour filled the air once more. As I followed Beth, I saw a steep slope ahead leading down toward the flowing water. I stopped and watched as she stepped into it. Her skirts were trailing in the brown water, but she made no attempt to hitch them up.

She turned to face me. "It ain't nothin' to worry about," she said. "It's only shallow."

The stink in the air assaulted the back of my throat and I held my breath as I stepped into the cold, filthy water.

"Welcome ter the River Fleet," said Maria. "Ain't hardly no one as knows it's still 'ere."

I knew the Fleet to be an ancient river which had been covered over by London's streets. "And it's now become a sewer," I commented.

She laughed. "Yeah. Yer'll get used to the 'orrible smell in a bit."

The tunnel we were now standing in was far wider and higher than the previous one, and the arched brick ceiling looked to be about seven or eight feet high. The water was bitingly cold and the chill quickly crept up my legs. The sediment on the bricks beneath the water felt slippery, and I had to tread carefully to avoid slipping. Ahead of us the river ebbed away into the darkness, and I could only assume it was heading down toward the Thames.

Josephine and Margaret had been found in the river. Was this how they ended up there? Was I to share the same fate?

My steps slowed as I considered this, and after a while Beth turned to look at me. I decided to adopt a cheery disposition so she wouldn't notice my fear.

"I hope it doesn't take too long to make our way out of here," I said. "I'm to be married in five days!"

"Ter that p'lice inspector?" asked Maria.

"Yes, Inspector Blakely. How did you know?"

"I've just 'eard about it."

"Did Mrs Sutherland tell you?"

"Proberly."

"How long have you worked for her?"

"A fair while."

"I had no idea she was involved in any sort of criminal activity," I said. "She doesn't strike me as that sort of woman at all."

"She ain't no criminal."

"Did she ask you to bring Josephine and Margaret down here?"

"Yer askin' too many questions, Miss Green."

Foul-smelling water flowed into the main tunnel from several smaller side tunnels at various intervals. Further along it forked into two narrower tunnels. I followed the women through the one that led off to the left.

"Inspector Blakely is looking for me," I said. "He'll have worked out where I am by now, and he has a lot of men with him."

If talk of the police unnerved the two women, they didn't show it. In reality, James would have no idea where I was. I felt a sudden surge of panic in my chest, but I knew I could do little more than follow the two women through the water for the time being.

The two tunnels soon reconnected to form a much wider one. High up on the wall to our left was a row of arches. I wondered whether they would open up into an overflow chamber should the water levels rise too high. Slightly further downstream we came across a number of other tunnels, some of which could be accessed by ladders fixed to the wall.

Others had sluice gates; some lowered and others raised. Maria and Beth continued on through the main tunnel, which was heading downstream. The water came up only as far as my knees, but the dampness had seeped up to my waist. I was cold and tired of wading through the filthy, stinking water.

"How often do you travel this way?" I asked them.

"Often enough," replied Beth.

As the tunnel grew ever wider, I sensed we were almost at the end. I felt a churn of dread in my stomach again.

The only way out for me would be via the river. Were they planning to push me in?

"The tide's comin' in," said Beth as the tunnel broadened into a wide chamber.

I saw bright, dazzling daylight in a wide rectangular opening up ahead of us. We had reached the Thames. The water in the chamber reached my waist and I shivered uncontrollably from the cold.

"This chamber's completely filled at high tide," she added.

"Am I destined for the river?" I asked. My skirts were heavy and sodden, and I staggered several times as I waded through the water.

Maria and Beth exchanged a glance but said nothing. I tried to quell the rising panic in my chest as we waded ever closer to the outlet into the river. The water moved slowly in toward us, lapping at the brick walls of the chamber. I tried to fathom whereabouts on the river we were, what place lay directly south of Ludgate Circus?

I glanced up and saw that the walls and ceiling were damp and slimy. There was no doubt the river would fill this chamber completely at high tide. Through the rectangle of light I saw a stone wall, and it occurred to me that it could be a bridge support. At that moment a loud rumble resounded through the chamber. It sounded like the rumble of a train and now I knew where we were.

"Are we beneath Blackfriars Bridge?" I asked.

Beth nodded.

I looked at the water around me and felt an even greater sense of panic. I had swum in a lake a few times as a child in Derbyshire, but swimming in the Thames with its strong currents was a different matter indeed. I felt sure my clothing would weigh me down, and being fully immersed in the cold water would come as a complete shock.

Where did my fate lie? In the water or at the mercy of the knife Maria held?

My body began to shake and, once again, I thought of the poor girls whose throats had been cut before their bodies were thrown into the water.

"Did you bring Josephine and Margaret down here?" I asked. "Is this how they ended up in the river?"

Beth's face had an ugly sneer to it, but she said nothing.

"Did you murder them?" I asked.

Beth took a step closer to me and tossed the lantern she was carrying into the water.

"You did, didn't you?" I continued. "You cut their throats and threw them into the river."

Before I had time to speak again the two women were standing either side of me. Beth pulled off my bonnet and grabbed a clump of my hair. The swiftness of her movement caught me by surprise.

"Don'tcha worry, Miss Green, it's almos' painless. Yer won't know nothin' about it," said Maria.

I saw daylight flash on steel close to my face. A strange calm descended and I closed my eyes as I waited for the inevitable to happen.

They were about to slit my throat and drown me. An instinctive urge for survival seized me.

"No!" I cried out, my voice echoing around the chamber.

"Quiet!" hissed Beth, still holding my hair.

I tried to struggle free, twisting my head around so the knife stayed as far from my throat as possible.

As I pushed an elbow into Maria's chest, my spectacles fell into the water. Hands grabbed at my arms. I squeezed my eyes shut and fought with as much strength as I could find. I pictured James at St Giles' church on our wedding day. I could see his smiling face as strong hands pushed me down into the water.

My head dipped under the surface but I continued to fight, lashing out blindly with my arms and legs. I knew they would eventually overpower me, but I was desperate to keep the knife at bay.

James was still smiling at me, and I fought for that moment with everything I had. I fought for the day when I would become his wife. My lungs ached for air, but I resisted the urge to open my mouth and take a breath. With my face underwater I knew it would mean certain death. I had to hold on for as long as possible, but my strength was fading. There was no hope of escape.

I stopped struggling and allowed my body to remain still.

Perhaps they would believe I was dead if I stayed still. Perhaps I could pretend I had drowned.

The pain in my chest intensified, and my head felt as though it were ready to explode. I continued to fight the urge to breathe.

How much longer could I hold on?

I felt sure that if I kept James' face in my mind I would somehow reach that day.

My wedding day.

His blue eyes were fixed on mine. I tried to return his smile, but then I felt water in my throat.

It was too late.

CHAPTER 49

Despite the sharp pain in my ribs, I couldn't stop coughing. I felt aware that I was moving up and down but, when I opened my eyes, all I could see was a blur of damp wood. It took me a moment to realise I was lying in the hull of a boat. Turning my head, I saw a bridge looming over me beneath a cloud-filled sky.

"Try to keep still, Miss Green," said a man's voice.

A hand was resting on my shoulder, and I realised I had been covered with something that appeared to be an overcoat.

"We just need to get you ashore," he added.

How did he know my name?

I wanted to ask the question but my throat was too sore. I also felt an intense pain in my eyes and at the back of my nose. I ignored the instruction to remain still and pushed myself up.

I was sitting in a rowing boat. Two men were seated in the centre, each holding a long oar, while another sat behind them. The one who had spoken was by my side. Each of the four men wore a dark, peaked cap and a buttoned-up double-breasted jacket.

I finally recognised the man who had spoken to me as Sergeant Bradshaw from the Thames River Police.

"Where's James?" I asked.

The sergeant pointed toward another rowing boat nearby, and there I could make out the unmistakeable form of James, still in the labourer's clothes he had worn to visit The Queen's Head. Thankfully, he'd removed his false beard.

I waved at him and he waved back.

"Penny!"

I could just about hear his voice across the water.

"She's all right!" Sergeant Bradshaw called over to him.

I glanced back at Blackfriars Bridge, and at the dark arch in the wall of the river embankment beneath the bridge. Although my eyesight was poor without my spectacles, I could just about detect a rowing boat moored beside it.

"What happened to Beth and Maria?" I asked.

"The women who were trying to drown you?" he responded. "They jumped into the river. My men are out searching for them, but the current's strong. You're lucky to be alive."

We rowed toward Thames Police Station and alighted at Waterloo Pier, where I was helped out of the boat. Almost as soon as I had set foot on the pier James was by my side.

As I embraced him I recalled how I had pictured his face just at the moment when I had thought I was drowning. Tears began to flow down my cheeks and my body shook with relief.

He held me close. "I should never have let you do that, Penny, it was so foolish of me. You should have had someone with you."

He led me into the police station, where I was given dry clothing to change into from the store they kept for people who were rescued from the river. I sat beside the fire with an overcoat wrapped around my shoulders and told James what had happened. He listened intently.

"That will have been E Division paying The King Lud a visit," he said. "Hopefully they've apprehended Mrs Sutherland by now. I'm quite astonished to hear she was connected to the Twelve Brides."

"Probably not as astonished as I was when I saw her! How did the river police know where to find me?"

"Five minutes after you disappeared beyond that door we decided to spring ourselves on the publican. He was quite alarmed, I can tell you! I asked where you'd gone but he refused to tell me. We arrested him, along with a young man and lady who also work there. Third Division summoned a Black Maria to take them to the station at Bridewell Place.

"Then we broke down the door you'd gone through and discovered the trapdoor. When we lifted it and saw the long tunnel beneath it, we really had no idea where you'd disappeared to. Some of the men went down into the tunnel, while I ran to catch up with the Black Maria to ask the publican where the tunnel led. I still couldn't get anything out of him, so I told the man that by withholding information he was endangering a human life. I told him he'd receive a much lighter sentence if he told me where the tunnel led. He took a bit of persuading, but eventually he relented and told me it ended up at The King Lud.

"I felt sure those tunnels somehow had to connect with the River Fleet, as we knew smugglers had taken advantage of those routes in the past. We alerted Sergeant Bradshaw and his men, who brought their boats around to where the Fleet joins the Thames. We realised then how Josephine Miller and Margaret Brown must have ended up in the river. The outlet for the River Fleet is well hidden beneath Blackfriars Bridge, so the girls could have been deposited there without anyone seeing a thing."

"They tried to do the same with me."

"And they would have succeeded if we hadn't got to you just in time."

"Perhaps it's just as well I'm leaving my profession," I said. "There have already been too many attempts on my life!"

"I imagine most news reporters have a rather more sedate time of it," he replied. "There's something in your character that seems to crave danger, Penny."

"Not at all," I protested. "It seeks me out, I feel sure of it."

"I'll head over to Bridewell Place later and find out how they're getting on," said James. "I hope Mrs Sutherland hasn't eluded us."

"She hasn't," said a lady's voice. "They've got her."

I looked up to see a lady in a blue flannel dress. She had brown hair and a freckled complexion.

"Mrs Worthers?" I asked, shrinking back in my seat in fear of another encounter with a gang member. "How did you get in here?"

"Don't worry, Miss Green, they let me in."

"What's this all about?" asked James, getting to his feet.

"I can explain, Inspector Blakely. Please don't worry, there's nothing to be concerned about. I've been watching the Twelve Brides gang for some time, you see. I've been working for a lady who lives near Piccadilly. She's been robbed twice and is tired of all the criminal activity in the area. I'm a private detective."

"Goodness, how interesting!" I exclaimed. "I'd convinced myself you were a criminal. I kept seeing you everywhere, and my assumption was that you were up to no good."

We both laughed. "You must have suspected Mrs Sutherland, then," I continued. "Is that why you were present at the London Women's Rights Society meeting?"

"No, I attended that meeting out of my own personal interest. I had long admired the work Mrs Sutherland had done with the Women's Rights Society in north London and talk of the new organisation intrigued me. I'm as shocked as you to discover who she really is. And I'm so sorry to hear about your ordeal, Miss Green. How are you feeling?"

"A little tired, but I'm extremely pleased to hear that Mrs Sutherland has been apprehended."

"You're not the only one. I was carrying out one of my regular visits to St Bride's earlier – I've been frequenting the area to identify gang members, you see – and today I was surprised to witness a large group of police officers outside The King Lud. I hung about with the rest of the crowd until the building's occupants were marched out. I assumed there had been a mistake when I saw that Mrs Sutherland was among them, but she was taken to Bridewell police station."

"With hindsight, it would have been useful for us to work together," I said.

"I suppose it would have. I'm careful to keep my work secret, however, as it wouldn't do to have too many people knowing I'm a detective."

"It would hamper your activities, that's for sure," said James. "Thank you for sharing some of the useful information you gleaned with us. I'm grateful to you for that."

"My pleasure, Inspector."

"Is Mrs Worthers your real name?" I asked.

She smiled. "I couldn't possibly say, Miss Green."

CHAPTER 50

"**A**nd finally, it is my great pleasure to present to you, Miss Green, in honour of your excellent service to our fine newspaper, the *Morning Express*, a personal gift from myself."

Mr Conway, a large man wearing a baggy, brown tweed suit, gave a bow and presented me with a leather-bound box that fitted neatly into my palm.

"Thank you for the gift, sir," I replied, "and for your extremely kind words."

We were gathered in the boardroom of the *Morning Express* offices, a room I had stepped inside only a handful of times during my eleven years of employment there.

"And congratulations on your impending nuptials!" Mrs Conway leaned forward to say brightly. "May you enjoy a long and happy marriage together."

"Thank you, Mrs Conway."

"Right then," said Mr Conway. "We'd better be off. Good luck in your married life, Miss Green, and do pass on my regards to the lucky fellow."

The proprietor and his wife bade everyone farewell,

leaving me in the boardroom with Mr Sherman and my colleagues.

"Aren't you going to open your gift, Miss Green?" asked Edgar.

I lifted the lid to reveal a silver pocket watch resting on a little cushion of green satin.

"A gentleman's watch!" laughed Edgar.

"It's the same watch everyone receives when they leave the *Morning Express*," I replied.

"Only if they've served for at least ten years," added my editor.

"But why did Mr Conway give you a watch intended for a gentleman?" queried Edgar. "He could have given you a locket instead."

"I presume he has a little store filled with silver pocket watches," I said. "Besides, I'm probably the first long-serving lady to have left her employment here. I'm sure James will be very happy to wear it."

"He'll get a much nicer one when he retires from the Yard," said Mr Sherman, "but I suppose it'll serve him well until then. We shall miss you, Miss Green."

"I shall miss you all too," I replied, my voice cracking a little. "Very much indeed. You'll all be attending the wedding, won't you?"

"Mrs Fish and I wouldn't miss it for the world," said Edgar cheerily. "And you can visit us here any time you like."

"Thank you. I hope to do so from time to time."

"I'll also make sure Mrs Fish sends you an invitation to her next ladies' luncheon."

"That would be lovely."

"I must confess I'm a little pleased you're leaving, Miss Green," he added, "because that means I'll be able to report on the trial of Mrs Sutherland and Miss Gold myself!"

I sighed. "Yes, I should have liked to report on that."

"You could follow the proceedings from the public gallery," suggested Frederick.

"I could, but it wouldn't quite be the same, would it?"

"Don't tell Mr Sherman, but I'll happily allow you to write my court reports for me," said Edgar with a grin.

"I'm standing right here, Fish," said the editor with a rare smile. "And besides, Miss Green, I think you already know what will most likely happen during the trial. Miss Gold will freely admit that she arranged the murders of Miss Miller and Miss Brown, implicating Mrs Sutherland as deeply as possible in the hope that her prospective death sentence will be commuted to life imprisonment instead."

"It's a shame that Beth and Maria won't be standing trial," I said.

The two women responsible for attacking me had thrown themselves into the river as soon as the police arrived and hadn't been seen since.

"Did they escape or are they dead?" asked Edgar.

"I wish we knew," I said. "I can't see how they could have swum to safety without being seen."

"It's a shame they won't face justice," said Mr Sherman, "but they were only the foot soldiers. Fortunately, the people they were working for have both been caught."

"I can only hope there's enough evidence to convict them," I said. "I hear Mrs Sutherland has excellent legal counsel."

"I'm sure she has," replied Mr Sherman, "but now she and Miss Gold have been captured, the gang members may start talking. After all, they have nothing left to fear. And if the police offer them leniency in exchange, their evidence could prove rather damning for Mrs Sutherland."

"James told me that's the plan."

"There you go, then. And you'll be able to keep a close eye on the case through the eyes of your husband!"

.   .   .

Back in the newsroom, I packed my belongings into my carpet bag for the last time and bade my colleagues a swift farewell. My throat felt tight with emotion and I was keen to leave before any tears managed to escape.

I scurried down the stairs, not wishing to dwell on the fact that this would be the last time I ever left the building as an employee. I had almost reached the door which opened out onto Fleet Street when I heard a shout behind me over the rumble of the printing presses.

"Miss Green!"

I turned to see Mr Sherman standing halfway down the flight of stairs.

"It seems you can't get away from us quickly enough!" He smiled as he descended the remainder of the staircase.

"It's not that, sir," I replied in a choked voice.

He handed me his handkerchief just as the first tear rolled down my cheek.

"You're too good a writer to lose, Miss Green," he said. "I'd like us to come to some sort of arrangement. Mr Conway needn't even know about it. There may still be an opportunity for you to contribute here and there. Under a pseudonym, of course. As you know, I already have a number of contributors who write a few articles a month." He scratched the back of his neck. "Just have a think about it."

I smiled as I wiped away my tears. "I'd love to, sir."

"As I say, have a think about it. You may feel differently once you're married."

"I doubt it very much!"

"Good." He returned my smile. "Well, good luck, Miss Green. I shall see you at the wedding."

CHAPTER 51

"I've certainly never worn anything like it before," I said to Eliza as I surveyed my wedding dress, "and I don't suppose I ever shall again."

The cream gown hung at the side of my wardrobe, as it was too big to fit inside. The bodice was a gold and cream brocade with a lace trim at the neck and sleeves. The remainder of the dress was a flowing cascade of silk skirts, the overskirts bunched and folded to reveal underskirts that were pleated and trimmed with lace. The lace veil hanging beside it trailed onto the floor.

"It's absolutely beautiful, Penelope." Eliza dabbed at her eyes.

"Are you all right, Ellie?"

"Yes, I'm fine." She walked over to my bed and sat down. "It's been an odd sort of week. I've been reflecting on my own marriage, which has proved to be rather a failure, and then there's this business with Mrs Sutherland..."

"What she did to you was awful."

"At least she didn't attempt to murder me!"

"No, but I don't like to imagine what might have happened if you'd continued your association with her. I feel rather responsible—"

"Oh, but you shouldn't!"

"I was the one who introduced the two of you."

"You assumed she was a well-meaning individual. We both did. And to think that I spent so much time with her working on the development of the London Women's Rights Society. The gall of the woman! She was so convincing. Utterly convincing, in fact. I simply don't know who to trust these days. I'm beginning to wonder whether I'm rather a poor judge of character."

"You're not, Ellie." I sat beside her on the bed. "She fooled everyone, and has evidently been doing so for years. To a certain degree I don't even think she believed she was doing anything terribly wrong. She was making a good income from her street robbery gangs and was using the proceeds to support various charitable works. We took her at her word because, most of the time, people are who they say they are. And perhaps we're both guilty of always wanting to see the best in people. I made the same mistake with Sarah, didn't I? Perhaps we both need to be a little warier in future."

"I'd say that you need to be a *lot* warier, Penelope. Thank goodness you've given up that wretched news reporter job. Perhaps you can help me salvage what remains of the London Women's Rights Society now. I think we need to change the name to remove any hint of association with that Sutherland woman. But given that we'd managed to gather such a formidable group of ladies it would be a terrible shame if all our efforts went to waste."

"I've love to help, Ellie."

"Thank you." She rested her hand on mine and gave it a squeeze. "I'm looking forward to whatever the future holds,

Penelope. With your marriage, my divorce and this new society on the horizon it feels as though a new and exciting chapter is about to begin."

"It does." I smiled.

"Now, I shall have to leave if I'm to meet Mother at the train station. I'm so terribly excited about tomorrow."

We were interrupted by a knock at the door. I rose to answer it.

"Any old iron?" called out a jovial voice, followed by raucous laughter.

I saw that it was Francis who had spoken. Beside him stood James, who was grinning widely.

"You're not allowed in!" cried Eliza, running toward the door. "You mustn't see the bride tonight! What are the pair of you doing here, anyway?"

"I'm supervising the inspector here on the eve of his wedding," replied Francis.

The two men giggled again.

"You're not drunk, are you?" scolded my sister.

"No, not at all," replied James, straightening his jacket. "We've just been to visit a friendly hostelry. There's one on every corner, you know."

"Don't ever mention a word of that riddle to me again!" I said with a groan.

James gave me a wink before continuing. "And young Francis here is to protect me from the men down at the Yard. They've been known to play a few tricks on a groom the night before his wedding."

"They'd better not," warned Eliza. "Francis, I think you should escort James home immediately so he can get a good night's rest. He's getting married in the morning! Keep him away from any trouble, especially with the police. They're the worst of the lot!"

"I will do," replied Francis solemnly, "just as soon as we've met with his colleagues at a public house near Scotland Yard."

Eliza tutted and shook her head disapprovingly.

"What are you two gentlemen doing here?" called Mrs Garnett, who had climbed the stairs behind them. "The bride needs to rest before her wedding day!"

"We'd better go, Francis," said James. "It turns out that coming here was a bad idea." He turned to me and grinned. "See you in the morning, Miss Green."

I returned his grin. "See you tomorrow, Inspector Blakely."

"And be careful, both of you!" ordered Eliza.

Mrs Garnett escorted James and Francis down the stairs.

"It'll ruin things completely if that fiancé of yours has a headache in the morning!" said Eliza as she closed the door.

"So long as he doesn't call the whole thing off I don't mind what he does," I replied.

"Oh, Penelope, he never would. You're not that Charlotte woman. Oh goodness, I hope she doesn't turn up with a mind to put a stop to things! I wouldn't put it past her, you know."

"She's found someone else to marry, so I think we'll be safe."

"Thank goodness for that." Eliza retrieved her coat from the cloak stand and put it on. "I'll go and meet Mother now. Hopefully Uncle Herbert has accompanied her. Do you think you'll be all right having him walk you down the aisle? Mother was very insistent about it, wasn't she? I suppose it's because he's the only brother she has left."

"I haven't seen him since I was eleven years old, but I recall him being perfectly nice."

"He is. Remember to walk slowly, though, as he has that awkward limp." She stepped forward and embraced me. "Get plenty of rest, won't you? Mother and I will be here in the morning to help you get ready."

"See you tomorrow, Ellie."

I could feel bubbles of excitement jiggling around in my stomach. I wasn't convinced I would sleep a wink with all the nerves and excitement I felt.

CHAPTER 52

I felt as though I were in a dream as I turned toward the sea of smiling faces. I squeezed James' arm just to make sure it was all real, and he glanced at me and grinned. He looked so handsome in his top hat and smart suit with the tall collar and white bow tie. It was difficult to believe that he was finally my husband.

With the vicar's blessing we walked slowly down the aisle toward the church door. My smile widened as I saw Eliza standing next to Francis. My sister gave a happy sob and Francis beamed. My mother was dressed in lavender blue and an extravagant hat. She looked happier than I'd seen her for a very long time. Beside her stood my laughing nieces.

I acknowledged Mr Sherman and my other colleagues, who had attended with their wives. Mrs Garnett had swapped her apron and bonnet for a pale green dress and a hat adorned with ostrich feathers. James' parents watched us proudly, no doubt relieved that their son had successfully made it to the altar on this occasion.

My face began to ache from smiling so much, yet I

couldn't have stopped if I'd tried. I felt as though I were walking on air.

All the familiar faces were filled with joy. There was a cousin whose name I couldn't remember and a great-aunt who looked so elderly I felt astonished she had managed to attend at all. Late spring sunshine was shining in through the church door, we had been blessed with a warm, beautiful day.

A figure appeared to my left, standing awkwardly behind the row of pews. He was leaning on a walking stick and pulling at his collar, as if the smart suit he was wearing felt uncomfortable. His skin was dark and his face, covered in trimmed grey whiskers, was heavily lined.

I stopped and stared. His eyes were large and dark, just as I had remembered.

He stopped fidgeting as he returned my gaze. There was a slight smile and then his face crumpled, as though he were trying to suppress an overwhelming emotion.

Was it sadness or joy? I couldn't tell.

"Are you all right, Penny?" James whispered into my ear.

"I think so," I replied, still staring at the man.

"You look as though you've seen a ghost."

"James," I said, turning to face my husband. "Meet my father."

THE END

HISTORICAL NOTE

Nineteenth century London saw its share of criminal women as well as men. The Forty Elephants was an all-female gang which operated in London for an astonishingly long time: from the eighteenth century until the 1950s. The gang was named after the area of London in which it originated – Elephant and Castle in south London. During the nineteenth century, the gang specialised in shop-lifting at high-class shops. They hid their loot in the cumbersome clothing of the time which was adapted with hidden pockets. The Forty Elephants were led by charismatic women such as Alice Diamond and Lilian Kendall – also known as the 'bob-haired bandit'. Gang tactics expanded to include posing as maids to steal from wealthy households and blackmailing men who its members had seduced into compromising situations.

In nineteenth century New York, 'Marm' Mandelbaum set up a criminal empire fencing stolen goods, bribing officials, financing bank robberies and even setting up a school which trained street children to become criminals. One of Marm's most successful students was Sophie Lyons who became known as the 'Princess of Crime'.

In researching the buildings for this book, I've noticed that most were damaged or destroyed in at least one of the following events: the Great Fire of London in 1666 and The Blitz in 1940-41 during WWII. Thankfully, many of the locations Penny visits in this book are still surviving today in one form or another.

The church where Penny and James marry, St Giles Cripplegate, has a long and fascinating history. Oliver Cromwell was married there in 1620 and John Milton was buried there in 1674. Cripplegate was the name of one of the Roman gates into the City of London and a fragment of the Roman wall still stands close by to the church. Its original name was St Giles-without-Cripplegate because it stood outside the city walls. There was a Saxon church on this site in the eleventh century and the Normans soon replaced it with their own version. It was rebuilt in its current Gothic style in the fourteenth century and the tower was added in the seventeenth century.

Although the church survived the Great Fire of London in 1666, it was damaged during the Blitz in WWII. The area of Cripplegate around it was decimated and much of the area is now covered by the Barbican development which was built in the 1960s-80s. This part of London has changed dramatically over the centuries, but the church still stands. It was restored in 1966 and now sits in the centre of the Barbican development.

Wapping, just east of the City of London, has a long maritime past. The Thames River Police was founded there in 1798 to tackle thefts from ships in the Port of London. The force was based at Wapping Police Station on the banks of the river and - incredibly - it still is today. I haven't yet found another police station in London which has been in continuous use for that long. Many of the Victorian police stations in the capital have been demolished or redeveloped for another use. The river police merged with the Metropolitan Police in 1839. Today Wapping Police Station is the headquarters of the Metropolitan Police Marine Policing Unit which polices forty-seven miles of the Thames. There's a little museum on site which tells you the history of the river police, apparently it's worth a visit.

Also situated at Wapping was Execution Dock where pirates were hanged. Their bodies would remain in place until three tides had washed over them and the remains of the particularly troublesome ones were then tarred and hung in cages at Blackwall Point (where the O2 Arena now stands) as a warning to others. The last pirate hangings took place in 1830 and since then the exact location of Execution Dock on Wapping's riverfront has been lost. For good measure though, a replica gallows stands in the riverbank by the Prospect of Whitby pub.

St Bride's Church on Fleet Street, and close to Ludgate Circus, was founded in the sixth century. In 1501, a merchant, William Caxton, established England's first printing press in St Bride's churchyard and the church's association with the printing industry began. St Bride's was destroyed in the Great Fire of London and rebuilt to a design by Sir Christopher Wren. The church reopened in 1675 and its famous steeple completed in 1703. With the rapid growth of the newspaper industry in Fleet Street, St Bride's became the parish church of journalism. The church suffered extensive bomb damage in the Blitz in WWII and services were held in the bombed out remains until the church was rebuilt and re-dedicated in 1957.

The Hanwell Schools in west London were known as the Central London District Poor Law Schools and opened in 1857 to house and educate destitute children. The schools were also known as the Cuckoo Schools as the two schools (one for girls, one for boys) were built on land called Cuckoo Farm in Hanwell, west London. Charlie Chaplin had a poverty stricken childhood and joined the school in 1896 when he was just seven years old. He spent two unhappy years there before moving to another similar school in south London. At the age of 14 he registered with a London theatrical agency and his life took a different turn. The schools closed in 1933 and the buildings still stand and are now a community centre.

Blackfriars Priory was established by the Dominicans in the thirteenth century. The location was south of Ludgate Hill, where the River Fleet meets the Thames. The priory was closed in 1538 during Henry VIII's dissolution of the monasteries and the buildings were used as a theatre and a base for the Society of Apothecaries. The buildings were destroyed during the Great Fire of London a century later, the Society rebuilt their part of the site and Apothecaries Hall remains standing today.

Blackfriars Bridge was first built in the 1760s and was the third crossing over the Thames at the time. The quality of the bridge was considered poor and it required extensive repairs before being rebuilt and opened by Queen Victoria in 1869. The adjacent railway bridge was constructed in 1864 and rebuilt twenty years later. Both these 1860s constructions still stand today.

The mysterious London Stone in Cannon Street is estimated to be around a thousand years old, possibly older. No one knows its true origin, there's speculation that it was once a

Roman milestone – possibly a location from where all distances in Roman Britain were measured. It has also been suggested that the stone is prehistoric and was an object of Druidic worship. It was first referenced in a list of London properties written around the year 1100. In medieval times, London Stone was a popular place to visit and countless stories were concocted about its origin.

In 1598 the historian, John Stow, described London Stone as "pitched upright... fixed in the ground verie deep, fastned with bars of iron." Some event (perhaps the Great Fire of London) caused the stone to reduce in size and in the eighteenth century it was placed in a protective cupola in front of St Swithin's Church. There it stayed for two hundred years until the church was destroyed in The Blitz in WWII. An office building replaced the church and a new protective alcove was built for the stone. When this office building was replaced in 2016, the stone moved to the Museum of London for a while. It returned to its location – in a shiny new case – in October 2018 and was unveiled in a ceremony by the Lord Mayor of London.

Sadler's Wells Theatre was first established in Clerkenwell by Richard Sadler in the seventeenth century and has been rebuilt a number of times since then. The theatre enjoyed a period of success in the mid-nineteenth century under the actor-manager Samuel Phelps who put on a number of Shakespeare plays. After periods of rise and decline over the years, the theatre today is a world-renowned venue for dance performances.

Temple Church was built in the 12th century by the Knights Templar as their English headquarters. The Knights Templar were a rich and powerful Catholic military order, better described as 'warrior monks'. The Knights Templar was dissolved by Pope Clement V in the 14th century, but the church is still going strong. Badly damaged during WWII, it's been fully restored and open to visitors. It was famously a location in Dan Brown's Da Vinci Code - both the book and the movie.

Shakespeare's Globe Theatre was built in Southwark by the Lord Chamberlain's Men in 1599. It was rebuilt after the building caught fire during a performance in 1613. The theatre was closed in 1642 and demolished. Subsequent development obscured the foundations of the theatre and by the late nineteenth century it sat beneath the Anchor Brewery operated by Barclay Perkins & Co. The brewery was demolished in the 1980s and excavations later that decade revealed part of the Globe's foundations. A plaque on Park Street, Southwark, now marks the spot where the Globe once stood. A modern reconstruction of the Globe was built in 1997 on the riverbank close by.

St Paul's Cathedral is one of London's most iconic buildings, it has hosted events such as the funerals of Lord Nelson, the Duke of Wellington and Winston Churchill, and the wedding of Prince Charles and Princess Diana. Famous people buried here include Lord Nelson, Christopher Wren, John Donne, Joshua Reynolds, Anthony van Dyck and Alexander Fleming. St Paul's was founded 1,400 years ago but the first long-standing building was built by the Normans in the 11th century. The spire made St Paul's Cathedral the tallest building in the world until the spire collapsed in 1561. Sadly, the rest of the cathedral was destroyed a century later in the Great Fire of London.

Sir Christopher Wren was commissioned to design the new cathedral and the building, as we know it today, was formally declared complete in 1711. Its iconic dome is one of the largest cathedral domes in the world. St Paul's survived the Blitz in WWII, despite many buildings around it being completely destroyed. The cathedral has been a filming location for Mary Poppins and Harry Potter. It was the tallest building in London until 1965 when the BT Tower opened.

Ludgate Circus sits at a crossroads between Fleet Street and Ludgate Hill. Lud Gate once stood here and was the western-most gate in the Roman city walls. This area is supposedly the burial place of the legendary Welsh king, King Lud. It's not clear if King Lud actually existed or not - he features in the 12th century book 'History of the Kings of Britain' by Geoffrey of Monmouth.

Lud Gate was demolished in the 18th century and Ludgate Circus was constructed in the 1860s and 70s. The King Lud pub was built in the 1870s and sadly closed in 2005, the building is now a restaurant.

The subterranean River Fleet is one of London's 'Lost Rivers' which have been largely covered over by roads and buildings and integrated into London's sewers. The Fleet runs from Hampstead in north London down to its outlet beneath Blackfriars Bridge. Apparently you can still hear the river these days through a grating in Ray Street, Clerkenwell.

If *The Gang of St Bride's* is the first Penny Green book you've read, then you may find the following historical background interesting. It's compiled from the historical notes published in the previous books in the series:

Women journalists in the nineteenth century were not as scarce as people may think. In fact they were numerous enough by 1898 for Arnold Bennett to write *Journalism for*

Women: A Practical Guide in which he was keen to raise the standard of women's journalism:-

"The women-journalists as a body have faults... They seem to me to be traceable either to an imperfect development of the sense of order, or to a certain lack of self-control."

Eliza Linton became the first salaried female journalist in Britain when she began writing for *the Morning Chronicle* in 1851. She was a prolific writer and contributor to periodicals for many years including Charles Dickens' magazine *Household Words*. George Eliot – her real name was Mary Anne Evans - is most famous for novels such as *Middlemarch*, however she also became assistant editor of *The Westminster Review* in 1852.

In the United States Margaret Fuller became the *New York Tribune*'s first female editor in 1846. Intrepid journalist Nellie Bly worked in Mexico as a foreign correspondent for the *Pittsburgh Despatch* in the 1880s before writing for *New York World* and feigning insanity to go undercover and investigate reports of brutality at a New York asylum. Later, in 1889-90, she became a household name by setting a world record for travelling around the globe in seventy two days.

The iconic circular Reading Room at the British Museum was in use from 1857 until 1997. During that time it was also used as a filming location and has been referenced in many works of fiction. The Reading Room has been closed since 2014 but it's recently been announced that it will reopen and display some of the museum's permanent collections. It could be a while yet until we're able to step inside it but I'm looking forward to it!

The Museum Tavern, where Penny and James enjoy a drink, is

a well-preserved Victorian pub opposite the British Museum. Although a pub was first built here in the eighteenth century much of the current pub (including its name) dates back to 1855. Celebrity drinkers here are said to have included Arthur Conan Doyle and Karl Marx.

Publishing began in Fleet Street in the 1500s and by the twentieth century the street was the hub of the British press. However newspapers began moving away in the 1980s to bigger premises. Nowadays just a few publishers remain in Fleet Street but the many pubs and bars once frequented by journalists – including the pub Ye Olde Cheshire Cheese - are still popular with city workers.

Penny Green lives in Milton Street in Cripplegate which was one of the areas worst hit by bombing during the Blitz in the Second World War and few original streets remain. Milton Street was known as Grub Street in the eighteenth century and was famous as a home to impoverished writers at the time. The street had a long association with writers and was home to Anthony Trollope among many others. A small stretch of Milton Street remains but the 1960s Barbican development has been built over the bombed remains.

Plant hunting became an increasingly commercial enterprise as the nineteenth century progressed. Victorians were fascinated by exotic plants and, if they were wealthy enough, they had their own glasshouses built to show them off. Plant hunters were employed by Kew Gardens, companies such as Veitch Nurseries or wealthy individuals to seek out exotic specimens in places such as South America and the Himalayas. These plant hunters took great personal risks to collect their plants and some perished on their travels. The *Travels and Adventures of an Orchid Hunter* by Albert Millican is worth a read. Written in 1891 it documents his journeys in Colombia and demonstrates how plant hunting became little short of pillaging. Some areas he travelled to had already lost their orchids to plant hunters and Millican himself spent several months felling 4,000 trees to collect 10,000 plants. Even after all this plundering many of the orchids didn't survive the trip across the Atlantic to Britain. Plant hunters were not always welcome: Millican had arrows fired at him as he navigated rivers, had his camp attacked one night and was eventually killed during a fight in a Colombian tavern.

My research for The Penny Green series has come from sources too numerous to list in detail, but the following books have been very useful: *A Brief History of Life in Victorian Britain* by Michael Patterson, *London in the Nineteenth Century* by Jerry White, *London in 1880* by Herbert Fry, *London a Travel Guide through Time* by Dr Matthew Green, *Women of the Press in Nineteenth-Century Britain* by Barbara Onslow, *A Very British Murder* by Lucy Worsley, *The Suspicions of Mr Whicher* by Kate Summerscale, *Journalism for Women: A Practical Guide* by Arnold Bennett, *Seventy Years a Showman* by Lord George Sanger, *Dottings of a Dosser* by Howard Goldsmid, *Travels and Adventures of an Orchid Hunter* by Albert Millican, *The Bitter Cry of Outcast London* by Andrew Mearns, *The Complete History of Jack the Ripper* by Philip Sugden, *The Necropolis Railway* by Andrew Martin, *The Diaries of Hannah Cullwick, Victorian Maidservant* edited by Liz Stanley, *Mrs Woolf & the Servants* by Alison Light, *Revelations of a Lady Detective* by William Stephens Hayward, *A is for Arsenic* by Kathryn Harkup, *In an Opium Factory* by Rudyard Kipling, *Drugging a Nation: The Story of China and the Opium Curse* by Samuel Merwin, *Confessions of an Opium Eater* by Thomas de Quincy, *The Pinkertons: The Detective Dynasty That Made History* by James D Horan, *The Napoleon of Crime* by Ben Macintyre and *The Code Book:*

The Secret History of Codes and Code-breaking by Simon Singh, *Dying for Victorian Medicine, English Anatomy and its Trade in the Dead Poor* by Elizabeth T. Hurren, *Tales from the Workhouse – True Tales from the Depths of Poverty* by James Greenwood, Mary Higgs and others, *Sickness and Cruelty in the Workhouse - The True Story of a Victorian Workhouse Doctor* by Joseph Rogers, *Mord Em'ly* by William Pitt Ridge, *Alice Diamond And The Forty Elephants: Britain's First Female Crime Syndicate* by Brian Macdonald. The *British Newspaper Archive* is also an invaluable resource.

THANK YOU

Thank you for reading *The Gang of St Bride's*, I really hope you enjoyed it!

Would you like to know when I release new books? Here are some ways to stay updated:

- Join my mailing list and receive a free short mystery: *Westminster Bridge*: emilyorgan.com/westminster-bridge
- Like my Facebook page: facebook.com/emilyorganwriter
- View my other books here: emilyorgan.com

And if you have a moment, I would be very grateful if you would leave a quick review of *The Gang of St Bride's* online. Honest reviews of my books help other readers discover them too!

GET A FREE SHORT MYSTERY

Want more of Penny Green? Get a copy of my free short mystery *Westminster Bridge* and sit down to enjoy a thirty minute read.

News reporter Penny Green is committed to her job. But should she impose on a grieving widow?

The brutal murder of a doctor has shocked 1880s London and Fleet Street is clamouring for news. Penny has orders from her editor to get the story all the papers want.

She must decide what comes first. Compassion or duty?

The murder case is not as simple as it seems. And whichever decision Penny makes, it's unlikely to be the right one.

Visit my website to claim your FREE copy:
emilyorgan.com/westminster-bridge

THE CHURCHILL & PEMBERLEY
SERIES

Also by Emily Organ. A cozy mystery series set in an English village.

1932. Armed with a handbag and fuelled by cake, Annabel Churchill is a mature yet tenacious private detective. Together with her quirky sidekick, Doris Pemberley, she's determined to solve mysteries and chase down criminals in the sleepy Dorset village of Compton Poppleford.

Find out more here: emilyorgan.com

Made in the USA
San Bernardino, CA
25 May 2020

72306290R00207